# CURSED FOR KEEPS

# CURSED FOR KEEPS

*A Curse Keeper, Curse Breaker Fairytale*

## E.J. KITCHENS

Cover design by Victoria Cooper Art

Cursed for Keeps / E.J. Kitchens —1st ed.

Print ISBN: 978-0-9993509-9-7

❀ Created with Vellum

# CHARACTER GLOSSARY

❧

## The Royal Family of New Beaumont

King Patrick and Queen Marianne
Prince Rupert and wife, Princess Belinda
Robert, Duke of Pondleigh
Lyndon, beloved servant and godfather

## The Royal Family of New Grimmland

Queen Solstice and King Theodore
Princess Snow

## Residents at the Cottage for Retired Enchanters

Colors, Cello, Who, What, I Don't Know, Today, Blatherskite

## Others of Note

Lady Violetta, enchantress
Prince Dokar, prince of the Unseelie Faerie
Lady Lucrezia, who was banished from New Beaumont
Birch, Lord of the Mirror of Talvinen

# PROLOGUE

*Dear Lady Violetta,*

*I have seen some of your recent gown designs, and I must say how jealous I am of the ladies who wear them! Perhaps we could discuss a gown for myself and my daughter sometime? Speaking of my dear Snow, I am brought to the less agreeable reason for my writing you. I have heard of the recent events in New Beaumont and of the reappearance among mortals of that odious faerie Prince Dokar. I'm terrified he shall come to New Grimmland next. You know we have already had our share of misfortunes. Snow, being a beautiful princess dependent on her stepmother for her care, is a likely target for such a fey. Though I am both a stepmother and a queen, I am not that kind of stepmother and queen. I have always done my best to protect my daughter, and I shall do no less now. You are familiar with this fey prince and the world of magic. Is there a safe place where Snow can hide until this menace returns to his own realm?*

*Sincerely,*
*Queen Solstice of New Grimmland*

*P.S. If you have a dress that would be helpful to Snow, I will gladly pay whatever you ask. We still struggle to find a solution for The Secret.*

*My dear Queen Solstice,*

*How kind you are! I do so love designing gowns, and mine can be ever so useful as well as beautiful—I maintain there is never a reason to forsake the latter for the former. I do agree about the danger for Princess Snow. Oh, that odious Prince Dokar! How I loathe him! Despite his rather dashing appearance. His suits always show his trim waist and broad shoulders to advantage. Where was I? Oh yes. I know just the place for her! I will make arrangements immediately and send word where to send her.*

*Sincerely,*
*Lady Violetta, enchantress*

*P.S. I will most certainly work on a dress for Princess Snow and will take The Secret into consideration. I have a feeling we might be able to work out a happily-ever-after for her, after all. With my outfits, anything is possible.*

# CHAPTER 1

Once upon a time there lived a young man, the son of a king's widowed sister, who was raised as a prince. He was a brave, honorable man beloved by his family and kingdom; a worthy prince they called him. It was this "almost prince" status that led him to be cursed by the evil faerie lord Dokar and a young lady who wanted to be queen. He was forced into obedience to the young lady's and the faerie prince's every whim—if he heard their commands. However, the almost-prince had among his friends an enchantress—the great Lady Violetta herself—and a clever cousin (the real prince, Prince Rupert) and cousin-in-law (Princess Belinda). Through their efforts, he obtained a Selective Deafening Spell, which would allow him to *not* hear any commands given him by Prince Dokar or Lady Lucrezia, should he ever be so unlucky as to meet with them again.

Consequently, as soon as the wounds from his last encounter with the pair had mostly healed, the almost-prince set off in pursuit of them with the goal of freeing himself once and for all—after he paid a call on a certain beautiful princess whom he had pined after for several years. It was, perhaps, not the wisest plan, but after hearing nothing from the lady of his heart for some time and seeing his cousin so happy, he felt a need to do something toward securing his own happiness. Why not pursue the villains while he was out and about?

The reason, he was soon to learn, was another curse.

ROBERT, Duke of Pondleigh, nephew to the king of New Beaumont, tried not to pace like a schoolboy waiting for the bell to sound the beginning of summer break. It had been over four years since he'd seen Princess Snow of New Grimmland—since before he'd found out about that blasted curse Lady Lucrezia had put on him, since before his cousin Rupert had been transformed into a beast. He'd thought it necessary to keep away from Snow lest he be used against her kingdom in some way. But now that he was free, or free-ish anyway, and healed from a poisoned stab wound—well, mostly healed—he'd ridden off to New Grimmland to see her. His eagerness and usual confidence sank into pain and confusion. He'd come to find out why she'd stopped answering his letters.

"I'm so glad Prince Rupert is doing well." There was genuine warmth in Queen Solstice of New Grimmland's mellow voice. Except for the queen's lady-in-waiting and a guard, the two of them were alone in her reception room, an elegant, well-lit room hung with landscapes of New Grimmland and the queen's homeland, a cold kingdom in the far north. Incongruously he'd always thought, a large, gold-framed mirror, ornate and three feet tall, hung on the wall in a spot of honor. That particular part of the wall had once held a portrait of an ancient king and had, the late King Theodore once informed him, a peephole in it, for that was the spot where one could see the room in its entirety. But now there was only a mirror, with a bit of magic making it glow. Like the golden bracelet Queen Solstice wore.

"I am happy to hear such wonderful things of Prince Rupert's wife," Queen Solstice continued.

Robert forced his attention from the mirror and its reflection of the outer door to Solstice. She was a gracious, beautiful woman, one whose true age didn't show, which had led to many an unpleasant remark about the king marrying a woman nearly young enough to be his daughter. Robert had engaged in more than one round of fisticuffs in defense of her and the late king's honor.

"Yes," he said. "Rupert is better than well now, and Belinda, though a bit rough around the edges, is as sharp as a tack and devoted to Rupert, yet won't let him get away with any nonsense. She's perfect for him."

"I wish them every happiness." There was a wistfulness to Solstice's smile as her gaze landed on her husband's empty chair. The expression gave way to sorrow as she glanced at Robert, then disappeared almost as quickly behind a placid mask.

The door to the chamber opened, and Robert's heart nearly leapt from his chest as he spun around. *Keep it together, Robert. No need to make a fool of yourself in front of Princess Snow. Again.*

But it was the servant who'd been sent to fetch Snow, and he was alone. Robert suddenly felt very tired, and the wound in his side ached.

"Princess Snow is indisposed and begs to be forgiven," the man said.

With a quiet sigh, Queen Solstice dismissed him. She graciously didn't offer any excuses to Robert.

"Will Princess Snow continue to be indisposed, do you think?" Robert asked her, his tone heavy.

"I cannot answer for my stepdaughter." It was said in a resigned tone that didn't encourage him at all. Solstice laid a gentle hand on his arm, her dark eyes sorrowful. "You may inquire after her once each day for the next three days, if you wish."

Robert did so, but Princess Snow remained "indisposed." He didn't even chance to see her walking the castle grounds, nor did she attend any of the informal dinners held during his stay. Solstice had held few formal dinners since her husband's death, and it seemed Snow had a habit of being a recluse when not forced into company. What had happened to the friendly girl he'd known as a boy?

On the morning of the fourth day, Robert went to take his leave of Solstice in her reception room, praying for a miracle but not really expecting one.

"The queen is in a meeting," the servant said as Robert approached the room, "but she ordered me to announce you immediately." He did so and ushered Robert inside.

While somewhat embarrassed to be barging in, Robert's frayed soul was assuaged in that the queen at least valued him and the relationship with New Beaumont. Cared enough to give him time, even if it meant interrupting a meeting with several of the nobles of the land.

As Robert walked in, he studied the group of ten men with interest, as he had every time they'd met over the years. If he and Snow did marry, as her father and Solstice had hoped, and Robert became king, which nobles could he trust to help him guide New Grimmland in wisdom, justice, and love?

Duke Houen, an older cousin of Robert's brother-in-law, could play Saint Nicholas at any village play with a little padding. Despite the hardships of the past few years, which had left him frail and his purse diminished, his eyes still held the twinkle of joy and wisdom Robert always looked for in him. Duke Fredrich wore a sour expression but seemed a fair man. Guagin struck him as grasping, pompous, and in favor of marrying himself to Queen Solstice. Schwan, once a guard and now a nobleman, was shrewd and private. He'd killed the sorcerer who'd assassinated King Theodore and had received a title and lands in gratitude, gifts he'd somehow managed to turn into a sizable fortune. After marrying a high nobleman's daughter, he'd taken his wife's father's place at court when the man died, rather conveniently some thought. There was a trace of magic about Schwan, and that or something about him had never sat well with Robert. Schwan might be a man of the blade, but the former guard was no true and loyal soldier at heart, Robert suspected. He scoffed and quickly studied the remaining nobles as he bowed to them.

"Forgive me for intruding, gentlemen," Robert said as he walked around the group toward Solstice, who always sat near the mirror. "I came to take my leave of Queen Solstice."

"Leaving so soon?" The young Lord Bankor observed Robert with an undisguised arrogance that made Robert's jaw tick. "I'm sure *everyone* will be sorry to see you go." *Snow prefers me*, his piggy little eyes declared.

"I'll be back." *Queen Solstice would give me permission to pummel you if I asked for it. Don't think I won't.* Robert held Bankor's gaze until the young man looked away, doubtless aware of Robert's claims to the princess and Snow's avoidance of them both. Her avoidance of Bankor was something

Robert had been at pains to assure himself of after the pipsqueak's first digs at him two days ago.

Duke Houen stepped between them with a hearty laugh and an outstretched hand. "I hope your return will be soon, Robert. You'll spend the night with Anne and me tonight, won't you?" he urged. "You can wait another day to return to New Beaumont."

"Gladly, sir," Robert answered with the first genuine smile of the day as he shook the older man's hand. Houen, in addition to practically being a relative, was part of a small group of kings and nobles of faith who corresponded regularly to encourage one another and hold one another accountable, to keep them from the pride and other dangers men of power were so often prey to. It would be good to have and to give that encouragement in person, for while Robert had Lyndon, Rupert, and King Patrick often nearby, Houen had lost King Theodore.

"Excellent." Houen, his expression brighter even than usual, clapped him on the shoulder. "I'd better get along and warn Anne. Gentlemen," he said, glancing around the room, "I think it's time for a break." He patted Robert on the shoulder again and led the nobles out.

The others followed, Guagin, Schwan, and Bankor all giving Robert jealous looks as they passed him. The former two, men of an age with Robert's uncle, exuded jealousy of a different kind than the pipsqueak. Jealous of Robert's influence, perhaps?

"Good morning, Robert." After all the men had exited, Solstice greeted him with a smile, and he thought with pride, a lessening of the tension evident in her posture earlier. They spoke for a few minutes, and she gave him greetings for his family.

"I am sorry your visit was not as you'd hoped," she said after he bid her farewell and turned to go.

His steps faltered. *Everyone will be sorry to see you go.* "Me too," he said softly.

"When will you return?" There was a cautiousness to her question, and he wasn't sure what answer she hoped to gain from him. She clasp her wrist to her chest, her fingers tracing the charms of a golden bracelet, a match to one Snow had always worn. He wouldn't know if she wore it still.

Robert paused, letting the question settle into his mind. Without the aid of pride and possessiveness to goad him, did he plan to return? Should he? "I don't know." He started forward again. "Perhaps not until Houen invites me again."

Solstice said nothing, and Robert continued to the door.

As a servant opened it for him, he stopped and turned back. "Have you any news of the faerie Prince Dokar?" His failure with Princess Snow wouldn't stop him from succeeding in his other goal.

Solstice startled, and said with motherly concern, "I really don't think you should be going after him, Robert. Fighting a fey prince is more complicated than simply brandishing an iron knife, especially since he'd be expecting that now."

Robert set his jaw. He felt very much in need of a monster to slay at the moment. Fighting seemed all he was fit for. Relationships apparently weren't for him.

Pinching the bridge of his nose, Robert banished the thought and the familiar ache and called up the truth. *Rupert apologized for cutting you off, your parents couldn't help leaving you—they died—and your sister married a foreigner and couldn't help it either. Haven't Aunt Marianne, Uncle Patrick, and Lyndon always been there for you? You're tired and hurt.*

"I don't know where he is," she continued, drawing herself up. Robert wasn't sure if it was stern mother or stern queen he saw. "And if I did," she said, her chin high, "I wouldn't tell you. King Patrick and Queen Marianne would never forgive me if I did."

A weak smile briefly curved his lips, and he forced himself into a soldierly posture. "Then where can I find out how to fight Prince Dokar? It's said more is known about magic in the kingdom of your birth than anywhere else."

She paled. "I did not make a study of it."

"I didn't mean to imply the rumors about King Theodore's death were true," he amended hastily, mentally kicking himself for upsetting her, "but that you might know of something helpful or of someone who might have that knowledge."

"I can't help you. I'm sorry."

Surprised by the quickness of her reply but keeping his expression neutral, Robert bowed. "Thank you for your concern and your hospitality, Queen Solstice. I wish you and your daughter health and happiness."

He had just crossed the threshold when a hail from Solstice stopped him again.

"You might..." she said hesitantly, with an odd look at the gold-framed mirror, "you might try the Cottage for Retired Enchanters in the Dark Forest. Perhaps someone there could give you the answers you seek." She spun away and left the room through the door to her private chambers, her fast stride hinting at some unease in the communication she'd given him.

Robert smiled a grim smile and left. Lady Violetta had suggested this Cottage for Retired Enchanters. Despite Belinda's claims the air-headed enchantress had learned her lesson, Robert didn't trust her good sense completely. After all, it was Lady Violetta who had been tricked into giving

Lucrezia the spell that had brought him under her—and then Prince Dokar's—control.

But if both the enchantress and Queen Solstice suggested he go to the cottage, to the cottage he would go.

IT WAS several days journey to this Cottage for Retired Enchanters, he'd been told, and it was going to be an even longer one due to Lyndon's insistence on a slow pace since Robert was not fully healed from the stab wound Lucrezia had given him. Though feeling like a horse chafing at the bit, Robert let the man dictate the pace. Lyndon, his uncle's personal servant and Robert's godfather, was getting on in years, after all.

"What do you know about this Cottage for Retired Enchanters?" Lyndon asked the third morning into their journey.

*Not much, though traveling at this pace, I know what it feels like to be retired.* The morning sun was bright, the forest-shaded road inviting, and Robert and Firethorn, his horse, were aching for a run instead of their plodding pace ... but his dear godfather would chase him down and hogtie him if he tried so much as a canter. "There are seven enchanters currently living there, I believe," Robert answered. "They have a library they guard zealously, and while they esteem cataloguing their lives for prosperity, it seems they take rather odd names— more than one over their lifetime—so the history of their birth and family is obscured. Rather shady, if you ask me."

"Enchanters tend to live a very long time—and often do very foolish things—so perhaps the changing of names is because they like a separation from the reminder of the family they lost centuries ago and from the foolish acts they'd rather not be remembered for and would undo if they could?"

"Hmm," Robert intoned. Could he convince Lyndon that something startled Firethorn and sent him into a gallop? It might hurt the wound in his side, to be sure, but what was a little pain?

A flash of white drew Robert's attention to the strip of cleared land between the forest and road. Why was there a glow of magic about that slant of sunlight? A tall, thin, familiar figure began to take form within it, and Robert regretted his desire for a reason to gallop.

"Run, Lyndon!" Robert kicked his heels into Firethorn's sides.

But it was too late. As a bubble of magic surrounded him, freezing everything around him and pinning his arms to his sides, Robert couldn't help but wonder, that if they'd traveled faster, he might have avoided this meeting. For surely the Cottage for Retired Enchanters had wards against angry faerie princes.

Tall, trim, with a dark faerie handsomeness and a glow of magic about him, Prince Dokar materialized before them. Or Robert and Lyndon materialized in front of him, Robert wasn't sure, for now he and Lyndon faced a shadowy wood that looked as if it held any number of dangerous, magical creatures. Dokar eyed Robert like a cook choosing cuts of meat.

Robert grunted as he was jerked by magic from his horse to the ground, landing hard on his knees on a dirt road. Biting back a cry, he stiffened his spine, met Dokar's fierce gaze, and smiled lazily. "I'm sorry, were you saying something? You'll have to speak up if you expect me to hear you."

Dokar's lips moved quickly in snarled words, but Robert

heard nothing, felt only the tingle of Lady Violetta's Selective Deafening Spell. He shrugged insolently when Dokar's mouth stopped moving.

"Command him," Dokar growled at a frail, blonde woman, hunched and wringing her hands, standing beside him. *Lucrezia?*

Robert's burst of anger against the once-proud woman who'd cursed and stabbed him vanished almost as swiftly as it came. She had begged forgiveness and accepted her exile without complaint, and as he saw her now, wretched and with guilt in her expression, he pitied her. Cautiously. She'd always been tricky.

"Please," Lucrezia begged, yanking at the locket she wore, digging the chain into skin already raw at her neck. "I take back our bargain. I don't want a crown! Let us go!"

"*Command* him."

Lucrezia's hand tugged on the locket again, and despite a struggle, she turned to Robert and began to speak, though he couldn't hear her.

"No," he said simply, when her lips stilled. "Whatever you want, or whatever he wants of me, the answer is *no*."

Dokar and Lucrezia both gaped at him.

"You might as well let me go. I am no longer under your control." Well, so long as he couldn't hear them, but they didn't need to know that.

Eyes flashing dangerously, Dokar crossed to him in three steps, and Robert braced for a blow. Instead, Dokar pinched Robert's chin between long, thin fingers and studied his face. After a moment, he scoffed and stepped away, rubbing his hand on a handkerchief the same shadowy green as a dark forest.

"Lucrezia," Dokar said, still focused on Robert with a knowing look Robert didn't like, "he's being helped by that enchantress. He can't hear us talk to him."

Closing her eyes as if in grateful prayer, Lucrezia didn't respond, and Robert found himself hoping he could bring about her freedom as well as his own. This was not the exile they'd sentenced her to.

"But no matter," Dokar continued cheerfully. "I am a fey of many plans." He opened his right hand to reveal the crushed green handkerchief. It began to shift and glow, squirm and flicker, until a small frog sat in his palm.

Robert got a very bad feeling. The frog-kerchief blinked at him, which didn't help the feeling.

"How do you fancy your future husband as a frog, my lady?" Dokar asked Lucrezia, one eye still on Robert.

"I am not—" Robert began indignantly.

Dokar lunged forward, shoved the frog into Robert's open mouth, and forced his jaw shut. Robert, unintentionally, unavoidably, swallowed.

While Robert choked and shivered against a strange slimy coolness seeping through him, Dokar stepped away and smiled a thin, glittering kind of smile that matched the cruel mischief in his eyes.

"Did you know, Lady Lucrezia, that Robert, Duke of *Pond*leigh," he began mockingly as Robert doubled over, clutching his roiling stomach, "the most honorable of noble gentlemen, faithful friend and trusted advisor to his king and queen, has just been cursed? That he must gain a kiss from a lady every day or he shall greet the minute past midnight and each minute afterward, as a frog?"

Robert stilled, the settling of the curse settling his stomach and clearing his mind. His hands weren't pinned to his sides any longer, and while he had no pure iron blade, he had a steel one in his boot. He began carefully pulling it out. Killing the curser was one way of breaking curses, he'd heard. With Dokar here, he couldn't *not* try to free himself and Lucrezia.

"That ought to make court life more interesting, don't you think?" Dokar continued. "The duke gets two days of humanness if the lady he kisses is married. Three if she thinks he is Prince Rupert, for their resemblance is very great. And … ah … if it's the *first* kiss of a princess … a betrothed one … then he's free. This will be much more fun than simply marrying him off to you, Lucrezia."

Snarling a refusal, Robert staggered up and sent the knife spinning toward Dokar. The fey lord merely laughed. With a flick of his finger, he bowled Robert over, throwing him back against the hard-packed dirt and sending the knife who knew where.

"When he's tired of that," Dokar said as Robert's head spun and Lucrezia sobbed pathetically, "I might let him marry you. Marrying you, Lucrezia, or living a life of infamy, are his only choices … unless he wishes to live *hoppily*-ever-after."

Slowly, the sound of Dokar's laughter and Lucrezia's weeping faded, and the bubble of magic and light around Robert followed. As the noises of a forest, of his horse shifting nervously, crowded in on him again, Robert swore. A frog! Couldn't he at least be threatened with beast-hood? He could do the kingdom some good that way, and wouldn't have to worry about cats and being stepped on, if … well … if worse came to worse.

His gut tightened. Unless he'd missed some clause in the curse, he could tuck tail and race back home to New Beaumont, where his aunt would gladly greet him with a kiss each day—where he could goad Rupert by getting a kiss on the cheek from Belinda every now and then—or he could continue on to this Cottage for Retired Enchanters hoping there was a friendly little old lady there with a penchant for kissing young men. Or that there was an enchanter with knowledge concerning fighting Dokar and his curses. As much as he loved his aunt, he really didn't want to spend the rest of his life at her side. If only Snow would talk to him! He could really use a wife right now.

He looked past Lyndon, who was still blinking back awake, toward home, then back toward the New Grimmland palace, and finally, through the seemingly endless woods toward this cottage. He swore again. It wouldn't matter if a kiss on the cheek from his aunt would count or not: he couldn't make it home by midnight. He likely couldn't make it anywhere but a village before nightfall. A village sure to have a barmaid he could charm a kiss from.

Robert stared down the tree-shrouded lane, a sick feeling twisting his gut. He could either keep his human form or keep his honor in not being an idle flirt. Keep his kisses solely for the woman he loved. Which was it to be?

The sounds of falling trees and rough shouts around a bend in the road decided for him.

# CHAPTER 2

T he woods were deep, dark, and dangerous enough as it was. Were highwaymen required too?

Two booms shook the road. Princess Snow of New Grimmland bit back a scream as she tumbled to the floor as the carriage jerked to a halt, horses neighing and men shouting. Heart hammering louder than a dwarf in a ruby mine, she pulled herself up, lifted the edge of the oilskin window cover, and peered out the unmarked carriage. A sizable tree lay across the road ahead, another behind. Sizable, masked ruffians swarmed from the cover of the dark forest, yelling for the coachmen and guards to lower their weapons and hand over any valuables. She and her companions had a sizable problem, for she was their only valuable and she wasn't about to be handed over.

Snow's mouth firmed into a grim line. So much for traveling incognito—that brought its own dangers it seemed. Is this what her subjects put up with regularly? Highwaymen accosting and robbing them?

Lowering the window covering as her two mounted guards engaged with the highwaymen, Snow locked the carriage door and swiftly pressed a thick dowel in the top of the wall at the driver's back. It depressed, poking him. Not comfortable, but more discreet than yelling at a time like this. *Take care of yourselves. I'm alright*, the poking said.

She hoped the latter statement was true anyway. She had the distinct feeling the highwaymen didn't believe the coachman when he claimed to have no passenger.

Skimming the seat edge with her fingers, she found and triggered the latch hidden there.

The carriage door rattled and a rough voice called out, "Open up, ya coward. Don't waste our time. We charge for it in stabs!" The following raucous laughter had a slur to it.

Snow bit back a scoff. The seat edged up, and she threw herself into the empty space underneath it. A heavy, dirt-brown cloak fell from the seat bottom to cover her.

Just as the seat clicked into place again, the door burst open and a shot rang out from across the road. The fake bottom of the carriage seat opened, dumping her on the dusty road. She curled up, tucking her knees to her chest and checking that the magically camouflagic cloak was covering all of her. *Search the coach and leave. You've no reason to hurt anyone.* A hint of movement at level with her but nearer the edge of the road caught her eye. One of her guards lay on the ground, bloody but breathing.

"Stand down!" a man yelled, his booming voice commanding and tinged with a New Beaumont accent.

"Lookie there, men: it's a ransom!"

Stretching forward, Snow could just see through the carriage wheel spokes the ebony legs of a fine horse, the body of a highwayman, and the feet of several other horses and men. Was this newcomer mad that he should challenge all of these? She very much doubted he had enough loaded guns to take them all down, though she wished he did.

"No one's going to ransom you," the man retorted, and she got a terrible sinking sensation in her gut. She knew that voice. She'd hidden in her room for three days to avoid its owner.

Well, as long as he didn't get hurt, she wouldn't have to talk with him now. *Please, for his own sake, and mine, don't let him get hurt. Or any further harm come to my men.*

"You don't even merit a reward," he continued. "The standard of highwaymanship in this kingdom is surprisingly low."

The highwaymen's replies were not polite, but they were short. After a few moments of gunshot blasts and the harsh neighing of a battle-trained horse, everything went silent.

"That's all of them! That was impressive, stranger," one of her guards cried.

Snow let out a breath of relief, started to crawl out, then remembered their rescuer. She *could* stay hidden and walk the rest of the way to this Cottage for Retired Enchanters Lady Violetta had suggested she flee to for the summer.

She'd just decided it was a pleasant day for a long walk when a thud drew her eyes to the road ahead. A handsome man of about thirty, with a military bearing, light brown hair, and three thin scars on his cheek lay unconscious in the dirt to her right, and he was bleeding. Her own wounded guard staggered up and toward him. The coachman squatted before the carriage and looked straight at her.

"Poisoned apples," she cursed silently, and began crawling out from under the carriage, careful to avoid a frog squished by a previous traveler. "Get the medical kit and water canteen."

The coachman nodded, but waited to offer her a hand up before obeying.

Snow soon knelt beside the unconscious Duke of Pondleigh, examining him with her eyes and tentatively reaching toward him, cloth in hand to staunch the flow of blood from a gash in his side. She hesitated and looked to her hands. They were gloved, as always. What did he have to fear from her so long as she kept her gloves on? Setting her jaw, she pressed the cloth to Robert's bleeding side, checked his head for injury and found none, and then poked him on the shoulder. "Wake up, Robert. I am not taking you with me. You've got to wake up and go your own way." *I have enough to deal with without you staring at me moony-eyed or ignoring me when I need you, whichever Robert you are today.* An ache she'd rather ignore threatened to split her heart. *Ignoring me until the pull of a crown outweighed the ill of being married to me.*

"Your Grace!" A middle-aged man with a bearing somehow both fatherly and fierce charged into the clearing. He reined in his horse as he spotted them, and after dismounting, hurried to Robert's side. Snow backed away, sensing the man's determination to care for the duke. She motioned for her guards to leave the newcomer alone. "How is he?" the older man asked, a deep concern evident in his tone. She guessed him to be a personal servant, possibly the one Robert and Rupert were so fond of.

"I—" *I don't know.*

"The stubborn idiot thinks he's invincible," the man muttered as he yanked up Robert's shirt to expose his wound. To her shock, there was already a bandage around Robert's waist. Above that, on his left side, was the fresh gash, bloody but not deep. Her gaze skimmed Robert's frame again, noting he was thinner and paler than she'd ever seen him. His previous injuries must have been severe indeed if the exertion of fighting a few bandits had been too much for the famed warrior.

The coachman stepped to their side with the medical kit and canteen, eyes questioning. Snow nodded to the newcomer, who glanced up and then took the supplies.

"I'm Lyndon," he said as he opened the box and began to clean and dress Robert's wound. "Servant of King Patrick of New Beaumont. This is his nephew, Robert, Duke of Pondleigh. Is there a place nearby where we can take my lord?"

Snow stiffened, but she studied Robert's pale face again, her heart softening dangerously. "Yes," she said reluctantly, "there's the Cottage for Retired Enchanters."

Lyndon gave her a strange look before turning back to his patient. "Excellent. Thank you, miss."

Snow blinked. *Miss*, not *princess*. He didn't know who she was, and it had been some years since Robert had seen her. Perhaps *she* needn't meet with Robert at all.

◈❧◈

THE "COTTAGE" was a large three-story, thatched-roof home set in a clearing in a wood of towering evergreens. Lady Violetta had claimed the cottage and its residents were charming, so Snow was on her guard. Lyndon, to keep the stubborn Robert as still and quiet as possible, had given him sleeping medicine when he'd started to wake an hour or so ago. Consequently, Robert was being supported by two guards as Snow stood on the moss-covered flagstone before the door and rapped with the knocker. The younger two of her guards had flesh wounds, one a scrape across his hairline from a bullet and the other a crease in his arm, but they insisted they were fine and were now standing guard at the carriage. Their color wasn't bad, so Snow decided to believe them.

To give Lyndon and Robert more space in the coach during the remaining journey, she'd ridden Robert's horse—astride, to the shock of everyone—and now her muscles were making her regret it. She mouthed a silent "ouch" as she shuffled closer and knocked a second time. At her third knock, the door vanished. It was either that obvious invitation or the sudden sensation of moss brushing her boots and beginning to grow around them that urged her to hurry inside.

"Hello? Is anyone here?"

No one answered, but a silver-haired man in a dressing gown—a comfortable, plush crimson one with a fur collar and a stitched crest of some kind—padded past the entryway, whistling. His eyes met hers. The whistling stopped, as did his forward momentum. After a brief sweep of the group, his pale blue eyes settled on Snow with startling intensity. His face turned a bright red that went beyond any blush she'd ever seen. Were enchanters extravagant in everything?

"Oh ... *um.*" Laughing awkwardly, he snapped his fingers. He was swallowed in a burst of crimson only to reappear in an elegant suit with a sweeping crimson cloak. "Retired, you know," he said, backing slowly down the hallway as they blinked blinded eyes. "Don't really change until dinnertime usually. Just put on the robe then. Not really appropriate for company though. I'll ... *um* ... There was a letter from Lady Violetta I should probably read. ... I'll ... I'll just tell the others you're here."

"Wait!" Snow cried, but he vanished again, leaving a crimson glow to the hallway. Her heart sank as her eyes blinked away the dazzle. Were all enchanters this flighty? They had an injured man!

After a glance at Robert, still unconscious and draped between the two guards, his clothes covered in dirt and blood, Snow straightened her shoulders and marched on. "Come. We'll find a room for the duke ourselves."

"Allow me, miss." Lyndon hurried around her. "As we arrived, I saw a guest wing at the rear of the cottage."

Snow fell into step behind Lyndon, and the group bore to the left and indeed ended up at a doorway with the wide frame indicative of an outer wall that had become an inner wall after an expansion. Beyond it were two bedrooms, a small sitting room, and a stairway leading to a floor above. Suspecting the state of the bedrooms, Snow grabbed sheets and blankets from the linen closet under the stairs and followed the men into the closest room.

Under their wide-eyed stares, she deftly made the bed. As Lyndon helped the guards settle Robert into it, she inspected the room. At least the previous guest had left it fairly clean. All it currently needed was a good dusting, sweeping, and the windows washed. Not being a normal princess had some advantages: she wasn't merely a useless, pretty thing in these situations.

She peeped at Lyndon. That she must clean up after herself was one of the stipulations she'd agreed to in order to stay, that is, which Lady Violetta had agreed to on her behalf. So she was her own maid. Could she not claim to be the enchanters' new maid and stay away from Lyndon and Robert altogether? If she covered her hair and wore the plain dresses she'd packed, Robert might not recognize her at a passing glance. She'd not give him the opportunity for more than that.

"I'll find our hosts and get things sorted out," she offered.

*Tell them not to refer to me as Princess Snow.* After instructing the guards, who already knew she was traveling incognito, where to put the luggage and to help Lyndon as needed, Snow returned to the main part of the cottage, confident she would come to a sitting room eventually. The cottage was built for enchanters, and to guard their library, so its winding hallways didn't always make sense.

She soon found her destination, however, or it found her, she wasn't sure. Nonetheless, she was soon inside a large room with a cheerful fire and a multitude of seats, card tables, and musical instruments. Five men lounged about the room, their attire ranging from formal suit to wrinkled robe.

Before she could apologize for intruding, a short, round, energetic man scurried toward her. He was neatly dressed in a dark blue suit, so she hoped he wouldn't run away.

"I'm Cello," he said eagerly, bowing to her, his few strands of hair wafting at the movement. "I am the manager of the Cottage for Retired Enchanters. Let me introduce the residents."

"How do you do," Snow said quickly. "I'm afraid—"

Cello's smile shifted into the kind of sneer one gave a cockroach, and he pointed to the thin man sitting in the shadowed back corner. "This is *Who.*"

Snow gave the indicated man—whose face she couldn't see clearly thanks to the oddly thick shadows about him— the barest glance. The long-furred, gray cat in Who's lap meowed loudly, as if upset he'd been left out of the introductions. "Yes, but—" she began hastily.

"And *What.*" Cello's voice rose in pitch and desperation, as if asking, *What have I done to deserve this?* Snow was wondering the same thing, for Cello was pointing to an empty wingback chair. This was a house of enchanters, so was he implying *the chair* was the enchanter?

"Where is What?" a blond-haired, bespectacled man sitting, legs crossed and tea cup in hand, on the sofa's arm asked mildly. He wore a patched, ink-splotched scholar's robe over his clothes. Ink also stained his fingers, chin, and nose. "Has anyone found him today? I don't think I've seen him since he arrived."

"I haven't found him." The crotchety answer came from a pleasant-faced, plump man sitting a good ten feet from everyone else. The green-eyed man, who looked about fifty, continued in the same offended tone, "Why does everyone ask me that every day?"

What madhouse had Lady Violetta sent her to? Is this what magic did to one?

"Please—" she began. *We've an injured man!*

"I didn't mean you, Today," the unnamed, bespectacled questioner replied coolly. "I meant *today*, as in not yesterday."

"Of course, I'm not Yesterday," Today snapped. "We haven't had a Yesterday for years."

"Does anyone *else* know where What is?"

Desperate now, Snow searched the room for anyone with any semblance of sanity or care in their eyes.

*"I Don't Know."* Cello gestured forcefully to the bespectacled questioner before sighing dramatically and shifting his gaze to the slouched man holding down the other end of the sofa. *"I Don't Care."*

The man in a disheveled suit with untrimmed chestnut hair shrugged and gave her a half smile. "Don't mind him," he —I Don't Care—said, catching Snow's eye and rising. He straightened his wrinkled jacket and bowed to her. The frantic pace of her heart began to slow. This man was the youngest, possibly early forties in enchanter years. Mayhap the magic hadn't driven him completely mad yet, if that were the issue.

"He thinks he runs the place," the man continued, indicating Cello with a flick of his eyes. "I'm Blatherskite, by the way. And I *do* care. Just not about my appearance, which deeply offends Cello. Hence his attempt to rename me."

"It's nice to meet you, Blatherskite. Who runs the place?" *Someone sane, I hope?*

"No one runs the place," he said with an amused smile. "It just sort of sits here. I wanted to make it into a moving castle, but they said only eccentric, heart-eating wizards did that. I don't think that's true. I am not eccentric, and I detest cards."

Blatherskite continued on, but Snow, suppressing a scream of frustration, turned toward the door, and nearly walked into the silver-haired man previously in the dressing gown as he strode inside. He met her gaze, his face flushing crimson again, before he turned to the other occupants of the room.

"Do stop it." The silver-haired man held up two open letters. "Lady Violetta sent them. They're our guests." Bowing to Snow and ignoring Cello's mutter of "not finished with the act yet," he continued, earnestly, "I'm very sorry, Princess Snow. Behind on the correspondence. Retired, you know." He handed the letters off to Cello before focusing on her again.

"I missed it before in my shock, but you had an injured man with you, didn't you? Let's get him comfortable." He waved to the others, who were, either by sitting up or combing their hair, making themselves more presentable. Blatherskite was craning his neck to read the letters.

"Don't mind them," the silver-haired man continued. "People tend to come looking for us, trying to get us to do magic tricks and such for them. We put on a crazy act to keep them away. Well … that is, some of us put on an act. I'm

Colors. I won't trouble you with my true name." He gave Snow a significant look. "Those aren't necessary here."

"Thank you," she said genuinely.

"You shall be *January* so long as you are here, if that is agreeable to you?"

"'Tis an excellent name."

He smiled, and it was a kind expression that, along with his promise of aid, began to set her at ease. He motioned for her to go ahead of him into the hallway, then followed her out.

Soon, they'd collected water, medicine, and bandages; started a pot of water heating; and made their way to the guest wing.

"The injured man is Robert of Pondleigh, nephew of the king of New Beaumont, am I correct?" Colors asked as they knocked on Robert's door.

"Yes," she answered, surprised until she remembered the second letter. Was it concerning Robert?

"I thought as much."

"Were you expecting him?" she asked, working hard to keep suspicion from her tone. Had he followed her?

"Yes. He has some research to do."

Oh. Cursing her bad luck and stifling her curiosity, Snow followed Colors into Robert's room and was relieved to see he was still abed and no paler than before.

Colors introduced himself to Lyndon, and the three of them took care of Robert. Thankfully, Lyndon did the actual cleaning and stitching of the wounds.

As Snow took one bloody cloth from Lyndon and replaced it with a clean one, she chanced to glimpse Colors. She'd heard the expression "green in the gills," but he seemed to have taken it a bit far. He was positively grass-like.

"Do you need to sit down?" she asked him quietly.

"Hmm? Oh!" He touched his face and then glanced at his hand, which was also green. "I'm fine." He smiled at her, and the color vanished.

"Oh." She couldn't help drawing back, but she managed to return a smile, wary though it was, before shifting her attention back to physician and patient.

After a few more minutes, Lyndon put down his tools and let out a long breath. He sat a moment staring tiredly at Robert while Snow and Colors cleaned up. At last, he shook himself and focused on Snow.

"Please forgive me," he began, "but we didn't have a proper introduction earlier, did we?"

"I'm January. A maid." She said it quickly, placing the last of the used cloths into a crate Colors had brought as she did, as if that act of cleaning up could make it true.

"Thank you for your help, Miss January." Lyndon said no more, but Snow didn't like the odd tone in which he said it, or his examining look.

"You're welcome. I'll leave you to rest now." She took one last peek at Robert, intending it to be her last for the duration of her stay—her last ever if she could help it—and turned away. Holding the crate in front of her, she made for the door.

But the trim, spritely Lyndon dashed in front of her and divested her of her burden. "I'll take that, Miss January." Before she could protest, he backed away, moving and speaking too quickly for argument. "Would you be so kind as to stay with the duke while I return these and clean up? That would be ever so kind of you, a true act of gratitude. After all"—his gaze bored into hers, reprimanding and firm—"he did help save you from the highwaymen. And if you'd give him more of the water and medicine when he wakes? He needs rest and to regain fluids." Not waiting for a reply, he strode out as authoritatively as any king, despite the dirty rags.

Staring after him open-mouthed, Snow looked to Colors. He shrugged as if in apology for agreeing with Lyndon. She shut her mouth. Traveling incognito had its drawbacks.

"He does have a point," Colors said at last. "I'll see to a room for you. Good night, January."

Snow watched him go, then stiffened her spine. Grabbing one of the clean cloths left behind, she used it as a kerchief to cover her dark hair. She'd taken a few moments earlier to change into a clean, plain dress, since she didn't want to bring any more dirt into the sick room. Between the plain gown and kerchief, she had a feeling Robert wouldn't recognize her. He'd forgotten her for four years. Why would he remember her now? Well, recognize her away from the throne, something he apparently found appealing.

Telltale raven-colored hair concealed, she pushed a comfortable-looking padded armchair against the wall and settled down, hoping Lyndon wouldn't take too long.

Sometime later, Lyndon still missing, Robert began to stir. His face was a touch pink, so she dampened a cloth with cool water and wiped his face and neck to cool him. Instead of it easing him back to sleep, his eyes fluttered open.

"Who are you?" he asked groggily.

Heart pounding despite herself, Snow stilled and let his unfocused gaze roam her face. *Do you remember me, Robert? Without all my finery? Me, Snow?*

His eyes, such a beautiful, striking blue, swept over her face and then focused on her mouth and stayed there.

He wasn't even trying to see *her*.

Scoffing, she turned away and began mixing his pain medication and water in a cup. Apparently, he'd gotten worse rather than better with age. The thought, for some reason she didn't want to consider, hurt. Snow's hand fisted around the cup. Robert of Pondleigh—either the version her young self had idealized or the true one—had no part in her future life. Nor did marriage to anyone, and there was no point in repining.

Setting her jaw, she returned to Robert and lifted the cup to his lips. "Drink this and sleep."

# CHAPTER 3

There was something Robert was supposed to be doing. Not die? No, that wasn't it. That was generally a good thing though, so maybe he had more than one *something* he was supposed to be doing?

Water trailed from his forehead to his ear. Come in out of the rain?

Robert managed to open one eye to a face-like blur of black, white, and red. "Who are you?" he rasped, realizing at the same time she was likely a nurse, for he was in pain, a great deal of it, and the wetness was from a damp cloth. He blinked and tried to bring the face into focus. It lost a bit of its haze, and his heart leapt. Princess Snow?

He searched the face again, fearing he was dreaming. His gaze caught on her mouth. There was a strange luster to her lips. Not quite like lip rouge. Not that she had any reason to wear that. Her lips had always been a striking red. This was different, a bit like magic. Why? She needed no magic to make her beautiful. Perhaps he was dreaming still.

The lady scoffed and turned away. A moment later she

turned back with a glass, which she brought to his lips. "Drink this and sleep."

Her voice was commanding. Robert obeyed.

◈

THE LIGHT COMING in the open window was pale moonlight when Robert woke again, his mind cloudy still. He shifted and a moan escaped as agony cleared away some of the haze. A face-like blur hovered over him again, even less clear in the dim lighting than before. But it wasn't Lyndon, and that worried him. "Who are you? Where's Lyndon?"

"I'm the maid. Lyndon's resting for a few minutes in the next room. You're both safe. You're at the Cottage for Retired Enchanters."

"You're the maid?" He blinked as she moved a lamp closer to better inspect him. "You look familiar." There was something familiar about her voice too. If only he could wake properly. His mind kept telling him she was Princess Snow, but he didn't trust it fully at the moment. Not to confirm what he most desired. He kept blinking and straining against the lamp's glare and the glare's shadows.

"I am the maid," she said with a strange sternness just as his eyes confirmed what his heart wished.

"Pr—" he began excitedly as he struggled to sit up, but she pushed him back down.

"You may call me *January.*"

January? Robert's smile fell as confusion took him. "Of a frosty disposition, are we?" he teased, expecting her to laugh and cease her ploy.

"Yes," she said crisply, holding up a glass for him. "Drink this and sleep. You've lost a fair amount of blood and upset a previous injury."

Robert stared at her dumbly as she brought the cup to his lips. Did she really think to pass herself off as a stranger to him?

*She's going to drug you again, idiot. Did you learn nothing from the frog incident? Open mouths are dangerous.* Calling up his wits, Robert pressed his lips together and sank lower into the pillows.

Snow startled, then lifted the cup to his lips again. "Drink, my lord."

Murmuring a refusal, he gave his head a slight shake.

Her brows furrowed, and they repeated the process once more before she sat back. "Would you prefer something else to drink? You need liquids."

Lips still pressed tight together, he motioned toward a chair against the wall some feet away. It held a blanket, so he guessed it to be her chair of choice for when she wasn't actively "nursing" him.

Her eyebrows lifted, but she set the cup on the bedstand and retreated to the chair.

"I'm getting up," he said. "I'll find something myself." Something not drugged.

Snow crossed her arms. "No, you're not."

"Yes, I am," he retorted and began pushing himself up. Busted mirrors but it hurt to move. Not to mention it brought enough black spots for a murder of crows to his vision.

"No," she said with a certain amused smugness. "You're not because you're not properly healed, and you're certainly not properly clothed."

Robert froze, suddenly registering that the fabric brushing his lower half wasn't trousers but sheets. *Oh no...*

"And if you're not clothed and I'm here..."

Robert sank into the pillows and yanked the blanket up to

his chin. "Lyndon put you up to this, didn't he?" he growled. His legs were already beginning to ache from inactivity and he couldn't leave the bed, much less the room!

Snow's lips pursed and her fingers tapped a rhythm against the chair arms. "He may have reminded me that the safety of myself and my men is due to you and that the least I could do was force you to stay still long enough to heal."

"No thanks are required. Feel free to leave for your own chamber."

"I believe thanks *are* required." Lyndon stepped lightly into the room, ignoring Robert's glare, and pulled up a chair against the wall opposite Snow's. With a contented sigh, he settled into it, stretched out his legs, rested his hands on his trim stomach, and generally seemed as if he were settled in for a long visit. He smiled mildly. "Pleasant dreams, you two."

"How do you expect me to sleep with the two of you in here?" Robert protested. "It's indecent, I tell you."

"Miss January is your nurse, and I am here, and others are down the hall."

January again? Robert's gaze snapped to Snow but shifted to the cuckoo clock on the mantel at her glower. She really intended to be known as January, didn't she? A maid? Robert thought back to the carriage. It hadn't been the royal carriage, come to think of it. Perhaps she was traveling incognito for some reason. She'd said they were at the Cottage for Retired Enchanters. Had she come to learn something of magic to protect the kingdom from Prince Dokar? Or simply to get away from the palace—and possibly him—for the summer? Or was there some other reason?

As for the former possibility, he sincerely hoped this Cottage for Retired Enchanters held as many answers as it did questions. But first was the little matter of him turning into a frog at midnight.

"There's not an elderly lady here, is there?" he asked hopefully. He knew better than to try to talk about the curse. Or to ask Snow, sitting with her arms crossed and something of the look of a captured enemy general in her expression, for a kiss.

"No."

Robert bit back an ungentlemanly expression. "Well," he said after a moment's thought. "I guess I'll just have to bear the sight of a pretty nurse"—he risked a peek at Snow and then turned to scowl at Lyndon—"and an old mother goat."

Lyndon merely gave him that same infuriating mild smile. "Good night, Your Grace. Miss January."

❧

IT WAS TOUGHER than he wanted to admit, but Robert managed to look asleep but not actually, not quite, sleep for the next two hours. When the little cuckoo—cruelly a home to a menagerie of polished wooden frogs—chimed ten past midday, he heard Lyndon rise and softly leave the room. Finally, a useful trait in his dear Lyndon! Letter writing every evening.

Hearing nothing but Snow's steady breathing and the wind softly rustling leaves, he began to push himself up.

A lantern flared to brilliance, and Snow looked past it with a silent, but forceful scold.

"I have to go to the bathroom."

"Do you?" Arms crossed, Snow raised an eyebrow at him.

"Yes."

She kept that "You'd better rethink your answer if you're fibbing" look pinned on him. The woman had a formidable glare. He almost felt sorry for their future children. They weren't going to be able to get away with anything.

"Don't you ever have to go?"

Snow opened her mouth, then snapped it shut.

"Just as I thought. You are human."

With a huff, she rose and picked up the little bell on the side table to ring for Lyndon.

"Must you rob me of my dignity? I don't need help, much less witnesses. What do you think I'll do when you're not watching? Run circles around the room? I'm not a dog." *But if I don't get out, I'll be a frog.* He grinned sheepishly. "Please."

Pursing her lips, she put the bell down and walked out of the room and pulled the door to behind her. "I *will* come back in there if I think you're up to something," she called back through the ornately carved door.

"I don't doubt it, matron." Steeling himself and moving slowly due to the black spots afflicting his vision, Robert eased into a sitting position and began sliding the window behind him further up. He'd realized at some point after Lyndon called Snow his nurse that he didn't need a barmaid or any loss of honor. All he needed was to get to a farmhouse. There was bound to be one nearby with a little girl of about three or four. His niece was always playing doctor and giving out kisses as medicine, when she wasn't "sawing" off his toes, that is. All he had to do was find such a home, collapse on the doorstep with enough noise to wake them all, and give them a true story about a highwaymen attack. Children loved him. Naturally, a little girl would want to help her parents tend him and would offer him a kiss. He could do this all the way to New Beaumont to his aunt, then he'd bring her back and woo Snow and find out how to destroy Dokar.

As he paused to bite his lips against the pain in his side, a draft from the half-open window reminded him of his attire, or lack thereof. But there was bound to be clothes of some kind in the stable, possibly even his own in his saddle bags. All he had to manage was getting away from his guards. Tucking a blanket about his lower half, he slid his feet off the bed and sat up.

"Your Grace?"

"I'm still getting out of bed. Woozy, you know." He added in a mutter, "That's what lying in bed will do to you." Using the bedstand as a brace, he pushed himself up and then arranged the water pitcher so as to pour slowly into the bedpan. That done, he climbed back onto the bed, opened the blessedly quiet window further, and began climbing out.

He was half out when the door swung open.

"Robert!" Snow's screech of surprise and exasperation was followed by a decidedly upset, but unsurprised, cry from Lyndon.

Robert fell the rest of the way out, staggered up by pure adrenaline, and shuffled toward the stables, clutching the blanket to him. *I refuse to be a frog. I refuse to be a frog.* He countered his body's screams for him to stop and the yelled commands of Snow from the window and from Lyndon rounding the corner of the cottage behind him. *You can make it to the stables and Firethorn. He'll be your legs soon. Go, Robert.*

"Stop, Robert! Or we'll—"

"You won't tackle me! I'm injured!" *You can do it. Just one more step, one more.*

"We don't have to," said a voice Robert didn't recognize.

A blast of magic hit him from behind, and everything went as vibrant as a rainbow before being swallowed by a darkness that wasn't the night sky.

ROBERT BLINKED awake as a blaze of light filled the room.

"Oh dear." Lady Violetta, dressed in an enormous crimson gown, appeared beside the bed, and he couldn't help but wonder: Did doorways expand to let her and her dresses through? Or did she magically transport herself everywhere to prevent getting indecorously stuck in doorways?

He blinked again as the light faded to mere pale sunlight.

"Good morning, Lady Violetta," he said, vaguely aware that his voice sounded a little more croaky than usual, even for him in the early morning. "As I doubt 'Oh dear' was a greeting, I'd like you to know that despite a fainting episode yesterday, and despite what Lyndon likely told you, I am rapidly regaining strength." He tried to sit up but somehow ended up on his back staring at the ceiling. "I think." Perhaps his body hadn't woken yet. Or gotten over whatever magic the cowardly enchanter who had taken him down from behind had used on him.

"Yes…" she said, ignoring his greeting. "This does present a problem." She flipped through a small book that reminded him of a naturalist guide to something or other. His gaze fell to her dress, which was hard to miss, especially with the bits of magic about it.

When he'd been looking for the poisoners and enchanters possibly involved in the assassination attempt on his uncle—which had also injured Rupert and himself and led to him falling under Lucrezia's control spell—he'd had to teach himself to see magic. It had come in handy on more than one occasion. Now, it just made him wonder, for it seemed as if Lady Violetta's gown was pinned together rather than sewn, as if she were called away during a fitting and used magic to hold the dress together rather than take the time to change.

"Yes…" she said again as she flipped another page.

But the woman's attire was none of his concern.

Receiving her properly was. Robert began the arduous task of sitting up while continuing to use the blanket as his robe.

As Robert struggled, three things came to his attention. The first was that he wasn't in pain, and he rather thought he should be. Second, the bed was enormous. Had they moved him to a room built for a giant to make it harder for him to escape? And third, they'd apparently put him in green pajamas, for he kept seeing green as he moved.

Wait. Dokar had said he would turn into…

"A spring peeper," Lady Violetta announced, lowering the book to her lap, "one of the smallest of the frogs. Be sure to keep all birds, cats, and snakes out of the room, Lyndon. And give him the proper food."

Letting out an unmanly whimper—what did manliness matter anyway when he was a frog?—Robert lifted a long, green leg. He could easily lift the appendage higher than his head, but that didn't improve his mood any.

"Well," Lady Violetta said with fake cheerfulness as Robert flexed his webbed toes, "at least you can still speak like a man. I don't suppose you can tell us what happened when you met with Prince Dokar? He cursed you, obviously, but what were the terms of it?"

Not bothering to tell the enchantress one couldn't speak of one's own curses, Robert started talking, and wasn't surprised when his intelligence seemed as understandable to them as *ribbet, ribbet*. Which was probably what they heard.

If only he'd been made a beast instead. That at least was a respectable curse!

Lady Violetta held up a hand, and Robert shushed. "Would you mind starting over again? You speak as a frog when talking of your curse," she said, and then she disappeared. A lithe speckled blue frog appeared on the bed half a foot from him. Taking the sudden transformation in stride, he repeated his tale—and it occurred to him he didn't have a tail, which all proper beasts did. Rupert claimed it helped greatly with balance. Robert fancied it would be useful as a club or whip as well, if the need arose.

The blue frog bobbed its head every now and then, and when Robert was finished, it hopped off the bed and Lady Violetta reappeared.

"That is most frustrating," she said with a commiserating shake of her head as she sat, carefully arranging her skirts around her. "But don't expect me to come to your rescue every morning."

Rescue? "This isn't permanent?" he asked, almost afraid to hope.

"Well, yes, unless you do something about it every day." She scooped him up, kissed the top of his head, and quickly placed him back under the covers.

A green haze surrounded him, and he shivered as that slimy feel woke inside him, spread as if reaching to gather its scattered self up, then retreated. The haze vanished.

Robert—real, human Robert—breathed a prayer of gratitude and stretched out under the covers. "Thank you, Lady Violetta." He flinched at an unwelcome message from his side. The pain was back. A small price, however.

She smiled kindly. "Just remember: I can't come to your rescue every morning. You'll have to learn to fend for yourself—respectably—soon."

"Will someone kindly explain this to me?" Lyndon asked in evident frustration. With a laugh of apology, the enchantress obliged. "I'll send for his aunt," Lyndon said quickly as she finished.

"Yes. There is, of course, Princess Snow." She held up her hand as if to protest what she'd just suggested. "I'm afraid I cannot recommend asking her for a kiss, or even wooing her for herself. I'm positive she'd not be easily won, and that not without some danger."

Robert sat up, automatically pulling the blanket up with him. "Danger? Is someone threatening her?"

He almost thought there was something sly in Lady Violetta's eyes before she said, in a melancholy tone, "I'm not at liberty to divulge the issues poor Princess Snow and Queen Solstice are facing."

Robert narrowed his eyes at her, but she merely shrugged helplessly, so he turned his thoughts to the princess and queen. He'd never noticed any magic about the queen, despite the rumors she and not a jealous sorcerer had killed King Theodore. He did vaguely remember a bit of magic about Snow last night. No, he'd seen magic about *January*. The princess pretending to be a maid, who'd found another way to not acknowledge his presence. She'd not want assistance from him.

*You couldn't help your cousin. What makes you think you can help Snow, even if she wanted it? You'll be lucky to free yourself.* Robert winced and shut his eyes against the ache in his body and his soul. Rupert had been like a brother to him, but then he'd practically cut him off after his injury during the assassination attempt and during his curse. It had taken every ounce of Robert's loyalty and love to keep trying year after year to talk with Rupert in more than the occasional letter, to try to talk sense into him so he'd give up his curse and be prince and friend again. Rupert had since apologized, but Robert didn't want to go through that again. Snow had rejected him; it was time he forgot about her. He was a warrior, but while part of that made him want to keep fighting to win her, part of that was also knowing what battles to fight.

"*January*," he said bitterly, "doesn't want anything to do

with me. She'd not let me help. *She* would be the danger in trying to woo her."

"You're a fighter, Robert," Lyndon scolded. "If this girl is important to you, fight for her."

"She's refused me, and I must respect that."

"The queen gave you permission to try again by sending you here," Lyndon pressed. "You know your uncle and her father wanted the two of you to marry. Princess Snow, when she was fourteen, knew what it meant when she, a princess, agreed to correspond with you, a man of royal blood and the choice of her stepmother and late father. However such a thing might be worked out among the commoners, where relationships are less pre-decided, between the two of you, it requires an actual verbal or written declaration to sever the relationship all parties involved expected to lead to marriage. Princess Snow has rudely—cowardly—refused to give that. She hasn't *technically* rejected you."

Robert rolled his eyes. He was pretty sure her hiding in her room when he came to visit constituted a rejection. He wasn't even sure anymore why he wanted to win her, not the cold, ungracious Snow he'd met the previous day and hadn't met at all the four days he spent at her castle. The one too cowardly or cruel to officially break what Lyndon was right in calling a tacit engagement. She wasn't the only beautiful woman he knew. He could find a woman both beautiful and kind, virtuous and brave. One who *liked* him. One who would delight in his presence rather than one whose love consisted solely in keeping him alive if injured.

Yet … underneath the sting of her current behavior was the memory of the Snow he'd once known from visits over the years and from their letters. Was it possible to find her again? That was something worth fighting for.

"Of course," Lady Violetta began, her expression decidedly sly now, "*January* hasn't rejected you. She doesn't even know you yet."

"But—" January ... a time of new beginnings. *Are you telling me to keep fighting, Lord?* January... Robert grinned. Strategy was part of war too, wasn't it? They'd been thrown together. Why not take advantage of it? To win her heart, her freedom from whatever she and Solstice faced ... and his own freedom. Robert's breath caught. "January is a *betrothed* princess," he blurted. Dokar had said the first kiss of a betrothed princess would free him.

"So she is," she replied with a careless shrug.

His burgeoning hope flickered out. "But what if even January won't talk to me?"

"How you do worry!" Shaking her head fondly, Lady Violetta rose and offered Robert her hand. He took it. "A kiss is a precious thing," she said, her gaze surprisingly solemn. "A first kiss a powerful one." She gave his hand a gentle squeeze. "Be patient, Robert, as well as cunning."

When he nodded, Lady Violetta released his hand and smoothed out her gown, one finger resting momentarily on a magic-shrouded seam. The fingers of her other hand, wrapped around her wand, tapped thoughtfully, each tap sending a different color of light racing along the wand's silver shaft. The tapping stopped, the flares stopped. A violet glow engulfed her, and she vanished.

*A first kiss...*

Robert's grin withered under the scorching effect of a felt glare on the side of his face. "What?" he asked in confusion as he turned to meet Lyndon's glower head on.

"Just where *were* you going last night?" Lyndon demanded, his expression fierce father. "I'd assumed you were determined to have another go at Prince Dokar, but now I'm concerned—"

"I was hunting an Emmy!" Robert blurted his niece's nickname, feeling the heat of embarrassment rising to his cheeks.

"An Emmy..." Lyndon's confusion quickly cleared and turned into a burst of laughter. When it finally ended, Lyndon gave him another paternal smile, one more fond than fierce this time. "If only you had as much sense when it comes to taking care of your wounds." He pulled a long bronze key from his coat pocket and walked to the door. "You're still staying locked in here until I say otherwise, you know."

"Lyndon!" Robert cried, but the beloved bane-of-his-existence was already outside, the key clicking in the lock.

Grumbling, Robert settled back against the pillows. Some minutes later, a note with a slim blue ribbon wrapped around it appeared in his lap with a violet poof. Robert hastily opened it.

"I altered your Selective Deafening Spell so it would work while you're a frog too," he read aloud. Why would being a frog change the deafening spell's effectiveness? Robert shrugged but mentally thanked Lady Violetta for her thoroughness.

# CHAPTER 4

S
now left her upstairs bedroom early the next
morning to find one of the retired enchanters—
Today, if she remembered rightly—bouncing on his
heels on the seventh step from the top.

"*Um*, good morning, Today." She watched him warily
from the landing.

"Good morning, January." Despite his crotchety appearance the previous night, he seemed bright and cheerful this
morning, his pleasant, round face finally matching his tone
of voice. He moved up a step and began bouncing again. "In
case you're wondering, I'm putting a Squeaking Spell on the
stairs as a warning to you of anyone coming up. A lady
should have her privacy. They won't squeak for you though."

"That's very kind of you."

"Is anyone else staying up here I should include in the
non-squeak category?" He moved up a step and bounced on
that one.

"It's just me. I sent my guards to stay at the village. I know
you don't like many guests." She'd also instructed her guards

to handle the matter of the highwaymen and send a report to the palace. That sort of thing needed to be dealt with. Guagin insisted the roads were perfectly safe. Bankor told her not to worry her pretty little head over anything but him. Houen and some of the other nobles, those most likely to listen to her and Solstice, had suffered from various illnesses and setbacks over the past few years and weren't as active as they once were.

"No lady's maid?"

"No," she said, and was grateful when Today didn't comment on the oddness of that. It was likely evident in the simpleness of her hairstyles and gowns, so perhaps he was just confirming a suspicion.

"That makes it easy. Just a minute, then I'll show you to the kitchen." His eyes twinkled as he grinned up at her. "Hope you can cook. Everyone looks after themselves here. It's in the rules."

He soon met her on the landing and offered her his arm. She slipped her arm through his, and he escorted her down, his steps squeaking at every tread, making her smile.

After a few twists and turns and orders for the house to behave itself, he left her slack-jawed at the kitchen door. The kitchen was spacious and bright, and was as covered with dust as teacups.

Wrinkling her nose, Snow strode up to the counter that claimed over a quarter of the room's wall space. It was a lengthy surface whose granite top she barely saw under the quantity of teacups and saucers strewn about in singles and haphazard piles, some stacked as high as seven sets. A residue of coffee, and an occasional fainter one of tea, stained each cup and scented the air. She drew her gaze slowly over the counter and sink again. Eighty-seven. *Eighty-*

*seven* dirty cups and saucers! Plus three plates, a bowl, and the accompanying cutlery.

Tying the apron she'd brought around her waist, she set to work clearing a path to the sink. At least there was a worktable in the center of the room she could use for now.

From something Today said, she gathered the enchanters used magic to get their domestic needs taken care of by servants back at their own estates. Despite Today's implication, she strongly suspected one or more of the enchanters used this kitchen for coffee and tea. Grimacing, she set a cup with a dark brown smudge in its bowl onto one of the shorter piles, bringing the stack up to three. Could she politely hint they get these taken care of by magic at home too?

As Snow was kneading dough a half hour later, a flash of light behind her made her lose count of her strokes.

"What a delightful apron!" exclaimed a decidedly feminine voice. "I've always said there is no reason not to wear beautiful dresses for all tasks so long as one properly protects them."

"Lady Violetta!" Hastily brushing clinging dough and flour from her gloved hands, Snow spun around to greet the enchantress. Lady Violetta might be a bit flighty at times, but she'd always been kind to Snow and Solstice and wore such magnificent clothes. And gifted the latter as well.

This morning, the enchantress's gown was a deep crimson, wide and flowing. A silver fur shrug covered her shoulders. Snow wasn't crazy about moving about in a gown like that, but… "It's lovely," she said appreciatively as she admired it a moment longer.

Lady Violetta gave her a pleased smile, twisting to better show off the gown's shimmer. "I was thinking of adding gemstones to the front. What do you think? An accent to match the shrug? Perhaps in the shape of a rose?"

Snow considered the dress a moment. The skirt was broad and the fitted bodice of a rich material, but otherwise it was elegantly simple. "I like it as it is, but gemstones would make it even more striking." She shook her head. "Either way, I love it."

Snow, at her stepmother's suggestion, tended to dress in simple gowns so as to not attract any more attention to herself than necessary. Gowns that also covered more skin than was fashionable, more skin than pleasant on warm summer days. Snow understood why but still yearned for the chance to wear such frivolous, gorgeously feminine things. What would it feel like to have sun and wind on her bare arms and ungloved hands? To touch another without fear?

The enchantress gave her that pleased smile again and clasped her hands in front of her. "How are you faring, my dear?"

Snow laughed as she looked about the kitchen. "'Tis too early to tell." She may have dishes to wash, but she didn't have to put up with the advisors here. While she felt bad about leaving Solstice to deal with them alone, she had done what she could for her stepmother and the kingdom by reminding the widowed Guagin what she'd do to him if he tried to force a marriage with Solstice. It was a relief to be free of him and the few court men who fancied themselves in love with her—Bankor, in particular. The plain dresses and reclusive tendencies hadn't had enough of an effect. Speaking of, if only Robert weren't here she might have a peaceful summer.

Snow narrowed her eyes at Lady Violetta. "Did you know the Duke of Pondleigh was coming here?"

"Of course." Lady Violetta waved her hand dismissively. "I

recommended he come." Catching Snow's glare, she quickly added, "I suggested it for when he was well enough to do so. But as my dear Princess Belinda says, Robert's idea of 'well enough' is 'not dead.' So I didn't know *exactly* when he'd arrive."

Snow narrowed her eyes a little more, just in case Lady Violetta had any ideas about her and Robert. "I'm inclined to agree with Princess Belinda in that observation."

Lady Violetta returned her scrutiny with an innocent look before reaching into the cuff of her glove and drawing out a handkerchief. "Most people do agree with her, without compulsion too. Prince Rupert certainly does. I made an exceptionally lovely and useful dress for Princess Belinda, you know, once upon a time. Unfortunately, that odious Prince Dokar ruined it. But speaking of dresses, Queen Solstice asked me to make you one. So I need measurements." Lady Violetta held up the square of silky white fabric. "Kiss this for me, will you?"

Heart hammering almost too loudly to think, Snow backtracked into the counter, one hand covering her mouth.

Lady Violetta gave her a reassuring smile. "I'll be careful." Another layer of satin gloves materialized around Lady Violetta's hands and buttoned themselves at her wrist with elegant pearl buttons.

Snow glanced between the cloth, the gloves, and Lady Violetta's confident expression, then sighed. She pushed away from the counter and took the cloth. "I never knew one needed an imprint of lips for a gown." But what was one more failed attempt to uncurse her? It wouldn't work, and she could still help Solstice.

Lady Violetta shrugged. "My gowns are unique. I'm not promising anything, mind, but that they will be beautiful. But one never knows, does one?"

Snow folded the cloth in half and pressed her lips over the fold. A black imprint appeared. Grimacing, she carefully folded the cloth until the part she'd kissed was hidden. She handed it carefully to the enchantress. "I mean no offense, Lady Violetta, but I can't find it in myself to hope for anything, so you needn't worry about disappointing me. I've tried it all already. The anti-spell potions, the magic lipstick, the counter-curses, but still the spell seer says—that's what Colors is, isn't he?" she interrupted herself at the sudden realization. "He turns crimson whenever he sees me, and that's not because he's bashful and blushing, is it? It's because he's sensing the curse?"

"Yes, dear," Lady Violetta said, her face brightening. "How clever of you to recognize it! He's a special type of spell seer. Curses from envy and hate tend to show red, he says. The sorcerer who followed your stepmother to New Grimmland was certainly envious of and murderously hateful toward your father. Isn't he charming? Colors, I mean."

"Yes, he is very nice. Why does he turn green for Robert?" Not that she cared. Unless Robert's curse was catching, of course.

Lady Violetta smiled cheerfully and glanced about the room, sparing a moment to appreciatively pat the lump of dough and then wipe her hand of flour. "Yes, that is very curious," she said at last, stepping away from the counter to survey the backyard through one of the windows. "I wonder what color he would have turned before—" She cleared her throat and faced Snow again. "I'm afraid I am not currently at liberty to divulge Robert's ... challenges. But if he asks you to kiss him..."

Snow raised her eyebrows, then crossed her arms. "It would tempt me to say *yes*."

"Now, Snow dear—" Lady Violetta began, her violet eyes wide with alarm.

"I wouldn't, don't worry." Snow added softly, pain nearly stealing her voice, "I know better."

Lady Violetta eyed her a moment, then asked, "How are the gloves I made you holding out?"

Pulling herself back to the present, out of the cold horror of the day she took an apple from an old soldier and her father "died," Snow held up her hands. She wiggled her fingers in their thin, wonderfully flexible, easy-to-clean leather gloves, her constant companions. "They're still the best gift I've ever received."

Lady Violetta's expression brightened again, and her dress sparkled to match. "I knew they would be. I know you avoid touching others in case that draws out the poison, but have you ever touched an animal? Most spells are by nature only effective on humans." Her mouth snapped shut, and she blinked as if in sudden realization.

"Well, I must be going," she said quickly as a glow gave her wand a silver halo. "I must speak to Robert again for a moment and then be on my way. So many projects to work on! Oh! ... So do you." She tsked as she took in the stacks of cups and saucers before turning back to Snow.

"It was delightful to see you, Snow dear." The building glow of Lady Violetta's wand suddenly dimmed. "Oh! How is you-know-who? I was already considering an outfit for him when your mother wrote me about one for you."

"Please do! He's doing well. As well as can be expected, considering," Snow amended, a familiar guilt attacking her.

"Hmm. Do greet him for me when next you visit." Lady Violetta patted her arm before giving her a strangely serious look. "You may not have hope now, dearest, but you have persistence, and, sometimes, that's more important.

You've struggled so long, you can't see an end to your pain. It will come, and you will be the stronger for having waited and fought. And do think about the animal bit." She disappeared, and a square of paper fluttered to the floor in her place.

Blatherskite, in the same slouchy outfit as the night before, padded up to it from nowhere, picked it up, and handed it to her, all before Snow had finished her start of surprise. Was the sound of footsteps forbidden in some enchanter code?

"Goodbye, Lady Violetta. Good morning, January." He smiled lazily, set a coffee-stained cup and saucer on top of an overturned cup in the small row of clean cups drying, and left as suddenly as he'd appeared.

Frowning after him, January opened the note. *A song for enchanting the woodland animals into helping about the house.* Snow contemplated the pile of cups and saucers, then slipped the spell into her apron pocket. She had a feeling enchanted woodland animals would be more trouble than help.

❦

SNOW, breakfast tray in hand, paused outside Robert's door and took a few deep breaths. The image of Robert bloody and unconscious had been harder to dismiss from her thoughts the previous night than she'd expected. If Colors hadn't stopped the stubborn fool from whatever fool plan he'd concocted … She scrunched her eyes shut and took another breath. The brave, handsome, heroically injured man thrust into her care was also a crown-grabbing louse and deserter. The latter characteristics were what she needed to focus on. What *January* needed to focus on. Not on whether she'd gotten all the flour off her nose or whether he liked her cooking.

Imagining herself with a heart of ice, Snow rapped on the door. "Are you decent?"

"Ha ha." Robert's response bellowed moodily through the door.

Not bothering to restrain her chuckles, Snow balanced the tray in one hand and used the other to unlock the door with the key Lyndon had given her earlier that morning. "Then you have two seconds to get into bed."

She opened the door and marched in, cautiously glancing around, but Robert was actually in the bed, nearly hidden under the blankets.

"The prisoner is still here," he said sourly.

"I'm glad of it."

"Really?" he asked, his tone one of surprised pleasure. He cleared his throat and added gruffly, "I mean, why? It's more work for you. And you have that old nanny goat Lyndon bossing you around."

"I wonder how that charming old nanny goat ever got mixed up with the likes of you," she said drily as she placed the tray's legs on either side of him.

"Animals flock together, I suppose," he muttered.

"What?"

"Nothing."

She narrowed her eyes at him for good measure and retreated to her chair, in which she'd left a few dust rags. "Where is he?"

*Animals flock* ... A familiar ache twisted her heart. Could she touch animals without harming them? She didn't like to admit it, but she slept with a stuffed bear just so she could safely hug *something*, touch something with her bare hands.

"He went to the village to mail letters and get food

supplies. Are you going to watch me eat?" Robert asked in exasperation as she picked up the rags.

"I'm to remain here to make sure you eat and drink."

"I'm not the hunger strike type." Despite his annoyed tone, there was a clear distress in his gaze as he looked down at the blanket that would likely slip to his waist if he sat up to eat, uncovering a bare chest. She wasn't about to spoon feed him to avoid the issue. She also didn't care to have his chest, which was rather muscular where it wasn't hidden by bandages, in view.

"I'll get you another sheet to use like a shawl so you won't catch a chill."

"How about a shirt and trousers?"

"I think you know the answer to that."

"Yes?"

"No."

Snow procured another sheet and draped it over his shoulders and turned away to gather her cleaning rags, giving him time to make himself respectable, albeit ridiculous. Soon, he was eating and she was wiping away years of dust.

"So, are you new here?" Robert asked as she dampened a cloth with water from the pitcher to keep the dust from flying.

"Yes."

"If your position only entailed cooking delicious meals like this and cleaning, I'd say I'm eternally grateful you're here. I wasn't looking forward to cooking for myself and Lyndon. Or worse, eating Lyndon's cooking."

Her lips quirked. "So you're not grateful I'm here?"

"You are the bars to my prison, Miss January. Drop that part of your job, and I shall be."

"I believe you'll find, Your Grace, that I share that honor with January."

Snow jumped a third time that morning as Colors walked into the room, red and green flashing over his face as he glanced between her and Robert.

Robert nearly lost a piece of bacon as his mouth fell open. He quickly recovered and finished chewing in a polite manner, though his eyes, keen and suspicious, bounced between her and Colors. Colors's skin faded to a normal tone, and Snow noticed he held three hefty tomes.

"I'm Colors," the enchanter said with a kind smile that, added to the twinkle of his eyes and his gentlemanly demeanor, made her want to adopt him as a grandfather, or perhaps an uncle, for he didn't seem that old despite the silver of his hair. "Lady Violetta suggested you two might find these useful." He set the volumes on a table still slightly damp from Snow's cleaning.

"Is it just me, or are you a bit green about the gills, Colors?" Robert asked in a pointed tone.

Colors smiled wryly and slipped his hands into the pockets of an elegant suit she'd not noticed pockets in before. Had he merely put a glamour over his dressing gown? "It's just you, Your Grace."

Robert's expression suggested confirmation, which gave Snow an unpleasant feeling. Was Robert really cursed too? "Wh—" she began.

"If you don't find answers in those books," Colors interrupted with a slight shake of his head, "I can look for more, or take you to the library once you're well enough."

"I'm well enough now!" Robert protested.

"Some of those volumes are very heavy, Your Grace," Colors said with amusement. "You'd better build up your strength by eating a full breakfast." He looked meaningfully at the half-full plate, gave Snow a slight bow, and left, promising to check on them later.

Grumbling, Robert returned his attention to his meal. "It's not as if I wasn't already broken-hearted," he muttered between enormous bites of egg. "Must everyone convince me I'm a weakling now too?"

"No one is accusing you of being a weakling. We simply want you to exercise a little common sense." Snow added in a mutter of her own, "I can see by your appetite how broken-hearted you are."

The next bite stopped a hairsbreadth from his mouth. "Of course I'm eating! I'm being bullied into it! And you didn't ask," he said pointedly after she turned away to indulge in an eye roll, "but I'm Robert, Duke of Pondleigh, nephew to King Patrick of New Beaumont."

"I don't think that's any reason to be heartbroken." She couldn't stop a scoff. "Unless it's because Prince Rupert finally turned back up."

"*That*," he said with surprising sharpness, "is reason to rejoice. I am *not* a crown grabber. If you'll allow me to continue?"

Taken aback, she nodded and began washing a window to avoid the feel of his scrutiny.

"Thank you. Princess Snow—she is your princess, correct?" he asked, and when Snow nodded, he continued, "Princess Snow and I once corresponded. She hasn't answered my letters in over four years. Very rude of her, I think."

*What letters?* "During which time," Snow couldn't help retorting, giving her scrub of the window extra force, "rumor had it you might become heir to New Beaumont, since Prince Rupert was nowhere to be seen." *I'm no fool, Robert. The timing of the breaking of our correspondence and your visit coincide too well with the period you had reason to think yourself a future king without the need to marry me. Matches too well with the timing of when I told you about the real me.* Another bitter comment found its way to her tongue, and she didn't even try to stop it. "As soon as he turned up again in New Beaumont, *you* suddenly turned up in New Grimmland to court a crown princess." *Desperate enough for a crown now to marry a princess you could never kiss?*

The back of Snow's head felt decidedly hot, and when she finally turned around in the following silence, she was met with an intense glare in stormy blue.

"Do you know her?" he asked now that he had her full attention. "Or do you take up for her out of female camaraderie?"

Snow lifted her chin. Robert's glare might have the force of a gale, but she was not one to be blown about by the wind. "I served at the palace for years. I know an innocent party when I see one."

"Female camaraderie then."

Snow sucked in a breath. Ignoring her, he continued, "Anyway, during which time I was hunting for those involved in the assassination attempt on my uncle, which also injured my cousin and myself. I was also dealing with an … illness of my own. I am only now somewhat recovered."

Snow's building anger puffed out. Robert had been ill for four years? She shook herself. No. She'd heard tales of his exploits during that time. He might have been sick of her, but he wasn't sick all those four years. "You probably wouldn't even recognize her if you saw her," she said, barely keeping the sourness from her tone as she turned back to the window.

"Oh, I don't know about that. Her beauty is unmistakable."

*Her crown, you mean.* She scrubbed harder, glaring at the reflection of Robert, whose lips twitched suspiciously. Probably trying to curve into one of those sappy smiles of his at the thought of "his" beautiful princess. "You probably did nothing but stare dumbly at her during your visits ... to memorize her beauty so you'd always recognize her."

"The first time we met after she'd grown up a bit I was only seventeen!" he protested, rattling dishes as he straightened. He stilled and added with dignity, "And I was suffering from a head injury from a thwarted attack on the way over. If I did stare *dumbly* at her, it was due to a concussion and a respectful awe." He added in a mumble, "Can't a man acknowledge a woman's beauty without her getting self-righteously offended?"

"Don't you have a breakfast to eat?"

"I'm finished. Unless you want to make me another one?"

"No."

He shrugged. "It was worth a try."

Frowning at him, Snow cleared away the breakfast dishes and plopped one of the tomes onto the tray. "Your mouth has had enough exercise for the morning."

"Are you implying I should use my brain now?" he asked good-humoredly as he flipped open the book. His blue eyes, twinkling with merriment, caught hers unexpectedly as he looked up, and for a moment, Snow felt like her twelve-year-old self again, thrilled beyond words that the heroic duke had noticed her.

She turned away, sorrow at what could have been slowing her movements as she gathered the dirty rags. "That would be implying you had one, and I don't know if I want to do that," she said, but it didn't come out as pertly as she meant it too. "I have work to do."

She scooped up the dishes and walked toward the door.

"You're obviously alive. I should leave you to rest and do your research. Colors said he and the other enchanters would take turns visiting you today."

"January?"

The concern in his tone pulled her to a halt in the doorway, but she didn't turn around. "Yes?" she answered tiredly.

She felt him watch her, as if waiting for her to turn around, but when she didn't, he said, "You're outspoken, especially for a maid. I ... I could use your help."

"My help?"

"Yes. I need the opinion of a sensible female, especially one who knows Princess Snow. I don't know exactly what I did to lose the princess's friendship, but I'd like to win it back. And her heart. Yet..." He paused and Snow stiffened. "I don't seem to know how. If you have any ideas to aid my cause, I would appreciate them."

"I can't think of anything." Snow quickly brushed through the doorway.

"You will let me know if you do?"

Snow pushed the door shut behind her without answering.

❦

THAT AFTERNOON, Snow left Robert in the men's care, borrowed Robert's horse, and rode to the village. The footpath Colors had instructed her to take rather than the road was drenched in wildflowers and promising for blackberries in a few weeks. Despite the warmth of the day, the ride was pleasant, and by the time she reached the village, Snow's mood had improved. Robert's claims and behavior didn't match up in her book, but that was no reason to let him get under her skin. She flinched and slowed Firethorn's pace to a walk as they approached the village. No reason to be rude to him. She should remain quiet and aloof. Ignore him. That was what she needed to do. She had enough troubles as it was, as did he, apparently.

"Good afternoon, Miss January." Sutton, the oldest of her guards, practically ran from the inn to meet her as she slowed Firethorn to a halt before it. He covered an accidental bow by clearing his throat and taking Firethorn's reins. The other two guards and the coachman jogged up behind him. One man had a bandage on his head, the other his arm, but they appeared healthy otherwise, thankfully. "Everything is alright, I take it?" Sutton asked, his gaze inspecting.

She smiled. "Good afternoon. Yes, it is." She slipped off Firethorn to the ground. "I merely wished for a ride and to see about getting some meals prepared for myself, the duke, and Lyndon." She didn't wish to spend all her day in the kitchen, and she pitied the two men too much, despite herself, to leave them to their own, untutored devices in the kitchen. She'd cook two meals and have the third prepared.

"We'll accompany you." Brenner held out two letters. "These were left at the inn for you this morning."

Eyebrows high, Snow took them. Her stomach twisted as the handwriting registered as familiar. She slipped them into the pocket of her riding dress, then drew out a note of her own. "Brenner, I'd prefer you to take this to my stepmother. Sutton will accompany me on my errands. Gareth and Mays, you can watch from a distance." She smiled knowingly under Brenner's glower and lowered her voice, "Four guards, plain clothes or not, would spoil my disguise."

Brenner frowned but nodded and then excused himself. She didn't strictly need one of the guards to take a letter for her, but she had no lady's maid because Gaugin or Bankor or someone inevitably bribed or threatened them into being a spy. She needed to know if the same had been accomplished with her guards.

"What has been done about the highwaymen?" she asked as she and Sutton strolled through the quaint village. He was the most skilled at remaining alert without the appearance of soldierly watchfulness.

Sutton huffed. "The villagers didn't seem terribly surprised about the attack. I gathered the locals aren't so prone to such fates as travelers, though I didn't get the feeling they consider the highwaymen as part of the village. Tolerated outsiders, most likely. They let them be because they are let be. The men we left in the road were gone when we returned for them."

Snow pursed her lips, annoyed at the bandits and at the villagers' lack of concern for justice. "Well, I will not tolerate it."

Sutton grinned at her, then opened the door to a pastry shop. She pushed off her concern in favor of enjoying the rich smells wafting to her and savoring the anticipation of trying the local fare.

⚜

SUTTON AND MAYS insisted on accompanying her to within sight of the cottage on her return. After they left and she saw to Firethorn's comfort, she leaned against the stall door and pulled out the two letters. Her stomach tightened as she tore open the first. It was thin, something of a relief. No lengthy discourse ordering some policy or other—comply or she and Solstice would be exposed as sorcerers and king-killers. Comply or her stepmother's golden mirror would be broken.

Snow unfolded the single page of indifferent-quality stationery.

*You will never marry the Duke of Pondleigh.*
*Do not encourage him.*

Snow huffed. Was she being informed or warned? She knew she wasn't marrying Robert or anyone else, but she didn't appreciate Bankor or whoever had the nerve to pen the note attempting to interfere. If only her stepmother's magic mirror could reveal the letter writers! But the lord of the mirror could only reveal things of the present.

She crumpled the letter and opened the second. Different stationery, different hand. Not that that meant anything, she suspected.

*A broken mirror can bring more than seven years bad luck.*

Her jaw clenching so tight it hurt, Snow neatly folded the familiar warning, looked about the stable until she found a pile of horse manure, and stuffed the note in it. The Keeper of the Mirror of Talvinen would never allow it to suffer damage, for her heart as well as her duty was bound within its golden frame. Snow wasn't about to let anyone threaten it either. Or threaten Solstice.

*I will return for you.* Snow resisted the urge to wrap her arms about her waist as she remembered a different note, one sent to her stepmother years ago. The sorcerer who'd followed Solstice to New Grimmland wasn't dead, merely hiding somewhere regaining his strength. So she feared, despite the mirror's inability to find him. He was determined to claim Solstice—"the fairest of the fair"—as his own. Snow was equally determined to stop him. With his curse as her weapon, she could.

It may have been a foolish rebellion of her teen years she'd never shaken off, but Snow took pleasure in sending a warning of her own after receiving those notes. Grabbing her saddlebags with their warm food, she hastened to the cottage, deposited the food in the kitchen, returned to her room, and acquired ten sheets of paper, one for each of the advisors, the most likely people to have discovered what truly happened the day she'd been cursed and her father "died."

*~A broken mirror can bring more than seven years bad luck.*

*If you wrote this, then you know what I am capable of. Attempt any harm and I will find you, and no mirror will save you from your fate.*

She sealed the notes and planned how to mail them through the village post. Lyndon could do this for her, a proper payment for a meal well cooked.

# CHAPTER 5

There was a squeak outside Robert's door, and he, reading while shuffling about the room, scrambled into bed, pulled the meal tray over his lap, and quietly slid the heavy book down on it, counting as he did so. The door lock clicked just as he slumped back against the pillows. He smiled smugly despite the resurgence of discomfort in his side. He and Today had timed that out to perfection.

He dropped the smile to glare at Lyndon as his godfather entered with a book of his own.

Lyndon arched his eyebrow at him and settled into his chair. "And which of our kind friends added the squeak to the hallway floor?"

"I don't know what you mean. It's an old house. Old houses squeak."

"They don't develop squeaks in a single afternoon, during which time seven enchanters promised to pay their respects."

Robert merely raised an eyebrow back at him before returning to his book, the memoirs of an enchanter who'd claimed to have dealings with the faeries. Enchanters apparently retired every fifty years or so to this cottage to write their memoirs and books on magic to preserve them for prosperity and the help of cursed princes such as himself. "Only six came. Nobody has seen, or found, the elusive What since we arrived. Blatherskite thinks he's been trying out invisibility spells and lost himself."

"Invisible I can deal with," Lyndon said as he opened his book to the page marked by a blue ribbon. "As long as he doesn't show up as a teapot or clock or something. I don't like cups talking to me. Find anything useful?"

Sighing, Robert ran his fingers through his hair and vaguely wondered if Snow or Lyndon would trim it for him before it got too long. "Faerie curses can be second or third curses, but they rarely allow other magic 'to attach itself to the subject.' So no 'human form' glamour will work to make me look human and no secondary transformation spell will turn me back human. Iron has never been found helpful in breaking faerie curses either, especially not the powerful, sophisticated magic Prince Dokar uses, so I can't just prick myself with an iron blade. At least from what I can make out from the two books I've skimmed so far."

Lyndon frowned. "Thankfully, it's a large library."

There was a squeak in the hallway, and Robert grinned innocently at Lyndon's glower.

"The handwriting in some of these books is atrocious," Robert continued. "Not even a Legibility Spell could fix it, so yes, it is a good thing it is a large library."

"If a Legibility Spell can't make the writing clear, it means the enchanter didn't actually know what he was talking about." Colors padded quietly into the room, comfortable in pajamas, dressing gown, and slippers. Snow must still be gone for him to be so dressed. His face briefly turned green, but the color faded quickly as he summoned a chair, its upholstery a lush crimson to match his robe, and sat companionably next to him.

"I can skip all those bits?" Robert asked.

"If a Legibility Spell can't make it clear, then yes, I highly recommend skipping those bits."

"He made a rather generous friend today." Lyndon shot a significant look at Colors.

Colors smiled mildly at another squeak from the hallway. "So I heard."

"Speed Reading Spell and Legibility Spell." Robert grinned.

Colors smiled again, with knowing amusement this time, as the dapper, round Cello entered with the bespectacled I Don't Know, followed shortly by Who. Robert found Who's face and appearance difficult to remember—an unusual thing for an enchanter. Arms crossed, Who leaned against the wall in a corner, slipping into the shadows of a space not previously shadowed.

I Don't Know summoned a chair and sat near Colors. He leaned toward him with one eye on Robert, and whispered, "Is his color better today, do you think?"

"It is as you see it," Colors replied.

"I'm still green," Robert answered his true question, saving the spell seer from polite evasions.

"Ah," I Don't Know responded in surprise.

"Don't suppose you could tell me why January makes you turn red?" he asked of Colors.

"A curse, as you know," Colors replied.

"He'll be no help, the old information-skinflint." Blatherskite, coffee cup in hand, pulled up a chair to the foot of the bed, positioned it backwards, straddled it, and propped his arms on the back. "I don't know why he retired to write his memoirs. He won't put anything truly useful in them."

"By 'useful,' our friend means names and details associated with scandals." Today entered with a steaming, fragrant cup of coffee in each hand. He received a narrow-eyed look from Lyndon—the same as everyone else—but unlike the others, Today looked away guiltily to Robert and cleared his throat. Robert did his best not to respond to that look.

"I'm not writing for the gossips." Colors accepted the cup Today held out to him. Another cup replaced that, and Today offered it to Robert, who took it gratefully, then gave one to Lyndon.

"It's not gossip if it's true," Blatherskite retorted.

"Could you tell me what red means?" Robert asked, forestalling a discussion of ethics. "Or anything more about green?"

Colors studied him curiously, his skin turning an unfortunate shade of green—a decidedly froggish one—before it faded to a pale gold. "Common spell seers," he said at last, the colors fading, "associate colors with specific curse motivations and types: red with a murderous envy or hate and a spell designed to spill blood."

*Snow.* Robert stilled, his heart forgetting to beat. *Panic and anger don't befit or benefit a soldier.* Swallowing hard, Robert worked to calm his racing thoughts.

"But I suspect," Colors continued, "some hues are linked to the spells or the spell givers, or multiple things. I haven't figured it all out yet. I'm not even sure they can be accurately sorted."

Robert took a moment to process that but found himself only half relieved. "The red color about her—her lips in particular—doesn't mean she's dying?" He held his breath.

"You can see that?" Colors exclaimed, nearly spilling his coffee as the cup rattled to the saucer.

"Yes. I had to train myself to see spells a few years ago."

"You did *what?*" Blatherskite blurted as the others stared. Even Who gaped at him.

Robert fought down both amusement and smugness at their shock. "Taught myself to see magic. I was under a curse at the time, so maybe since I was already influenced by magic, the impossible became possible. I can't do magic, just see it."

"Perhaps that is why," Colors said slowly. "But in answer to your question, January is in no imminent danger. More than that, I cannot say. I haven't fully theorized the colors of magic yet."

"Tell us about yourself." Blatherskite leaned forward against the chair back and took a sip of coffee, the sludgy kind even Robert couldn't tolerate. "The green and the gold bits."

"My lord has nothing he can say," Lyndon intervened diplomatically. "His curses forbid it."

"You can tell them about the colors, Lyndon," Robert said, "since it might help Colors develop his theories." *And if any of you know something that would help...*

Lyndon pursed his lips but then nodded. "The gold resembles the golden hair of the young woman responsible for the first curse." Interrupting an excited "ahh" from the gentlemen, he continued, "She also wanted to gain a crown by it. Gold again. I might add that the spell was not meant for my lord, so please refrain from speculations regarding it." He gave a pointed look at Blatherskite, who merely smiled innocently and sipped his coffee, not that the action hid the eagerness to his gaze.

Robert would have laughed if it weren't his reputation at

stake. As it was, he could trust Lyndon with it. He had other worries. Snow had gone to the village earlier, but had not yet returned. Evening was fast approaching, and Robert was growing concerned for her.

"And the green?" Colors asked, catching Robert's gaze at the wall mirror positioned to allow him to see out the window behind him. A gift from Who. Incidentally, Robert could see the faint color of a spell on the glass to keep him inside. It had a different kind of reddish hue than Snow's lips. A symbolic color for "stop"?

"The second is from Prince Dokar," Lyndon said. "My lord has been threatened with … *ah* … frog-hood if certain conditions are not met."

"Got caught walking the forests with a pretty faerie, did you?" Blatherskite said, his eyes bright.

Cello slapped him on the shoulder. "None of your scandal mongering."

"I assure you my lord did nothing to deserve either spell," Lyndon said with an appropriately raised chin.

Robert felt he ought to take up his own fight at this point, but movement in the mirror caught his attention.

"Good grief!" Robert started to twist around to look out the window itself, but a sudden agony in his side convinced him to stay focused on the mirror instead. Or rather on Snow as she galloped into the yard from the footpath, slowed Firethorn to a walk, and walked him around the yard. Galloped! Astride. On *his* horse. All this time he'd thought her a delicate flower, and not without cause: it was well-established in New Grimmland. How many secrets did this woman have? Overprotective stepmother indeed. How he'd struggled on his visits to her because all the normal things he thought she'd enjoy, that she'd enjoyed as a child, seemed forbidden to him: riding beyond a plodding walk, archery, hikes.

But his grousing stopped as he caught the broad smile on her face, one such as he hadn't seen since before her father died. She was always beautiful, but this kind of beautiful, this was possibly his favorite.

A quiet chuckle came to his attention, and he cleared his throat and turned away from the mirror to Lyndon. "There's something fishy going on here," he said gruffly.

"She does ride awfully well for a maid," Colors said with a sparkle to his blue eyes.

Lyndon, who was standing beside the bed, watched likewise, brows furrowed. "She asked to borrow Firethorn, and since she rode him without a problem on the way here, I thought you wouldn't object. It didn't occur to me until later that—*ah* ... I'd heard maids aren't horsewomen. Were scared of the beasts."

Robert huffed. Probably some scheme of Snow's to convince him to lose interest in her. He preferred she could ride with confidence and not shy at shadows, but he also preferred her honest.

With a keen glance between Robert and the window, Blatherskite laid his cup on the nearest table and rose. He said, rather too casually, "I'll go see if she needs any help rubbing down the horse."

"You're getting back to your writing." With a scolding glower, Today caught him by the arm of his wrinkled jacket and tugged him through the doorway. Cello followed on their heels.

"I am not a gossip," Blatherskite protested from down the hallway. "I'm a hobby journalist, and yes, there is a difference."

The others soon followed, and Robert and Lyndon were

left to their research until Snow brought them dinner. Shortly afterwards, Lyndon left her on guard duty, and went, hopefully, to check on the horses. Snow obviously knew how to ride, but could she care for his precious Firethorn properly?

"You ride well, January," he said as he exchanged one book from the new pile Colors had delivered for another. Snow was sitting in her chair, reading also. Unfortunately, he had a feeling she'd gotten a Privacy Spell from someone, because he couldn't so much as tell the language of the book. It had a bit of haze around it that suggested a Legibility Spell wouldn't help.

Her gaze flew to the window behind him, and he pointed to the mirror Who had helped him situate. Returning her attention to the book, she said, "Thank you for the loan of your horse. I brushed him down and saw that he was comfortable."

"Thank you. I ... *uh* ... didn't know you rode?" *I've always heard you became a timid young lady during your teenage years. Hardly spoke to anyone and certainly never rode horses beyond a slow walk.*

"Why should you know it? Besides, a lady's maid is often required to ride with her mistress."

*Because we've known each other for years! We're practically engaged!* Robert swallowed down his frustration. This was *January*, a new beginning.

He let them lapse into silence, and was unsurprised when Snow made no attempt to break it. *What did I do to deserve her mistrust and disdain, Lord?*

Later, as he slipped toward sleep, he prayed for Lady Violetta to return the next morning and for Snow's icy heart to melt, at least enough to give him hope.

❧

THE NEXT FEW days were much the same: He woke as a frog. Lady Violetta kissed him back to humanness. Snow brought him breakfast and read awhile with him. She went for a ride in the afternoon, and the enchanters joined him for coffee. She, he, and Lyndon spent the evening reading. She spoke to him as little as possible. She was both the light and shadow of his days.

The only improvement the week's end brought was Lyndon allowing him to walk around the room a few times a day—the door locked and curtains closed since Lyndon still refused to even let him see his clothes. Robert was half convinced Lyndon just wanted to cut down on the laundry.

# CHAPTER 6

S now stared forlornly at the pile of laundry in her room. She could take it to the village and hire someone to do it, but then she'd have to explain the special washing process (the "just in case" anti-poison laundry detergent and no-touch washing method) her step-mother insisted be used with her laundry. Snow didn't think she was *that* poisonous. Still, she didn't like strangers doing her laundry, or dishes for that matter.

She peeked at the generous wall mirror. *You need to make sure the guard delivered your letter—unopened and unaltered. You could take care of both there.*

She hastily looked away and searched out the window for the clothesline. She could always hunt up the washing equipment here. Hanging her undergarments to dry outside a houseful of men wasn't so embarrassing, was it?

*Coward. There's a better place to do it, and you know it.*

The golden charm bracelet hidden under her glove weighted her arm like guilt as she searched her memory for the location of the clothesline. *Coward.*

Sighing, Snow gathered her laundry into a duffle. That done, she pulled the bracelet out to dangle at her wrist, pausing a moment to admire the charms, which glowed softly when this close to a mirror. Of the finely wrought, golden representations of a castle, a sword, a snowflake, twin mountain peaks, and an orb, the orb glowed the brightest. The incongruous bronze cube hanging near the clasp held a Switch Spell and remained dull. Snow touched the wall mirror, letting the golden ball hang against it.

*Mirror, mirror, hear me call, to the land past Fall, to the castle wall, take me and my all.*

The mirror chilled under her gloved touch. Ice spread across the silver surface and down the wall to form a path to her feet, soon freezing her in place.

*A daughter of Winter, a friend of the keeper, begs entrance.*

The glow about the golden ball brightened, and ice grew from the mirror's surface to swallow her. It pulled her and the duffle into the mirror, into the hidden land of Winter, the land her stepmother was keeper of, a responsibility Snow would one day inherit.

Snow shook loose of the clinging crystals and found herself in the verdant walled gardens of a castle nestled in a frost-bitten valley between snow-covered mountains. She stood in the rose garden. Men's voices carried in the clear air through the archway into the vegetable garden beyond, and she made out the precisely phrased terms of the trade agreement she and her stepmother had been working on before she left the palace. The speaker's accent was similar to her stepmother's, yet he often favored pronunciations and words that had long ago slipped into the category of *archaic*. This would be a surprise given his youthful appearance, but Birch, Lord of the Mirror of Talvinen, had looked about twenty for as long as she'd known him. And for a thousand years before that, or so she suspected from the bits of his history he and Solstice had shared with her. He was cursed as well.

Peeking through the archway into that chamber of the garden dedicated to vegetables, she found Birch leaning against a garden post, ignoring the bean vines twining up it, reading aloud from the trade agreement. His simple, practical clothes were hardly fitting for a castle, but it was difficult for Solstice to sneak men's clothes into her rooms and then into the mirror for him. And for Snow's father.

Gathering her courage, Snow hoisted the duffle and strode through the archway.

Wearing a broad-brimmed straw hat and dressed as a commoner, her father, the true ruler of New Grimmland, was kneeling in the dirt in the plot next to Birch's, weeding the tomatoes.

Stopping his digging to ask a question, King Theodore looked up at Birch and then saw her. His face brightened with a smile that warmed her heart. Birch looked around likewise and grinned.

"It's about time you showed yourself, Princess." Eyes twinkling, Birch crossed his arms, tucking the document against his side. "I was beginning to think you'd come to spy on us instead of visit."

"I'd never neglect to visit," she said, grinning in return.

King Theodore pushed up from the garden dirt and brushed off his pantlegs as she settled the duffle on the stone walkway and stepped up to him. "One day he's going to start telling me when people arrive." Theodore took off his gloves and greeted her with a firm hug. She'd given up resisting, of reminding him of the danger to himself. It was so tempting to relax and hug him back, as she did as a little girl, but she kept herself stiff instead, making sure no movement of hers accidentally brought her face—any exposed skin—against his.

"Why spoil Snow's view of your look of pleasure at her appearance?" Birch responded, his tone teasing but his look one of understanding. He knew only too well how much pleasure could be gained from the sight of others, how much pain from seeing but never touching.

*Thank you for keeping that for me, Birch.* She smiled her thanks to him as she stepped away from her father.

"What did you bring?" Theodore asked, rubbing his thick beard as he nodded to the duffle at her feet.

"My laundry. I didn't want it hanging about drying at a cottage full of men."

"What if I don't want a woman's laundry hanging up at my castle full of men?" Birch protested, eyes shrewd as he waved his hand at the castle behind him, empty save for himself and her father, both equally kings and servants. Birch's curse allowed him one day of freedom from the mirror a century, at the keeper's will. Her father didn't even have that. If he left the mirror and the protection of Birch's magic, he'd fall into the Sleeping Death again and never wake.

"Fresh baked bread for the use of your water and clothesline?"

"Deal, Princess." Rubbing his hands together like a little boy who'd made the bargain of his life, Birch walked off toward the castle, his metallic-silver hair brilliant in the sunlight, a blend of white and blue-gray to match the sky as it was then. "I'll get the tub set up."

Postponing the inevitable, Snow watched him disappear down the garden paths as her father watched her. She steeled herself for the moment Birch was out of hearing.

"Your stepmother tells me Robert of Pondleigh was

injured stopping an attack on your carriage." Fixing a stern look on her, Theodore pulled her note from his pocket and handed it to her.

Snow bit back an unladylike word. She *would* send the note with an honest, talkative guard. She'd neglected to mention Robert's identity in her letter, but she'd had a feeling Solstice would figure it out.

"He's recovering well," she said, opening the letter and skimming it to make sure nothing had been altered. No interference. Good.

"You didn't mention who saved you in your letter," he persisted. "Solstice had to get the information from the guard."

"Does it matter who did? We were attacked *in New Grimmland*. This shouldn't be happening."

"Highwaymen are like the plague, Snow. They're every-where, try as we might to stop them. And you know it matters. *He* matters. His health and his feelings."

*But what of mine? It's too hard to care for his and protect my own. I discovered a purpose for my curse, and I can't bear to want to undo it again. I'll never be free, and only with it can I protect Solstice—and so you.* "I know," she said tersely and made to walk around him.

He stopped her with a gentle touch to her arm. Calling up her respect for her father, she forced herself to meet his gaze, when she'd rather march on. She'd inherited his dark eyes, but where she'd always seen courage in her father's eyes, she too often saw fear in her own, felt it when he looked at her like that.

"You don't act as if you do," he said gently. "You—my brave daughter—hid from him for four days."

"And he from me for four years."

"Not visiting isn't quite the same as ignoring a visitor, but I agree that was surprising and unkind of him. Ask why."

Snow pressed her lips together, her heart aching. *I know why. Even if ... Does his reason matter in the end? I'm cursed. We tried fixing it, but it's too late now.*

Pursing his lips likewise, her father released her, then gestured to the laundry. "And get Robert to help you with the laundry. Or help him with his. It's a beast of a thing to learn to do for yourself, I can tell you."

She swallowed hard against the reminder of what her curse had cost him: to be his own servant in a lonely castle, a dead man with a mere magical reflection of himself in a crypt in his kingdom. But he had thrived despite that, managing without complaining. He did all that and was still concerned for her, Solstice, and the people of his land.

She gave a bittersweet smile as she noted the wrinkles of his coarse clothing. "Robert's on bedrest."

"He can still fold clothes or hand you things to iron."

"He's cursed, and I don't know what the affliction is."

That gave her father pause, and a seed of hope began to grow within her. It died quickly.

"Then find out," Theodore said.

"One curse in a couple is more than enough, Father." She started to walk away again, but he caught her gloved hand in his. She stopped, her shoulders slumping.

He tugged her hand gently until she looked at him. "Don't give up hope yet, Snow. And don't be a coward. To be uncomfortable, to make someone uncomfortable, is a better thing than you think. Talk with him about whatever happened four years ago. Maybe he has an explanation, or wants to apologize and beg for a second chance. He's a good man, Snow."

"How would you know?" she mumbled. "You've been trapped in a mirror for fifteen years."

"I have my ways." He laughed and chucked her under the chin, using his glove as a buffer. Her mood improved despite herself. "And I've always had a special reason to keep up with him."

"Just kiss him and bring him here." Birch sauntered back into the garden, his grin mischievous. "We could do with a third to break ties. Your father is exceedingly contrary and tries to gainsay me at every turn."

"Are you expecting me to say 'I don't always gainsay you,' and so prove your point?" her father said wryly.

"Your refusal to say so and fall into my trap *proves* my point," Birch replied.

As their banter continued, Snow's mind swirled with a thousand ideas, most set to a backdrop of bright blue eyes and a teasing smile that highlighted three thin scars in a handsome face. Her heart did a leap and plummet before she locked it up tight.

"No, Birch," she said firmly, interrupting them. *I won't condemn anyone else to a mirror prison, even if it's the only way for me to marry. I have another purpose now: protect Solstice and you both should the sorcerer return.* "Even if I did want to marry Robert, he might still be in danger from me on this side of the mirror."

"I think he'd be fine," Theodore said. "I think *I'd* be fine if you wanted to hug me without acting like a tree. It's not so bad here, Snow," he continued, not for the first time trying to make her feel better about poisoning him. "How many kings get to garden in the morning and fish in the afternoon? Be free of court politics? I'm freer now than I ever was before. And since my beautiful wife and daughter visit me—"

Birch scoffed. "Visit? Solstice practically moved in the day you did. You know a keeper's never done that before, right?"

Her father answered with a roguish grin. "Probably never had sufficient temptation before."

Birch rolled his eyes, then turned to Snow. "The laundry is ready when you are."

"Thanks, Birch."

He walked away again, and Snow picked up her duffle, deciding to try one last tactic, though it would be painful to her father. He and Solstice had hoped to have children, but the poison or the mirror or nature had prevented that.

"Besides," she said, straightening but keeping her gaze on Birch's receding figure, "if I married Robert—if he thought it worthwhile to give up his family and freedom to come here —it would be awkward for me, with a supposedly dead husband, to have children on the other side. If we could have children at all."

Her father cupped a hand under her elbow and gently squeezed her arm. "Some things are worth a little awkward-ness, even pain," he said, a touch of sadness in his voice. He took the duffle from her, the force of his gaze drawing her eyes to his. "Promise me you'll talk to him, Snow. Really talk to him. This has gone on long enough."

She recognized the command in his expression, and reluctantly, the love behind it. Slowly, Snow nodded, though her stomach roiled at the thought.

He smiled, the tension evident in his face easing. "We'll take care of your dresses and unmentionables here, but you can get Robert to help with the linens."

Sighing, Snow took his offered arm and followed him to the castle.

"When we've done that, do you want to go for a ride or have fencing practice?"

"Fencing. I've been riding Robert's horse."

"Have you now?" he said in an insinuating kind of way.

"Yes, and don't read anything into that. There are only two horses to choose from."

"I wouldn't dream of reading anything into the fact that you're comfortable borrowing Robert's things, as if he's at least a friend."

Snow bit back a sigh. Her father was incorrigible.

# CHAPTER 7

S o far, Robert had been a spring peeper, a little grass frog, a bullfrog, a barking tree frog, and a common toad. The latter had instigated a fight with Lyndon about whether frogs and toads were the same and if Prince Dokar's curse had broken its own rules by making him a toad. If the curse just happened to be green things, he was rather hoping for a lizard ... or a dragon.

But no such luck today. Robert stretched a long leg in front of him and twisted it to get a better look. It was more reddish than green, but dragons could be red too, right? There was hope for tomorrow?

"Well?" he asked Lyndon. At least he was a bit larger today. For a frog.

"Wood frog. You can freeze yourself in the winter. You can eat slugs and snails in addition to insects and things." Lyndon put the naturalist guide to amphibians down and glanced at the cuckoo clock on the mantel, then out the window and said nothing more. The rosy dawn was fast losing its softness.

"She's late, isn't she?" Robert said, working to keep his voice steady.

"Yes." Lyndon shot another look at the clock.

"Lady Violetta did say I'd have to take care of this myself eventually."

"She implied she'd come every morning until your aunt arrived," Lyndon snapped. He exhaled slowly, then added in a mutter, "I don't know what's worse—a full-time beast who won't give up his curse or a part-time frog who has to be kissed every day."

"I don't shed." It was his one advantage. Couldn't he at least have been a lion? An eagle? Even a opossum had more teeth than he did. He couldn't scare anybody into anything other than a worry about warts, and that was only some days. Or was that a myth? He'd heard some frogs were poisonous, but that wasn't the kind of mischief Dokar was after.

Ignoring him, Lyndon added in a mutter, "A flighty enchantress or a princess who pretends she's a maid."

Robert winced. "Lyndon, about Snow, what might I have done to damage our relationship? I thought Snow and I were friends, and willing to be more when the time came, and then..." *Then she cuts me off only to show up as a colder, different woman than the one I knew.*

Sighing, Lyndon ceased his watch of the clock and leaned back in his chair to rub the bridge of his nose again, a common sight when he had a stress headache. Robert had, unfortunately, been the cause of more of those than he cared to admit. "Did you read her letters? Respond to them? Visit her?"

"Of course I read them. Practically memorized them."

"Did she know this?"

"Yes—I don't know." A sense of his shoulders sinking caused him to lay flat. He was quiet for a moment, considering. "Sometimes it took me a few weeks to reply, but I always did. My visits weren't long or that frequent, but she never seemed to expect them to be. I do have duties of my own. ... My letters tended to be short too, I guess. I certainly didn't address everything she said. Am I supposed to? Girls can talk a lot. I had no advice or help to give for most of it. How does one nod and 'hmm' in a letter?"

One corner of Lyndon's mouth curved briefly, and he dropped his hand to his lap. "She would probably appreciate knowing you were 'listening' even if you aren't verbose in your response. You don't have to fix anything for her, necessarily."

"If she doesn't want me to fix it, then why tell me about it?"

Lyndon shrugged. "Does it matter?" He stared at him thoughtfully for a moment. "You weren't starting rumors by showing interest in another lady, were you? Those travel kingdom to kingdom, you know."

Robert shot him a glare. "You know the rumors better than I do, so don't ask me. I barely talked to any young lady because I considered myself engaged. I could have been married by now to a wonderful woman who would adore me and never hide from me, but *no*, I was faithful to a tacit engagement that was apparently all two-sided—me and her late father but never her. Actually, she did accuse me of being a crown-grabber, but our relationship was her parents' and my aunt and uncle's idea, so she can hardly blame *me*."

Lyndon raised an eyebrow at him, and Robert grimaced at his own bitterness.

"There may have been one young woman rumor-seekers paired you with," Lyndon said thoughtfully a moment later.

"With me? But who—?"

"They usually paired her with Prince Rupert. Her father made sure of it."

Groaning, Robert let his little body collapse onto the comforter. "I'm going to have to tell her about Lucrezia, aren't I? You think that's it?" He continued in an affected voice, "You know those four years I didn't visit? I'd been bewitched by a beautiful woman, and I've only now been able to, mostly, break free of her spell."

Lyndon chuckled. "You don't have to put it exactly like that. Be patient, Robert. Princess Snow isn't the type to make rushed decisions, and that's a good thing."

"Not when you're threatened with frog-hood. Can't I just tell her I was cursed and leave the details out? I can't talk about it anyway. I told her what I could in a letter years ago, but who knows if she read it?"

"She should know more in case Prince Dokar and Lucrezia get around the counter-measures, though I pray that never happens."

"Agreed."

Lyndon leaned forward to pat Robert's head affectionately. "Your castle of dreams may have tumbled, Robert, but it can be rebuilt. Don't despair. You can't talk about the curse, but I can. You just have to convince Princess Snow to come to me for the full truth."

"Sure you don't want to just blurt out my secrets over dinner? I don't mind."

"I don't think that will be as effective as her seeking out answers."

"I was afraid you'd say that." He'd almost thought Snow was contemplating talking to him last night, but always, just as her mouth opened, something stopped her. Lyndon would speak, the hallway squeak, a whippoorwill sing, and her lips would snap shut, his hopes dashed.

Sighing, Robert tried rubbing his forehead but only managed to swat himself in the eye with a webbed hand. Blinking, he sat up and took stock of his limbs. He needed to work on his coordination more than he needed to mope.

After a few minutes of getting his bearings, Robert began hopping around the bed, then simply hopping up and down, testing out today's legs. At least in this form he didn't have to worry about clothes or being told to stay still. The window didn't appear bespelled in this form either. Was the magical barrier only set to humans?

After a well-executed leap to Lyndon's head, his godfather left him to go to the village for cooking supplies for Snow. Their bargain was for Lyndon to deal with getting supplies and some meals from the village and for Snow to cook for them. Lyndon also took Robert's and his own laundry to the village. Snow preferred to do her own. She never ceased to surprise him: a princess who willingly did her own laundry. Why? Why no lady's maid either? She'd been helpful to him since arriving, but not friendly. Was her curse the freezing of her heart so that she cared for no one? Robert's heart ached at the thought. *Whatever her curse is, Lord, help me free her of it. Even a sacrificial love could be cold; help her, us, learn to delight in each other as well as love in deed.*

Watching in the mirror, Robert saw Lyndon take the same footpath Snow had. Once he was out of sight, Robert leapt for the windowsill and peered down to the ground below. Only a few feet down.

It appeared Lady Violetta had forgotten him for the day, so he might as well make the most of it. Feel the sun again, the grass, swim in a creek, catch his own breakfast. He was a good shot and knife thrower, but bug catcher? He was pretty sure he could be. Could he outsmart or out-hop a predator?

Get swallowed by a serpent and fight his way up and back out like a hero of legend?

He was pretty sure Dokar wanted him alive to cause mischief, which meant the fey prince had likely added protections to Robert in his "vulnerable" frog state. He might as well make the most of that too.

His thin lips curved into something like a grin. Oh, it was going to be a good day.

Robert leaned his rounded head out the window and looked left, then right, out of habit rather than need, given the lateral position of his eyes. Seeing no enchanter likely to bespell him from behind, he leapt onto the grass. He didn't take the time to categorize the feel of the thin blades, which were higher than he expected, or smell the dirt; he hopped again and went bounding through the yard, free at last.

The forest was ahead. Prey, predators, freedom, adventure!

The buzzing of a fly hit his membranous ears, and he spotted the possibly tasty morsel up and to the left. It was high enough for a challenge. Keeping his eyes on his prey, Robert put on more speed, pushed up with his webbed feet for all they were worth, and flicked out his tongue.

The buzzing of the fly was joined by a woman's voice wafting from a window across the yard. She was singing a clear alto, bewitching but not in the way of magic. *Snow.*

Robert smacked onto the grass. He lay there a moment, just listening. He'd managed to convince her to sing a duet with him during his last visit—successful visit, that is—to New Grimmland. It was a wonderful feeling, sharing something he loved with someone who cared for it as well, sharing *something* he cared for with *someone* he cared for. He'd intended to propose in a more official manner and set a wedding date that trip, but she kept talking about her twenty-first birthday coming up the next year. He'd assumed she was hinting he should wait for some reason, that maybe she was intending on claiming her father's throne then and preferred to, as queen, ask him rather than him, merely a duke, ask her?

Now that he thought about it, had she been talking simply because she was nervous? Had she been humiliated that he hadn't asked her? Angry?

"I—" *I wish I understood her.* His bewailing was cut short as his tongue flicked back into his mouth with a juicy fly in its grasp.

"Ha!" he cried as he picked himself up. He may not have the power of a beast, but he could take care of himself.

Sights set for the forest and its promise of adventure, Robert bounded forward, but a glimpse of movement through the kitchen window slowed him. One of the enchanters was with her.

Perhaps he could learn something of Snow's curse if she didn't know he was around. Perhaps that was part of why Queen Solstice sent him here.

Robert took a longing look at the forest, but then hopped to the kitchen and up to the windowsill.

# CHAPTER 8

Snow was a coward. She moaned as she opened her eyes to a view of the thick wooden beams in the ceiling above her head. She'd once heard if you counted the beams in a ceiling the first night you spent under them and made a wish, your wish would come true. Pity it was too late to wish for courage. Or a less meddling father.

She hadn't been able to talk herself into talking to Robert the day before. Hadn't even taken the duffle of laundry anywhere near him, but today she must. She'd promised. She was fairly certain Lyndon and Robert knew who she was, but somehow, she thought it might be easier to talk with him as January. A maid and a soldier rather than two royals.

Groaning, she pushed up from the bed, dressed, and hurried downstairs to prepare breakfast. The distinct sound of splashing water greeted her as she entered.

Blatherskite stood in front of the window at the sink-end of the pile of cups and saucers. *He* was washing dishes?

"Good morning, January," he said cheerfully with a glance

over his shoulder at her. His smile was rueful. "Didn't expect me in here, did you?" He was wearing a dressing gown and slippers, which were a faded blue and far less fine than Colors's, and his thinning brown hair was sticking up at odd angles.

"To be honest, I didn't." She took her apron from its hook on the wall.

"Yes, well, my servants object to having teacups appear out of nowhere at random times of day and night, so I'm left to do those dishes myself." His abashed look and charming smile had a disarming effect, and she found her mouth curving in return.

"You wait until they're all dirty to wash them?" she asked, but without censure.

"Oh no," he said, laughing. "I don't wash them until I've reached forty-seven cups. It's a nice number and gives me plenty of thinking time."

She raised an eyebrow at him, and he glanced at the pile again, then cleared his throat.

"Colors may have reminded me that even fewer than that clutters your kitchen. More than that certainly so."

"That they do," she said with a chuckle as she began collecting foodstuffs and bowls. She'd left the eggs Lyndon had bought in the village in a basket in a shaded portion of the counter, near Blatherskite. As she moved beside him to get them, she realized his attention was more on the guest room across the yard, visible through the window, than on the dishes.

"You know I wanted to be a journalist," he said, catching her catching him spying, "until my magical abilities showed up and I was whisked off into the world of enchanters."

"What does that have to do with spying on the duke of Pondleigh? Are you making sure he doesn't try escaping out a window again? I thought Colors and Cello bewitched them."

"They did, but animals can get through. No, I'm watching for Lady Violetta. I'm pretty sure it's her I've felt arrive early every morning this week. Has she visited you more than that once?"

"No," Snow answered in surprise. Why would Robert be getting early morning visits from Lady Violetta, especially since he already had a houseful of enchanters at his beck-and-call?

"I thought not. I wonder if it has something to do with his curse. Know anything about it, do you?"

"No." Snow found herself, to her embarrassment, leaning over the counter to see out the open window. She scolded herself back to the basket of eggs and from thence to the table. "I don't know what it is." She hesitated, but concern— no, curiosity—won out. "Do you?"

His cunning smile made her frown.

"Not everything," he admitted with a shrug. "Not the juicy bits anyway. But I'll let you know when I find out." He winked at her, earning another frown, which only made his eyes twinkle.

"Don't trouble yourself on my account," she said.

"Oh, it's no trouble." He winked again, then went back to drying cups and spying. She returned to preparing breakfast.

Snow loved singing; it made ordinary tasks go faster and brought pleasure to herself and, she'd been told, to others. So she began singing as she worked.

Before long, a thump turned her attention to the windowsill. A frog sat there calmly looking between her and Blatherskite. It was about three inches long, light red in color, and had black markings on its eyes, making it look almost as if it wore a mask.

"You're a bold thing," she said as its dark eyes settled on her. "Come to rob us of flies? That sort of thievery I don't mind."

It raised up, its little chest expanding as if to say it could if it wanted to.

Chuckling, she went back to forming the bread dough into balls for its final rising.

"I think the frog admires your beauty," Blatherskite said a few moments later. The frog was still sitting there, looking about the room but mostly at her.

"Are you used to being fed? Is that it? I don't serve frog food, I'm sorry," she told the frog as she placed the dirty bowls on the counter to be washed. It inched back as she approached. "I won't hurt you." At a soft padding of paws on the floor, she added, "But Charters here might."

The cottage's fluffy gray cat rubbed her ankles. When she gently shooed it away so she could safely walk by, it hopped onto the counter. The frog disappeared from the windowsill, and the cat followed. *Good luck, little frog.*

"Actually," Blatherskite said five minutes later from behind her, making her jump. She spun to her right, where she'd been hearing the rhythmic sounds of cups being washed and dried. Cups were floating in and out of the water under the impetus of soap bubbles, the drying cloth by an invisible breeze. Blatherskite stepped up to the sink, caught a cup in one hand and the cloth in the other and gave her a conspirator's grin. "I think I've figured it out."

"What?" she managed as she steadied her nerves.

"Robert's curse, the second one."

"Oh!"

"He had a run-in with Prince Dokar on the way here— not his first I'll wager—and got zapped with a transformation spell. Guess what he turns into?"

Snow hissed a breath through her teeth. Prince Dokar! *What did you do, Robert? Weren't your other injuries enough?* "I've no idea. He looks himself to me, but perhaps the transformation hasn't taken effect yet."

"Are you sure?"

Snow frowned at him.

"Perhaps," he said, his brown eyes twinkling again. "But it has a very interesting daily requirement for preventing or reversing the transformation." He paused expectantly, and Snow didn't make him wait long.

"Which is?" She didn't care for the smug twist to his lips but also didn't care to keep her pride at the expense of answers. Not that she truly cared for any reason other than relieving boredom.

"I hesitate to say in front of a lady. It's rather scandalous." He leaned toward her and whispered, "But the duke's nobleness may cause a permanent change in his ... *ah* ... status and eating habits. I don't know the exact conditions of his curse, but for some transformations, if it doesn't get reversed in a few hours, well then ... he might have to *kiss* his humanness goodbye." He waggled his bushy eyebrows. "Well, time for me to run along and get to writing. Have a good day, January." The last cup settled itself in the cupboard, and Blatherskite disappeared.

Snow barely heard his last few sentences. A strange mix of a cat's meowing and a male voice jerked her attention to the window. There was the cat scampering through the yard with a reddish frog riding on its head, going straight for the forest. Colors stepped suddenly from the footpath, and the cat with its rider curved back toward the cottage. At his appearance, the frog had slunk back to the thick fur of the cat's neck, almost as if not wanting to be seen.

What a curious thing that little frog was. Listening on

windowsills and riding cats. Was it someone's pet got loose? Or perhaps the mysterious What?

Snow sucked in a breath.

*Got zapped with a transformation spell. Lady Violetta didn't come this morning. I think the frog admires your beauty.*

"Robert!" The startled cry escaped her as cat and rider disappeared around the corner of the house. He would go escapading as a frog! Probably thought it a grand adventure!

She started to take off her apron to go after him, but stopped herself. He was an adult and could take risks if he wanted to. It wasn't her right to stop him. He wouldn't be the same brave Robert if she did. She forced a deep breath and went back to cracking eggs, but as the first golden yolk slipped into the bowl, nausea threatened to overwhelm her.

An image of the frog crushed under the carriage wheel after the highwaymen attack flared in her mind. Frogs were such fragile things, and Robert hadn't the sense—the desire, really—to keep out of danger. He didn't have the skills as a frog that he had as a human to take care of himself. Could he even get himself back human? What had Blatherskite been hinting at?

*If it doesn't get reversed in a few hours, he might have to kiss his humanness goodbye.*

Kiss.

Her knees buckled, and Snow grasped the counter with one hand and covered her mouth with the other. *Oh, Robert, I can't. I can't help you. You know I can't.*

But he only had a few hours. Or less. Lady Violetta had been late some time ago.

*Kiss him and bring him to the castle.* No, she didn't want him there. That was her haven, her true home. He could find someone else to reverse his curse. She'd call Lady Violetta.

Drag some girl—some *little* girl—from the village. That's what she'd do. She'd—

Did Robert even know how little time he had?

*Oh, what can I do? I poison everything I touch!*

Do you?

*Most spells are naturally set to humans.* ... Hadn't Blatherskite hinted Robert could get through the window as a frog while not as a human? It had been her and Solstice's fear rather than solid proof that had kept her from touching living creatures with her bare hands all these years. What if they'd been overly cautious?

Snow bolted out the kitchen, through the cottage, and out the front door, racing for the stables. Robert's horse was the only creature there. She hated to endanger him, but what choice did she have? She needed to know for her own sake as well as his.

She skidded to a halt in front of Firethorn's stall. Neighing a greeting, the gelding walked eagerly up to her and bumped her arm with his muzzle.

She grabbed his face between her ever-gloved hands. "If this doesn't work, I'll take you into the mirror, alright?" She lowered her lips toward him, then jerked back. Hands trembling, she yanked off her glove, kissed her fingers, squeezed her eyes shut, and, before she could talk herself out of it, shot out her hand and slapped him on the muzzle. *Please don't die!*

When no thumping of a heavy body followed, Snow opened her eyes. Firethorn stared at her reproachfully.

"You're—I didn't..." She swallowed back a sob, then a laugh, and brushed her hand gently over Firethorn's muzzle before putting her gloves on again. "Sorry, boy, but I'll give you a proper rub later. Without gloves!"

Snow darted out the stables and into the backyard, but

the cat was sitting demurely on a bench, no rider in sight. *Where did you go, Robert?*

Halfway through a frantic search of the garden, she spun around and ran back into the house. What if he were looking for Lady Violetta? Or her?

Robert's room was empty, but there was a lumpy something on the kitchen windowsill, facing out.

Snow slowed her steps. Moving lithely, she slipped off her glove and crept to the counter under the window. The frog started to turn around. She kissed her fingers, closed her eyes, and smacked him on the head. *Please don't die!*

A very un-frog-like "Ouch!" came bellowing through the window, shortly followed by an "Oh no…"

The horrified statement only added, incongruously, to her relief. Opening her eyes, she found no frog on the windowsill but heard movement in the rosebush underneath it.

Climbing on the counter to do so, she leaned out the window, found the tousled head of brown hair among the red roses, dark green leaves, and thorny vines below, and started to call out. She choked on a gasp instead. It was definitely Robert in the rosebush, and there was far more of him in view than proper for her to see.

Snow scrambled back into the kitchen, searching it with her eyes until they landed on a tablecloth covering a breakfast nook table. She swept it off and tossed it out the window.

"Put this on. I'm coming out."

"What? No! January, wait! I'm fine, really!"

Snow opened the window by the breakfast nook and crawled out, careful to avoid the rosebushes.

When she neared the other kitchen window, Robert was still huddled in the rosebush, half the tablecloth uselessly caught in the thorns as he tried desperately to unstick it. Something about the scene—Robert alive and in such a predicament—touched something in her she hadn't felt in a long time. She started to laugh.

"Go away, January! I'm fine! Go get Colors! Today! *Anybody* else!"

"Why, Robert," she couldn't help saying, taming the laughter into teasing as she strolled to the opposite side of the rosebush as Robert cowered in it. "Stop to smell the roses on the way to the creek for a swim, did you? Don't you think you're a little old to be going swimming in the buff?"

"No! I can explain!"

"What's to explain?" She began unsticking the tablecloth thorn by thorn. "It's a hot day, and we did hide your clothes. … But not in the kitchen."

"January! If you'll just listen—"

"Of course, with exposed wounds like that, you might be trying to get an infection." She loosed the last thorn and released the tablecloth. He hastily pulled it to him, the movement exposing long scratches on his arms and shoulders. "Hoping to become a pathetically ill figure, are we? Planning on sending for Princess Snow as a dying wish? That's not a tactic I'd recommend, by the way."

"No!"

She gestured for him to rise, and when he wouldn't, she rounded the rosebush, made a sweeping glance of him to make sure the tablecloth was in place, grabbed him by the arm with her gloved hands, and half hauled him to his feet.

She held his arm until he steadied and then began dragging him toward the front door. Still suffering from an inexplicable level of relief—she could touch animals without hurting them! she could help Robert without killing him!— Snow couldn't manage to stop herself from mercilessly teasing Robert until he was safely back in his bed under the covers.

"Or were you planning on posing as David for a new statue for the garden?" she asked as she tucked him in, noting the scratch on his shoulder was already turning red, a different shade of red from his face and neck.

"January!"

"Is that all you can say?"

"No! I—"

"We need to check your wounds for dirt and rebind them, plus do something about all those scratches," she interrupted, finally getting the desire to laugh under control. "I'll get Colors to help." She turned to go, but he caught her hand in his, his other hand carefully holding the blanket up to his collarbones.

"Let me explain. Please."

The laughter in her heart faded at his desperate look. She tugged her gloved hand free and nodded slowly. *You could get him to explain what happened four years ago too while he's at it.* Her stomach knotted. "Alright, but quickly. We need to clean your wounds."

His shoulders sank in relief, but then his mouth twisted in a silent oath. "You'll have to wait until Lyndon gets back," he said in defeat. "He can explain. I can't. Curses, you know."

"What do you mean: curses, you know?"

"Most curses don't let you talk about them."

"They don't?" She didn't have a problem talking about hers, not that she wanted to. That was a good way to get Solstice and herself beheaded as a sorceress and a king killer. Or get her father killed. "Well, he can tell me later then. I'm going for Colors."

Robert didn't protest again, and she didn't even bother

shutting his door. She found Colors in the kitchen heating water. Today was pulling bandages from a drawer.

"It'll be ready in a moment," Colors said without turning to her.

"You saw?" she exclaimed, coming to sudden stop just inside the room.

"Yes." Today put the folded bandages into the crate. "Colors has been trying to keep the young lord contained in the yard while still letting him have a bit of exercise."

"But—" *You knew he was in mortal danger from the curse but did nothing?*

"That was rather risky, don't you think, January?"

She jerked around to find the speaker.

The mysterious Who leaned against the counter, his arms crossed, his thin face shadowed by the cabinets. "Wasn't it?"

"My curse doesn't affect animals." She turned to Colors, making a conscious effort to keep the mounting anger out of her voice. "If you saw, why weren't you doing something about it? Blatherskite said his condition might be permanent if his transformation lasted more than a few hours!" Her voice rose despite herself.

Colors raised his silver eyebrows, his skin for once remaining its natural, nearly colorless appearance as he looked at her. "Did he now? He sometimes takes a 'headlines approach' to explaining things."

"A headlines..." *Letting him have a bit of exercise.* "You mean it doesn't?" She'd gotten upset and kissed a frog all because of an overdramatic coffee drinker!

Colors's lips twitched, and he turned away to the steaming water kettle. "Not his, but it does return every day. Unless he gains a kiss as a human, that is."

"I'm not kissing him as a human."

"I wouldn't recommend it."

"I'm glad we're agreed."

Colors used a towel to transfer the kettle to the crate, and they made their way to Robert's room. Was there any chance he hadn't realized what had happened to him? Were spontaneous uncurses a thing?

A lovely perfume announced he had a visitor even before the squeaky floor announced their arrival.

"What happened to my clothes?" Robert's voice thundered down the hallway. Lady Violetta was seated beside him in an elegant silver-and-violet chair. Lyndon stood behind her, both patiently listening to Robert's fit.

"Granted, in your cruelty, you only left me with drawers, but I want them! I even lost my bandages!"

Colors drew up short, his lips pressed together as if trying desperately to keep laughter inside. Having already done all her laughing, Snow now felt her color rising, but she lifted her chin and marched on.

Rather than be distressed, Lady Violetta, scooting forward in her chair, said with interest, "That's been a matter of some study actually. The current theory is that they get lost in the ether and eventually turn up somewhere or other. Some claim that's where all the socks without mates come from. The pairs get separated in the ether during transformations and end up with other socks, just not the right ones. They don't know where the outer clothes go though. Perhaps it's only the socks that get out since they're smaller?"

Snow stepped lightly into the room.

Robert groaned, then as he met her gaze, pulled the blanket closer to his chin, his cheeks flushing red, highlighting the three thin scars there. He'd promised to explain those one day, but never had. Just one of many things she would ask him about. Just not at the moment.

"Darling!" Lady Violetta cried, rising as she spotted them.

She greeted Snow with a squeeze of her hand while talking to Colors and Today. Colors was now wearing a dashing crimson suit and cloak, and Snow fancied Lady Violetta's cheeks were just a bit pink when Colors complimented her dress. It was the same style she'd worn before, only now in the striking blue of Robert's eyes, with a rose outlined in gemstones on the skirt. What would it be like to wear a dress like that and dance the night away at a ball? Be kissed under the moonlight? All without worrying about killing someone.

Snow gave her head a slight shake and imagined herself with a heart of ice. She'd gotten over that romantic nonsense years ago, and she wasn't about to let anything drag her back. Her curse had a purpose. She wouldn't forget that or bemoan what could never be. Setting her jaw, she claimed her chair. The others soon produced their own and sat.

"Don't worry about the clothes, Robert dear," Lady Violetta said, turning back to him, drawing his attention from Snow. "That's actually why I'm late." She tapped her wand on the edge of the bed. A tailored suit in dark-blue-and-gold appeared on it. "Sticky suits aren't difficult to make if one knows how," she continued, smoothing out the jacket with her hand like a fond parent. "But yours needed to be handsome, and since you're going to be sleeping in it too, wrinkle-free. That took extra time. I didn't bother making it impervious to moths since I figured you could take care of any of those fluttering about. Knowing you, and having had a ... *uh* ... *conversation* with Prince Rupert and Princess Belinda, I did make it so that blood stains wouldn't show and so that weapons would not get lost."

"A sticky suit...?" Robert repeated, bewildered. He slid one arm from under the covers to tentatively prod the jacket sleeve. It released him without effort on his part.

"Very sensible, Lady Violetta," Colors said. "And I can tell from here it's excellent craftsmanship."

His compliment was echoed by Today. Lady Violetta's cheeks pinked again.

"Lady Violetta…" Lyndon glanced worriedly between the suit and Robert.

"I believe once we've clean him up"—Colors patted the crate in his lap—"we'll find him healed enough to leave the bed. And I think he's grown sensible enough not to run away."

"I am always sensible," Robert protested. "But I still don't know what a sticky suit is."

"It's exactly what it sounds like," Lyndon said. "It sticks to you in the transformations and doesn't get lost."

"Translation: there will be no more need for tablecloths," Blatherskite said. He, Cello, and I Don't Know stood just inside the doorway.

"There will … *ahem* … be more need for kisses. That won't change," Today added.

Everyone turned to Snow and Lady Violetta.

"I haven't eaten breakfast yet. I need to do that before it gets cold." Working hard to keep her steps slow, Snow strode out the door.

"I don't even know what happened earlier." Robert's comment followed her out. "One minute I was on the windowsill a frog, the next I was in the rosebush a man, and whatever happened in the interim was not a kiss."

"Fortunately, your curse is a bit lax in its definition of *a kiss* for the daily requirement," Lady Violetta said.

"That was more of a slap than a kiss." The amused comment sounded distinctly like Who's, though she didn't remember seeing him in the room. "But it's a start."

Snow groaned and walked faster.

# CHAPTER 9

Four flies, a slug, and a snail may have filled up a frog, but human Robert was still hungry.

"I never got breakfast," he said after bathing, suffering further doctoring at Lyndon's hands, and struggling into his sticky suit. Who knew clothes were such a blessing!

Taking the hint, Lyndon left for the kitchen, stating they had cold cuts and fresh bread if breakfast had been put away.

"If you happen to see January," Robert called after him, "I told her you'd tell her about my curses."

"I gather she knows about the frog one."

"Tell her anyway."

With Lyndon gone, Robert eased himself from the bed. Slowly, he straightened and walked to Snow's chair. Blatherskite had given him a Glide Spell, and Cello an Anti-bump Spell. If Lyndon didn't want him up and about for fear of overtaxing his strength, that didn't mean he had to stay in bed. Robert slipped his hand between the seat cushion and the arm and fished out the spells, then read them aloud while keeping one hand on the chair arm. Done, he hid the spells again and gave the chair a slight push. It slid easily over the floor—wood and throw rugs alike.

Robert sat and quickly guided himself into the hallway. He set his sights on the doorway into the main house with its long hallway, took firm hold of the chair arms, and pushed off. He whooshed down the hallway, glided over the raised entryway, and went sailing along the main cottage's hallway. A wall loomed ahead as the path turned.

"Stop." The chair eased to a halt just before the papered wall. He didn't even lean forward or have to grip the arms as the chair stopped—the chair wouldn't lose him.

Chuckling in glee, Robert stood, turned the chair around, and pushed off toward his own room again. He stopped there, ordered the chair to turn left twice, then raced down the hallway again. The third time he approached the turn in the hallway, he caught footsteps over the slight brush of air from his speeding conveyance.

"Stop," he whispered. Not taking the time to turn around, Robert pushed off with his feet and sped back to his room, abandoning the chair just inside it. He barely regained his bed before the hallway floor squeaked.

"Food?" he asked hopefully as Lyndon entered with a tray.

Lyndon stopped just inside the doorway and glanced around. "I heard a squeak in the hallway before I reached it."

"You have my word of honor I have not been walking or running the hallways."

Lyndon eyed him narrowly, then shook his head and gave him the tray. Robert hid a grin.

"Did you talk to Snow?" he asked as Lyndon chose a book from the pile and settled into his chair.

"No. She went for a ride. I'll find her later, don't worry."

"Thanks," Robert said genuinely, then began to eat his human breakfast. "I'd like to go to the library, and—" *I don't even have to walk, if that worries you.*

"Tomorrow. You've had enough excitement for today."

Robert started to protest, but in truth, he was a bit tired. "Old nanny goat," he muttered, but in good humor.

"*Bah,*" Lyndon replied, opening his book.

SNOW'S EXPRESSION was exceptionally grim when she joined Robert and Lyndon later with their lunch and, oddly, a duffle. After a curious glance at Robert, she set the duffle in the corner.

Lyndon must have noticed her demeanor as well, for they were both quiet, except where politeness demanded conversation, until Snow rose to remove the plates and trays.

Robert cleared his throat as she took his empty plate. "Ladies generally only slap men who steal kisses." He risked a brief glance at her.

She gave him a quelling look and turned away to stack his plate with hers on the desk. Lyndon, a hard-won frown on his face that didn't match the twinkle in his eyes, brought her his dishes and returned to his seat.

"I'd be happy to earn the slap, just so you don't have to apologize," Robert continued.

"That is unnecessary, Robert, but your thoughtfulness is recognized." Plates arranged to her satisfaction, Snow searched the pile of library books beside the dishes.

"How do I look?" Robert sat up straighter and gestured to his torso, which was, thankfully, covered by the sticky suit. The magical suit was surprisingly comfortable and well-tailored. He'd have to be more specific in his praise of it to Lady Violetta, rather than merely giving a lazy, *It's nice*.

Book in hand, Snow faced him again, and he continued, "Some combination of handsome rogue and mortally ill hero?" Robert waggled his eyebrows at her.

One corner of her mouth twitched, but the smile died before being born. "You look like a cheeky duke who never learned that maids should be ignored."

"It's hard to ignore a pretty maid who calls you by your first name."

He bit back a grin as Snow winced. *Forget that in your disguise, did you? The curtsy too?*

"As an equal might…" he continued.

"It was my impression," she said frostily, "that titles are not used here. *Book* titles are what we should be concerned with." She lifted the spine of her book toward him: *The Poison Curses.* He made a mental note of it.

"Then it doesn't matter that you're a maid," he retorted. "So if being deathly ill isn't a way to win Princess Snow's heart, what do you suggest? Does she have a dragon I can slay for her? A treasure to find? … A curse I can cure?"

Snow hesitated, but then moved toward her chair. "Shouldn't you be worrying about your own curses?"

"I am, but I can add hers to my research without straining my mental abilities."

She began lowering herself into the chair, yet not so carefully as when she'd held her dinner tray. He'd not thought about it before, but the chair still had a whitish glow about it from the Glide Spell.

"You needn't concern yourself with the prin—Oh!"

Just as Robert began to mouth the spell end spell, the chair fled from under Snow's touch the two feet back to the wall. She tumbled to the floor, the book to her lap.

"No," Robert hissed, terrified lest the chair continue its way up the wall and fall on Snow. He threw back the covers and rose to help her, but Lyndon beat him to it. "Spell end," he mouthed as Lyndon reached her.

With a suspicious glare at him, which Robert was unequal to receive properly—not with a silent "ouch" forming on Snow's lips—Lyndon helped Snow up and into the now spell-less chair.

"Back in bed, Robert," Lyndon ordered.

"Are you alright?" Robert asked as he obediently returned to his prison. "My apologies for the … state of my furniture."

With a strange look at him, Snow cautiously settled into the chair. "Yes, I'm fine."

"I'm relieved. And truly sorry. *Um* … If you have a moment, there is something Lyndon has to say to you." Robert gave Lyndon a significant look.

Lyndon merely stared with intentional blankness at him a moment, before returning to his seat and facing Snow. "Yes," he answered at last. "Prince Dokar cursed Robert to be a frog unless he gains a lady's kiss each day. He thought he could force my lord into mischief and dishonorable conduct. Prince Dokar's design of causing trouble at court failed. However, we also failed to secure a suitable cure before the end of the first day. Consequently, each morning his grace wakes as a frog. Lady Violetta, and now you, have been kind enough to lend aid."

"Lady Violetta was late today," Robert added, fairly certain a blush was coloring his cheeks, "so I decided to explore until she arrived, since I am quite well in that form. I heard you singing."

"Ah."

It wasn't the response Robert wanted, but to tell the truth, he wasn't sure what he wanted or expected. Perhaps for her to blurt out why she'd stopped talking to him years before this incident even occurred?

"Tell her about the other one please, Lyndon."

Maybe that would do the trick.

Lyndon gave Robert a pointed look, flicked a glance at Snow's chair, and said, "As for the other curse, its color is *blonde*. A shapely, bewitching blonde."

"Lyndon!" Robert exclaimed. "That is *not* helpful!"

His godfather's lips curved as if trying to smile before flattening out. "If you'll excuse me, I must see to something."

"Lyndon! You promised!"

His godfather ignored him, and as he strode out, Robert turned to Snow, fearing what he might see. The satisfaction of confirmed suspicion? Anger? Or worse, indifference?

Instead, hurt flashed through her eyes before being swallowed by a blank mask.

"January, it's not what he implied. I mean she—" His words vanished, his mouth still moving, but, as Rupert had once informed him, more in the manner of a fish than anything else. He couldn't even summon the aid of a lipreader! As Snow's frost transformed to a wide-eyed stare, he forced a cough. "I mean, there is a blonde aspect, but it wasn't my fault! It wasn't even meant for me but for Rupert! And I'm mostly over it now!"

*Please be jealous! Please don't be hurt ... too much. Please believe me.*

"How fortunate for you." Posture stiff, Snow rose and strode to the door.

"January, please believe me! I was never unfaithful to Princess Snow."

Two feet from the door, her shoulders falling, Snow stopped. She didn't turn but seemed to be staring at the duffle.

"January?" he asked worriedly.

"What do you mean by 'mostly over it'?" she asked, a slight catch in her voice.

"I—I'm not over it at all, to be honest, but Lady Violetta found a loophole which effectively frees me from it."

"How long?"

"We discovered the loophole only a month ago."

She turned back to him. "I mean about the curse."

"Oh … life became complicated, quite complicated in many ways actually, after the assassination attempt on my uncle."

"Oh." The single word sounded strangely disappointed. Her shoulders, which had started to rise, fell again.

*I wrote you what I could, but you'd already stopped answering me.*

She turned away again, and his heart fell.

"Why does Princess Snow hide from me?" he blurted, unable to stop himself.

Snow stilled, then spun around, a wild wind in the movement warning him of a brewing storm. "Hide from you!" she cried. The hurt he'd glimpsed in her eyes earlier had returned in full force. "She bared her heart to you! Told you her deepest secret, the one that nearly drowned her, that could cost her her kingdom and even her life, and you never spoke to her again! When the beautiful face became a real person—with real flaws and deep struggles—you left!

"She thought you were friends, hoped that when she told you the truth, you could at least remain that, but you decided the two of you couldn't without even consulting her. Yet you wonder why, when you suddenly show up four years later, after your chances of ruling New Beaumont are gone, she refuses to see you!" Chest heaving, Snow spun away from him and brought the back of her hand to her mouth.

Robert stared at her, almost afraid to move lest she flee from him again. He was angered by the lie of his abandonment, but also caught by her pain, and struggling in the face of that pain with the joy that she was actually talking to him. But what deep, dark secret had she told him?

With a quick prayer for guidance, he said slowly, calmly, "She did mention blaming her stepmother for her father's death once. She also once mentioned lying about something she did and getting a maid into trouble, but she apologized for both those, and those are hardly kingdom-costing sins."

His eyes narrowed, and he added, barely keeping a sharpness from his voice, "And I'm not the one who ended the correspondence—and I don't consider the friendship ended even now—she did that. With no reason whatsoever, she stopped replying to my letters, and I sent many *over those four years.*"

Snow went still again, almost as frozen as her name implied. "That was the worst she ever told you about herself?" she said a moment later, her voice raw.

"Yes."

"When did she stop writing to you?"

"A few months before her twenty-first birthday. I didn't even get an invitation to her birthday banquet. I was going to propose that night!"

Snow listed to the side but caught herself and straightened before Robert made it to his feet.

"If you don't believe me," he said, forcing himself to lean back against the pillows again, "you can ask Lyndon. I've badgered him about the post often enough over the years for him to give you an honest answer."

Snow slowly turned to study him, as if wanting to see the truth of what he said in his eyes. He held her gaze and nodded.

"I wrote you too," she whispered. Eyes shimmering, she fled the room.

*She wrote him...*

As his gaze followed her out, the likely reason for her reaction, for the years of pain both had endured, clicked into place, and he found himself very much wanting to pummel whoever had been diverting their letters. Who would do that? Had it been Lucrezia wanting to keep him free as a backup plan? That pipsqueak Bankor? Who would gain by Snow not marrying him?

By the time Lyndon joined Robert, his fury had cooled into a cold anger that kept him pacing his small room, and a joy that occasionally had him staring stupidly at Snow's chair. She'd written him! She was really talking to him now!

"Did January ask you anything?" he queried, accepting the coffee Lyndon offered him and sitting down in Snow's chair.

Lyndon smiled sadly and took a sip of his coffee. "About you posting letters to her and waiting for the mail like a puppy for its owner every day?"

"I was not that bad."

Lyndon didn't reply to that specifically. "She did. I also explained about Lucrezia."

*Thank you, Lord, and you, Lyndon.* "And?"

"I doubt she made it to her room before tears flowed."

Robert set his cup on the bedside table and stood. "I should check on her."

Lyndon waved for him to sit. "Give her time to finish her cry and think about what you said. Some ladies don't like to be caught with red eyes and a runny nose—and I suspect she is one of those."

Remembering his sister in her teenage years, Robert returned to his seat. "What do you think happened? Why would anyone block our communication?"

"If Snow married, she might claim the throne. Something she's hitherto appeared unwilling to do. You trust the queen?"

"Yes. And Snow has always seemed to. Queen Solstice is beautiful, but her appearance and charm are free of magic, at least as far as I can tell. If Lucrezia was responsible, then Snow should have received the recent letter I wrote telling her I was coming."

"Unless Lucrezia had an agent in the palace who didn't know to quit the interception."

"True. It could also be one of the advisors. The nobles might be afraid I would not be as easy to overrule as the queen and princess."

"But which one? Or ones?"

"I'm for Bankor. He needs a pummeling."

Chuckling, Lyndon set aside his coffee and picked up a book. "It's a good thing for the young men of New Grimmland that Princess Snow made herself scarce over the years."

"I wouldn't beat up everyone who talked to her," Robert protested. "Just those who annoyed her or challenged me."

Shaking his head fondly, Lyndon scooted his chair closer to the candelabra on the table next to him. "Let's figure out your curses, then worry about the letters." His smile was sly. "Those aren't needed now."

Robert grinned back, then stretched out in the chair to enjoy his coffee, but a slight movement of the chair reminded him of his earlier escapade. He cleared his throat, drawing Lyndon's attention. "Yes, I got a spell to make the chair glide. I went on several exhilarating—but effortless and painless—rides down the hallway. Figured it would be a good way to get around the moratorium on walking. I did forget to remove the spell from the chair. I'm sorry." As Lyndon shook his head again, in exasperation this time,

Robert continued, "But you didn't have to do that to me—a blonde curse!"

"I think it had the desired effect," Lyndon answered with a return of that sly smile, "as painful as it may have been for a few moments." His tone softened, and he leaned forward to grip Robert's shoulder. "I wasn't being vindictive, Robert. Venting frustration, yes, but no more so than you calling me an old nanny goat, which I am compelled to be by my own affection and your aunt and uncle's orders."

Robert patted his friend's hand. "I know, and I am glad you're here, Lyndon."

CHAPTER 10

As soon as Lyndon was out of sight, Snow ran for her room, not stopping until she stood in front of the mirror and rested the golden orb of her bracelet against it. A tear froze on her cheek as the mirror sent out its icy arms and pulled her into the dark of the castle gardens.

Robert hadn't abandoned her! He still wanted *her*, not the throne.

The tear melted, and the crystals vanished, freeing her from their hold. By starlight and memory, she found the garden bench hidden under a willow's curtain, threw herself on it, and wept, four years of pain, confusion, and anger in those burning drops.

When the storm clouds darkening her soul had given up their power, she lay quietly for a few moments, daring to dream about a future with the friend she thought she'd lost. Then the dream shattered.

Robert hadn't abandoned her it was true, but he also didn't know about her curse—someone had stopped their communication at that letter to prevent him knowing the truth, or because it was a likely time for Robert himself to stop their correspondence. He wasn't seeking her affections despite the curse, but in ignorance of it. Would he abandon her now, if she told him? Would he even be willing to stay her friend when he couldn't be more? She'd given up hope for freedom from her curse years ago, which was why she'd written the desperate letter to Robert, knowing she'd put off his proposal as long as she could and that he needed to know why she couldn't marry him. She'd vowed then to make her curse useful. She'd bought a Switching Spell from an unscrupulous enchanter for the day the sorcerer came back for Solstice. Snow would switch places with her, kiss the sorcerer, then make sure he never woke. No one was taking Solstice from her father. Not the sorcerer or Guagin or anyone else. To ensure that, she needed her curse.

An ache settled in her heart. She wanted what Solstice and her father had, but she couldn't condemn anyone to life in a mirror.

"Princess?" A lantern, its brilliance magnified against Birch's mirror-like hair, followed the hail into the secluded garden chamber.

"Here, Birch." Sniffling, Snow pushed herself into a seated position and used her handkerchief to dry her face.

Birch stopped in front of her and raised the lantern to better see her. His expression darkened as he took in her tear-streaked face. "I can't curse anybody for you, Princess," he said with feeling. "I wish I could." His eyes searching hers, he sat beside her, an invitation to talk if she needed to.

Chuckling, Snow gave her face a final wipe and put away the sodden cloth. "Sometimes, I wish you could too," she said, her voice rough. She cleared her throat. "Is Solstice here? I have something I need to tell you all." She bit her lip as a final tear burned her eyes. "It's … I'm not sure how good it will be in the end, some of it, but there are parts for certain you won't like. There's also something you could do for me, Birch."

"She's here." Birch rose and offered her his hand. When Snow took it with her gloved one, he gave it a gentle squeeze and met her gaze. "I would do anything for you, Princess."

*I have only three people to love, and you are one of those. Let me help you. Let me feel alive once more.* Snow heard again in her mind Birch's declaration and plea, voiced many times over the years, and was reminded of Robert's request to fight a dragon or cure a curse for her. She gave a wet laugh. *Oh, Robert, I love your adventurous, generous spirit.*

Birch looked at her strangely, and she shook her head and let him lead her inside to her parents' sitting room.

Theodore and Solstice, sitting next to one another on a low couch, looked up as she entered.

"Darling! Whatever happened? Are you alright?" Solstice cried, rising. "Is it Robert? Did his wounds become infected?"

"You talked to him, didn't you?" her father exclaimed with more excitement than distress. He reached her first, and Birch released her to him.

Soon, Snow was seated beside Theodore on the couch, with Solstice on her other side and Birch seated across from them.

"Well?" her father prodded.

"Robert has two curses, one of which involves him turning into a frog if he doesn't gain a lady's kiss each day."

Her father paled. "Oh."

"I can kiss a frog without harm," she continued, not bothering to be embarrassed at the excitement in that odd declaration. "He was cursed by Prince Dokar right before we met on the way to the Cottage for Retired Enchanters, and Lady

Violetta has been helping him since. He stopped a high-waymen attack on my carriage rather than go look for some flirt to kiss so he could stay human."

"Prince Dokar!" Solstice exclaimed. "Queen Marianne will never forgive me. I sent Robert to the Cottage. I—" She cleared her throat as Theodore grinned approval at her and Snow scowled at her for the fun of it. Birch laughed at them all. "I warned him about engaging with Dokar," Solstice continued meekly.

"Lady Violetta had already told him to go there," Snow confessed, dropping the glower. "And Prince Dokar was hunting him." She explained Robert's "blonde" curse.

"That's why he stopped visiting then?" her father asked.

"That's part of it." Snow paused, her heart torn between happiness, anger, and fear. What if he deserted her now? Gathering her courage, she met her father's gaze. "A few months before my twenty-first birthday, I wrote Robert and told him about the curse. You always said it was my choice when to tell him, that I should, yet I always put it off, hoping for a cure. I'd given up on that by then and didn't want him to propose, which I knew he planned to do soon." She paused again, then finished softly, "I never heard back."

She was quiet a moment before shaking herself and noticing her father's gaze on her. His expression was pained. "I realize that would be hard for anyone to take," she continued, "but I'd hoped to continue our correspondence as friends, and I told him that. That's what hurt so much when he never responded. Why I wouldn't see him when he came. He finally showed up, and I assumed it was only because he was desperate enough for a crown now that Prince Rupert had returned to have a pretend marriage with me, and probably a mistress on the side."

"Snow, please cut to the chase," her father pleaded as he

rubbed his scrunched brow. "Have I been fooling myself and misleading you about him all these years?"

Laughing, Snow shook her head. "No, you were right. *He* thought *I'd* stopped talking to him, and because of the curse and some kingdom business, he was afraid of coming to New Grimmland lest he be used against us. Someone had been monitoring our conversations and saw my confession as an opportunity to justify the breaking of our relationship. I don't know who or why exactly—"

"Someone who fears a strong leader," Theodore growled. "Robert could not be pushed around like a queen of foreign birth with a mirror to protect and a distaste for arguments." Theodore gave Solstice an understanding smile in return for her rueful one.

"You want Robert to write you another letter then," Birch said, finally joining the conversation, "and for me to watch to see who intercepts it?"

"Yes."

"Consider it done."

"Thank you, Birch."

"My pleasure, *Princess*." He cocked an eyebrow at her, and she suspected he'd been watching her on occasion, doubtless at Solstice's instigation, and knew of her maid ploy. "But first, you must ask him to."

"I will," she answered with a meek nod.

"Perhaps the two of you can find a cure," her father added. "Young men in love tend to be a force to be reckoned with."

"Yes…" Ice threatened to overwhelm her again, to freeze her heart to protect it from a repeat of the agony it had already borne. Did Robert love her enough to be that whirlwind force for her? To stay her friend at least?

*Some pain, some risks are worth it.*

*Please come through, Robert. I don't want to go through that again.*

⬥

ONE WOULD THINK she was about to face Prince Dokar herself, not her almost-fiancé, the man who'd still seek her after four years of silence. Snow focused on that last bit as the door to Robert's room opened.

"Good morning, January." Lyndon smiled fondly at her as he held open the door. "That squeak to the hallway has some good uses."

Snow's laugh as she entered with the breakfast tray sounded mostly normal. "Good morning, Lyndon. Good morning—"

No Robert was visible. A motion in green, like a little green ball bouncing up and down on the bed, caught her attention, and she paused to watch in disbelief. Robert … Not only would she have to kiss a frog every day, he wasn't even the same frog every day! What if she accidentally kissed a real frog? If Robert did that to her on purpose…

"Here I am!" a cheerful voice cried.

Despite herself, she startled at the human voice coming from the little tree frog, and despite herself, her nervousness shifted to amusement. "Good morning, Robert." *Or should I say, Sir Ribbet?* Turning away from both Robert and the keen-eyed Lyndon so they wouldn't see her smirk, Snow set the breakfast plates on the desk. Robert the warrior, a tiny tree frog, and not even a poison dart one!

"Go ahead and laugh," Robert said as he settled down on the covers. "It's a pathetic transformation."

"Far be it from me, Your Grace, to laugh at your plight."

Robert snorted. "Rupert got to be a terrifying beast for years! I can't terrify anything larger than a snail."

"Prince Rupert was a beast?" Snow asked, aghast, as she spun around.

"Yes, those years no one saw him, he was cursed and hiding out in the summer castle. That was his fault though. *I* am an innocent victim."

What on earth did Rupert do to deserve that? "Did Prince Dokar curse him too?"

Lyndon cleared his throat. "No. It was something of a private matter. I'm afraid its beginning and end would be of no value to the case of any other curse. Perhaps we can find something of use after breakfast in the library."

"Oh. Well, I assume from his recent marriage he is well now." Straightening her shoulders, she gave Lyndon his food and then turned reluctantly to the little frog, who was watching her hopefully now from a chair beside the head of the bed.

"I don't want to insult you," began a voice entirely too big and masculine for the little frog, "by eating flies rather than the meal you so kindly prepared, but I can't consume it very well as I am. I want you to know I won't take it personally if you kiss me. And Lady Violetta already had me test out the sticky suit—it works."

"Of course, Robert." Telling herself it was ridiculous to even think about blushing for kissing a frog, Snow tugged off her right glove. The golden bracelet bumped her palm as it slipped further down her wrist now that the glove didn't impede it.

"That's a beautiful bracelet," Robert commented as she kissed her fingers. "It reminds me of one Queen Solstice wears."

*Yes, and it doubtless looks like magic.* Snow merely smiled and leaned forward to gently touch his head. There was a bit of a flash, and then it was human Robert under her fingertips, sleep-tousled soft brown hair to be exact, his face nearly at level with hers, his blue eyes focused on her. Snow jerked away so forcefully she would have fallen if Robert hadn't caught her by the elbows.

Regaining her balance and looking everywhere but at him, she backed away, slowly this time. "I'm fine. Thank you." He let her go. Heart still pounding and ridiculous butterflies fluttering in her stomach, she backed away another step and tugged on her glove. "Let's eat before breakfast gets cold."

"Thanks for the kiss and the meal, January." Robert had the goodness not to wink. Instead, he picked up her tray and moved to her seat. "I should have warned you to stand a little further away."

After she sat, he handed her the tray. "You're welcome," she managed as she took it. "I'm glad I can help you." She gave him a small smile and turned her attention to the meal. She felt Lyndon and Robert watching her, as if waiting for her to bring up yesterday's revelation. "Robert," she said at last, daring a quick glance at him, "will you write one more letter to Princess Snow?"

Robert stared at her, his mouth trying to curl at the edges despite the large bite of eggs bulging his cheeks. He finally managed to choke down his food. "I could do that. Do you think she'll respond this time?"

Snow glanced at him through her lashes but didn't look up. "No," she said archly, "but it might enable her to discover who's been intercepting your letters."

"In that case," Robert said, "I'll dictate the letter. Maybe if I speak loudly enough, she'll hear me. Do you think she'll listen?"

"She might," Snow said, peeking up at him before returning her attention to her meal.

When they'd finished eating, Lyndon left to speak with Colors. Gathering her resolution into courage, Snow put her tray back on the desk and went for the duffle she'd left in the corner.

"January—"

"I'm not leaving, Robert."

She picked up the duffle, strode back to him, and dumped the contents—napkins, hand towels, and other linens—on his bed. "Will you help me with this?" She grabbed a cloth napkin.

His eyebrows went clear to his shaggy hair. "Gladly," he said, quickly recovering. He started to move the meal tray from his lap, but she took it from him and set it aside. When she turned back, Robert caught her gloved hand, his eyes intent on her and as pleading as they were the day before, and she found she couldn't move even if she'd wanted to.

"January, my heart has always been free from the curse— the blonde aspect, that is. She—" He cleared his throat again and let her hand go. It fell rather sadly to her side. "I've always been more a fan of raven hair than blonde. Don't let me forget to include that in my letter." He held her gaze a moment longer, then picked up a napkin and began folding it. "How should I fold this? A fancy swan or something? Or should I iron it first?"

Snow's traitorous face couldn't stop a smile, and her dazed heart couldn't come up with a witty reply. "A simple fold will do," she managed at last. "Perhaps we could work on your letter now."

"What do you think I should include?"

"How about what you've been up to the last four years?

Hearing about you only through rumors and news headlines was never quite the same."

"Alright. Do you think at some point Princess Snow will trust me with her secret again?"

Snow stilled, a half-folded napkin in her hands. *Trust.* She hadn't thought of it like that before. She'd only thought of her own fears and the hurt of a rejection. Did she trust him? To be faithful? Resourceful? He'd already proven his kindness and loyalty despite thinking her—knowing her—to be angry with him. Could she trust him with her heart and her family, to help her guard Solstice? Reason and their history said she could, but...

Fear and guilt both twined round her heart, creating an unpleasant sort of mirror. She'd said she wanted what Solstice and her father had—they had no secrets. Solstice never belittled Theodore by assuming he couldn't help, even if only by being a listening ear and a caring heart. Robert was a warrior. How could she dismiss his abilities to protect Solstice, especially if coupled with what she knew?

"January?"

"I think so, Robert," she hastily answered, starting to fold the cloth again so she wouldn't have to look at him. *Help me trust where trust is wise rather than fear, Lord.* "How about this: you rest in the cottage three more days, and then I'll talk Lyndon into letting us go for a ride or walk? By that time, I'll have gotten the secret from Princess Snow, and the blackberries will be ready to pick." *By that time, I'll have rebuilt some of what I destroyed, enough that you'd at least want to stay my friend.*

Robert took the napkin from her and placed it on the pile. "It's a deal. But can we at least have tea out in the garden one day? I don't want the sun to think I've been neglecting her too."

Snow laughed and gave him one end of a sheet to help

her fold. "I wouldn't want that. You've been maligned enough. So, the last four years? How many monsters did you slay?"

"Oh, lots," he said with a dismissive gesture followed by a mischievous grin. "None held my missing princess captive though, which was rather disappointing. I was always hoping to find her."

THE NEXT TWO days passed quickly. Robert and January seemed to talk more freely than Robert and Snow had the last year of their correspondence. They talked about their lives, books and music, shared about Robert's research, played card games in the garden, folded laundry, did the dishes, and even began joining the enchanters and Lyndon in the evening for music, conversation, and games.

On the second day, Robert received a note informing him Queen Marianne would be unable to join them, as she'd twisted an ankle in her haste to tell his uncle about the new curse. Rupert refused to let Belinda go in her place, saying Robert could find his own curse breaker. Snow suspected Rupert, who loved Robert like a brother, knew she was with him.

She was somewhat ashamed of how relieved she was— not that she was glad about Queen Marianne's injury—but she was quickly finding herself possessive of a certain green amphibian, and ridiculously happy at being able to kiss something without harming it. Always, though, the shadow of what she had to tell Robert dimmed her smiles, requiring frequent reminders that he was worth the risk of another heartbreak. That love involved trust.

The morning of the third day dawned bright, with just

enough clouds for a pleasant shade. It brought no worries of rain, which the cowardly part of Snow wished for, as today was the day for the outing and the second attempt at explaining The Secret. Burying her face in the pillow, she said a prayer for courage. If only she were half as brave as Robert.

"Do you wish to kiss Robert this morning, or shall I?"

Jumping up with a muffled scream, Snow's attention flew to the elegant woman sitting beside her bed.

"Good morning, dear." Lady Violetta, dressed in a magnificent silver gown with amethyst stones worked into it, smiled kindly and waved toward the end of the bed. A crimson gown and a lightweight shrug were draped over the comforter. It was the one she'd worn during her first visit to the cottage, only now with sparkling crystals in a rose design on the skirt.

"Good morning," Snow managed, unable to take her eyes off the gorgeous dress. If only she had a reason to wear it! She scooted over to it to rub the smooth satin between her fingers. "I'll kiss him."

Lady Violetta's silence held a knowing smile, Snow suspected.

"I've brought it for a fitting. It might make you feel tired for a while, but don't let that worry you."

"I don't mind." Would Robert gape at her if he saw her in it? If she admitted it, she really wasn't annoyed at his tendency to do so, not now that she remembered he'd never done that to anyone else. How had she forgotten that? Why did she always assume ill of him?

"You'll have to wear it all day, every day, of course. Treat it like your own sticky suit."

Snow looked up at her, eyebrows raised.

"Don't worry. It's self-cleaning for up to one hundred

days, and you have that lovely apron downstairs to protect it."

Smiling to herself, Snow brought the dress to her lap and began examining it for clasps and hoping it was something she could get in and out of by herself.

"Have you been using my spell?"

"Spell?" Snow asked, looking up to find Lady Violetta's eyes an unusually mellow violet that made her think of contentment. "Oh, the song for the creatures. No, but I think I will soon. And thank you for the dress. It's the loveliest thing I've ever seen." Would it help with her curse? Could she put off telling Robert until she found out?

*Coward. Tell him today.*

Lady Violetta just smiled, her eyes brightening. "I'll step outside a moment while you change. Remember—it might make you feel tired." She disappeared in a swirl of silver and violet.

Snow rose, and after brushing and braiding her tangled hair, quickly donned the dress. It fit to perfection. She stood still a moment, one hand out toward the dresser to catch herself should she feel suddenly tired.

She waited, flexed her fingers, studied each message from her legs and arms and the rest of her. She felt fine, better than that: it was a beautiful morning, and she, for once, was dressed to match! "You can come in," she called. "I don't feel tired at all."

Lady Violetta returned, through the door this time.

Snow spun slowly for her to see, her cheeks aching with a grin. "It fits perfectly! However did you manage it with only a kissed handkerchief?"

"Oh, well, that's a guild secret." Lady Violetta gave one of her elegant shrugs before examining Snow again, her expression almost concerned, or perhaps confused. "You're sure you're not tired?"

"No."

"*Hmm.* Perhaps it's the excitement, or it may not take effect immediately." She tapped a thin finger to her lips, then shrugged, though less elegantly than before. "If the stones on your dress turn red, tell Colors. I'll check on you soon. Remember, you must wear it continuously."

"I shall resign myself to being beautiful."

"*Hmm.*" Lady Violetta eyed her again and shook her head. "I'll be back in a few hours. In the meantime, enjoy and don't forget to kiss Robert. In your slapping method."

"I will and I won't. And thank you."

With a sly smile, Lady Violetta patted her arm and left in another burst of silver and violet.

Snow quickly finished her morning routine. Biting back a yawn, she went downstairs to fix breakfast.

She gave the cat a good rub and then put him out the kitchen window, leaving the window open. It felt unusually warm this morning. She put the kettle on to boil and started gathering ingredients, her footsteps dragging. What should it be this morning?

The cuckoo clock announced the quarter hour, and Snow shook herself. How long had she been gazing into the pantry? She pulled out a few items and set them on the table.

She removed the whistling kettle from the heat and headed back to the worktable, but stumbled as her eyes closed by themselves. Her feet suddenly lead weights, she staggered the remaining few feet to the worktable. Clutching its solid wooden top with both hands, she struggled to force her eyes to remain open. Lady Violetta hadn't exaggerated when she'd said the dress would make her tired. Was it because it was fighting her curse? Perhaps she should sit for a few minutes. Robert and Lyndon would be gracious about a late breakfast.

Snow took one careful step toward the chair and then clutched her throat, gasping for air as a familiar burn of magic choked her. This wasn't sleep—it was the curse all over again. She hit the floor, and the world went black.

# CHAPTER 11

**E**ven if Robert weren't currently a frog, he had a suspicion he'd still be bouncing around like one. Today was the day Snow was going to finagle a walk for them and tell him about her secret. That bit of magic about her had something to do with her secret, he'd stake his life on it. Who had done that to her? The same one who'd diverted their correspondence? If only he were a ferocious beast! He could terrorize *and* pummel the blackguard.

"You look very intimidating, for a frog," Lyndon said with a hint of a smile. "A moment ago I thought you were about to bounce to the ceiling."

Robert settled onto the pillow and made an effort to let go of his desire for vengeance. "Snow and I are going for a walk today, and she's going to tell me about her curse." At Lyndon's raised eyebrows, he added, "I'll behave, don't worry. No running, jumping, or fighting bandits unless unavoidable—running from them would involve running, after all, so I might as well fight."

Laughing, Lyndon caught him up in his hand and brought

him before his face. "Do I have your solemn oath as a prince of New Beaumont that you will endeavor, as much as depends on you, to neither overexert yourself nor acquire another injury or curse? As well as be a gentleman in your behavior to Princess Snow?"

"You have my word, good sir." Robert tipped forward in a bow.

"Then I shall let you out of the house. However, you will remain a frog until the outward journey is over."

"What!"

"You may walk around the blackberry patches and carry Snow's basket back for her. That way you won't overexert yourself but will have some opportunity for wooing. You may hop or ride in her basket on the way out."

Frowning, Robert drummed his webbed right fingers on Lyndon's hand, trying very hard to keep his thoughts to himself.

Lyndon's eyebrows rose again. "That feels exceedingly odd. Stop that."

Robert drummed all his fingers and toes on his godfather's hand. Lyndon threw him back onto the bed.

Laughing, Robert bounced from the pillow to the windowsill. He sat some time beside the open window, watching the dawn turn to morning and indulging in a snack of fruit flies, wondering if Lyndon, whose stomach had started growling, envied him the latter. Snow was a bit late today. Dare he hope she'd spent more time than usual getting dressed and ready for their walk? Not that he didn't already care for her and think her beautiful, but the extra effort would make him feel princely. Pity he couldn't do anything special to show his desire to be handsome for her. He couldn't even brush his hair until after she kissed him. When would they be ready for the true love's first kiss that would break his spell and start them toward their life together?

"I'll see if Snow needs any help." Robert bounded off the bed and out the door, Lyndon's warning for him to make enough noise so that people didn't step on him following him out.

"And watch out for the cat!" Lyndon added.

"We're on good terms, don't worry!"

Hopping through the house wasn't as fun as hopping over soft grass, not to mention the house liked to play with him: traces of magic that were on a hat rack one day were on a painting the next, a kitchen door after that. Ignoring this morning's odd magical aura about the hallway curtains, Robert made it to the kitchen without mishap.

"Snow," he called as he entered. A large red puddle stained the floor at the foot of the table. "Snow!"

Panic clawing at him, Robert leapt forward, only partly relieved to realize the red puddle was a dress rather than blood. Though she bore no obvious signs of injury, Snow lay still, eyes closed.

"Snow, wake up!"

Her face was too pale. Forcing himself to make use of his military training to stay somewhat calm, Robert slid to a halt just shy of Snow's outstretched hand. He couldn't hear her breathing. Her chest wasn't moving.

*No.*

*No!*

"Colors!" he yelled. "Lyndon!"

*Keep calm, Robert. You of all people know curses can be deceiving. Colors told you Snow's curse wouldn't kill her.*

Robert forced down the panic and made himself study Snow, his gut clenching at the sight of her so still.

A ruby glow of magic suffused her body, a fainter version

of that previously concentrated in her lips. No sign of a wound marred her, no sign of poisoned food on the counter. It had to be a curse. Curses could be cured. Not all were fatal.

"Colors!" he yelled again. Snow never flinched at his bellowing.

Frantic, Robert hopped back and forth in front of Snow's head, his gaze on her closed eyes, her ruby lips no breath crossed. If only he could touch her! Hold her, get her off the floor, carry her to a bed. Do something! But he was only a frog.

Swearing at Dokar, Robert forced himself away from Snow, determined to find Colors since his yells hadn't worked. He was halfway across the room when Lyndon charged in. Colors and the other enchanters materialized behind him in the doorway.

"She's not dead!" Robert cried. "She can't be! You've got to do something." Robert bounded back to Snow and nestled against her neck at her shoulder.

"Get away, Robert!" Lyndon warned as the group surrounded them.

"The curse won't hurt me as an animal, and Dokar's spell is a jealous one," he protested. She was already cool to the touch. *No, Lord, please, please bring her back to me.*

"He's fine, Lyndon." Colors knelt beside Snow, and after a pair of gloves materialized around his hands, he gently tilted her face toward him. His skin blushed the same terrifying red as the curse.

"Your color for her hasn't changed," Cello exclaimed, wringing his hands. "What happened then? Why is she dressed like that? Did she know? Did she choose her own funeral gown?" he cried, his voice rising in distress, its notes screeching.

Standing beside him, Today patted Cello's arm. His naturally cheerful face was clouded with concern as he watched Colors as much as Snow. Even Blatherskite had lost his usual eager gleam, as if this news bore no pleasure for him. Who was less shadowy and more solid than normal, weighted by a grief Robert could understand.

The glow about Snow didn't fade as did that on Colors as he continued to study her and probe her head for injury. The sign of magic about her wasn't the tempting red of a rose. It was the red of warning, the red of poisonous berries, of serpents and spiders.

*The red of poison...*

The reason Snow always wore gloves and rarely touched anyone, why she didn't kiss him directly even as a frog, burst on him: her curse had made her a poison to others. Something had turned that back on her.

Colors traced his hand down to Snow's wrist, feeling for a pulse there and then fingering the voluminous skirt at the gemstone rose. The stones were as deep a red as the dress, as the curse itself.

With a sigh of relief Robert couldn't understand, Colors sank back on his heels. "She's alive. The curse spread, that's all. I think we can make it retreat, with time."

"She's..." Eyes closing, Robert trailed off into a silent prayer of gratitude.

"Today," Colors said, his tone calm and commanding, "summon Lady Violetta. Lyndon, help me get January upstairs. Blatherskite, Cello, you might as well make coffee. All writing projects are off until we've researched the princess's curse and found answers. Who, tell I Don't Know to search the library catalogue again. Give him more terms to hunt."

*Alive...* While Robert blinked back tears, Lyndon scooped him up and placed him on his shoulder.

"Stay put so you don't get stepped on," his godfather ordered, his own eyes shimmering.

Colors carefully lifted Snow and carried her back to her room. Lady Violetta was already pacing the small chamber, her usually flamboyant gown a subdued, simple gray frock. Her expression was so distraught, so guilty, Robert didn't know whether to pity or suspect her.

"Oh, my darling!" she cried, covering her mouth with her hand. "I only brought it for a fitting, but she seemed so fond of it, I hated to take it away from her so soon. I should have known the lack of immediate effect was a bad sign!"

"There's no use fretting, Lady Violetta," Colors said firmly but kindly as he lowered Snow to the bed. "I trust all we need do is change her dress?"

"The dress caused this!" Robert blurted, his recent shock too much to keep his thoughts in check.

"Yes," came a small, broken reply. Lady Violetta seemed to fade before him.

"My lady!" Colors stepped to her side. His own arm briefly fading, he caught her round the shoulders, and they both re-solidified.

With a shy glance at Colors as he stepped away, Lady Violetta cleared her throat and regained her elegant posture. "Yes. I'm terribly sorry. I'll bring it back later, toned down. I'll have to drain the Poison Stone first, however. It worked too fast."

"Those are Poison Stone!" Colors exclaimed. His look at Lady Violetta was one of awe mixed with concern, though why that latter emotion was directed at the enchantress rather than Snow, Robert wasn't sure.

"The last few enchanters who tried for a Poison Stone died," Who said with more interest in his tone than usual.

Cello, Blatherskite, I Don't Know, and Today crowded into the room behind him.

Regal posture now fully regained, Lady Violetta gave an elegant shrug. "The Lady Octavia is not so fearsome if one knows how to approach her: I made an outfit for her. She gave me a Poison Stone in return." She glanced at Colors, and her cheeks pinked as Colors stared at her, surprise and admiration in his expression this time.

She tapped one of the stones on Snow's skirt. "I believe the princess's trouble is caused by a lingering poison-curse. Poison-curses can be drawn out or broken. I don't know how to break it, so I thought, why not extract it? The dress was made to take advantage of the Poison Stone's ability to draw the poison to itself. It was supposed to draw it slowly enough not to harm her, which is one reason the stone is split, for now, into the smaller gems making up the rose. When it is full, I can remove the poison from it easily enough. Eventually, we can draw out all the poison-curse. Theoretically, of course." Her brow furrowed, and she looked to Colors, as if expecting him to understand what she was about to say. "If we don't get trapped in the 'half of a half of a half' mathematics. No one has ever tested exactly by how much the poison reduces each—"

"Forgive me," Robert interrupted excitedly, hopping from Lyndon's shoulder to Lady Violetta's, "but how long will this take?"

Lady Violetta's smile blossomed, her violet eyes glimmering with their usual shine. "Robert dear, I didn't see you before. How well you look! I really don't know."

"This has never been done before," Cello put in with an official kind of nod, pride in the gesture. "*This* will be something to write about, along with the young lord's spell seeing. You must take your retirement soon, Lady Violetta."

"Exactly so," Today added with a nod of his own.

"Perhaps," she said modestly.

"The dress?" Robert nudged.

"Unfortunately," Lady Violetta said, taking back over the discussion, "it doesn't work if she's fully asleep. Her own movements and wakefulness help. I'll change her into a nightgown and bring back a weaker dress in the next day or two."

"How long until she wakes?"

"Two or three days?"

"I'll stay with her," Robert said firmly.

"Robert dear, of course you will." Lady Violetta's violet eyes sparkled with amusement. Robert, being held close to her face, was reminded how beautiful eyes were, and how different gazing into Snow's eyes was from anybody else's.

"Somewhere in the house anyway." She arched a thin eyebrow. "You certainly will *not* be in here while I change her. Not even as a frog. I'll do something about that in a moment, by the way."

"Give him a Pocket Spell, Lady Violetta," Who urged, drawing everyone's attention to his shadowy corner of the room. He leaned comfortably against the wall. "He can keep kisses in it and so can do more than yell for help when his lady love is dying."

Bristling, Robert glared at Who before remembering the man was trying to help him.

"How clever of you!" Lady Violetta exclaimed with a clap of her hands, which engulfed Robert and left him tingling with magic and a headache. She kissed him three times and sat him on the chair beside the bed. He felt that green slime in him shiver three times, but no change overcame him. He looked up at her questioningly, and she nodded at him, the kind of nod telling him to go ahead.

Assuming that was her way of indicating he should figure it out for himself, Robert focused on that slimy feeling inside, noting how it seemed to spread out, having one long "handle." Catching it, he yanked it out of his core.

Head spinning, he found himself, human Robert, sitting in the chair, Lady Violetta clapping her approval of his skill.

"Well done, Robert," she said, and then began shooing everyone out.

Later, after Lady Violetta had left, having promised to return that evening and tell them of her gaining of the Poison Stone, and Lyndon had gone to the village for food and the enchanters to the library for research, Robert sat, a book in his lap, watching Snow as she slept. A reddish glow still shrouded her, but her heart was faintly beating now. How long before she would fully wake?

Robert brought the back of her gloved hand to his cheek. "Oh, Snow, I wish the curing of your curse was as simple as a kiss." He pressed his lips to the back of her hand, placed it at her side, and prepared for a long wait and a lot of studying.

# CHAPTER 12

"**Y**a wouldn't disappoint an old soldier, now would ya? Especially not one who lost 'is leg in yer father's service?"

Ten-year-old Snow did her best not to grimace at the soldier's appearance, all wrinkled and scarred and telling frightful tales of suffering and death. But there was something more about the stooped, jagged-toothed man in a faded uniform blocking her path through the castle gardens that alarmed her. She couldn't say what, but it was worse than the physical ugliness she knew she shouldn't be frightened of or repulsed by.

He lifted the apple toward her again. It was a deep red and so tempting it made her stomach rumble. "'Tis my best apple, the only thing I've left to give my king afore I die. Give it to 'im, would ya, princess?"

Despite herself, Snow inched back. "I'm sorry," was all she managed before his expression fell and she began to feel sorry for him. The guards had surely allowed the old man in, or else he wouldn't be here, so perhaps it was alright? She'd been warned about accepting things from strangers, but if the guards thought the man, a loyal old soldier, acceptable … She fisted her hands. Surely

138

*her father knew better than the guards. Stiffening her resolve with the help of assuming a proper princess posture, she said, kindly, "I'm sorry, but I'm not allowed to take anything from strangers."*

*"Ya wouldn't be taking it for yerself but for yer father. I was planning on dying in 'is service afore my wound sent me home. The apple 'tis the last service I can give." He lifted the apple higher and closer, bringing it near enough for her to smell. It smelled as appealing as it looked, a total opposite to the old soldier. "Please."*

*Obedience warring with pity, Snow took another step back. Her heel slipped off the edge of the walkway, and she teetered. The old man caught her in a spry movement. She shivered at his touch to her elbow. Letting her go, he backed away and pressed the apple into her hand.*

*"Thank ya, princess. Ya gave an old soldier 'is dying wish."*

*"But—" she protested, struggling to get her balance.*

*But the old man was gone.*

*"You didn't tell me your name," she called to the empty garden, all distaste for the old man and his gift strangely gone. Father would be happy to receive such a present from one of his soldiers.*

*Snow skipped through the garden and hunted her father until she found him in his study, sitting with Queen Solstice, who smiled quietly at her as she entered. Her stepmother was kind, though reserved, as if she liked Snow but didn't know what to do about it. Snow was determined to like her if only to please her father, and she had a feeling Solstice felt the same about her, and that made her like her all the more. Solstice was also her mother's cousin, and though they grew up in different kingdoms, she could tell Snow about her and their family.*

*Her father rose as she raced inside.*

*"Look what the old man in the garden gave me! Gave you, I mean," she blurted, her stomach rumbling again. "May I have a bite too?"*

*Laughing, her father caught her up in a bear hug. "You may* have the first bite, darling," he said, swinging her around before setting her on her feet again.

Snow looked at the bright red apple, saw her reflection in its shiny peel, took a bite, and found she couldn't breathe. Couldn't spit out the bite nor swallow it. Her insides burned, her eyelids dragged themselves down in sleep despite the battle raging in her for air. Her father and stepmother cried out, but she couldn't see them. Then their voices faded. Everything faded, except a harsh voice she'd never heard before.

A crown can't give you everything, can it? Not love. Not life. You're dead! She'll carry on without you—with me. No crown can save you. Only love, and that you never had. It was only the crown, and that failed you. You're dead!

Cruel laughter followed this, and the taunt began again.

◔◍◑

SNOW WOKE SLOWLY. A middle-aged man in flamboyant clothing stood over her, his expression satisfied in an arrogant kind of way. She didn't know him and didn't like him.

She forced her head to turn away from him. It was as sluggish as her mind. What had happened? Why did her lips tingle so, burn with cold? Where was her father?

King Theodore appeared at her side and scooped her up in the tightest hug she'd ever had. She opened her mouth to ask what had happened, but she couldn't get it to work.

"What is it, Snow?" Solstice asked, placing a gentle hand on her back. "Don't squeeze her so tightly, dearest," she scolded her husband.

Snow's father loosened his hold and watched as she tried again to speak. He looked over his shoulder at the man.

"Shock. She only needs to rest," he said confidently. "You're lucky I was here. She's a child and not the curse's intended victim, *but still, she would never have awakened had I not been able to draw out the poison."*

*"Or had my wife not realized the true cause and sent for help,"* *her father said, a different kind of pride in his tone.*

❦

THE REST *of the afternoon was mostly a blur, with Snow lying on a sofa in her parents' sitting room, them hovering over her. By evening, she'd gained enough mobility to rise and ask for dinner.*

*Her father laughed and said, "Only in exchange for a kiss."*

*Happy with that bargain, and though her lips still burned with cold, Snow kissed his cheek. His eyes rounded, and he clutched his throat. Snow screamed as her father collapsed.*

*"Theo!" Solstice cried, falling with him as she tried to catch him. They both hit the floor, but while he didn't move, she scooted out from under him and began examining him for a pulse. "Theo!"*

*Snow fell back onto the sofa, staring at her father, frozen with horror. What had she done?*

You're dead! You're dead! She'll carry on without you— with me. No crown can save you. Only love, and that you never had. It was only the crown, and that failed you.

*She heard again the cruel laughter, forgotten and remembered. Touching a hand to her burning lips, she dragged her gaze from her father to Solstice. Solstice watched her closely, the panic gone, her gaze sharp.*

*Snow's breathing grew frantic as she realized what she'd done. "I didn't—I—"* I didn't mean too! I didn't know!

*"Hush, child," Solstice said hastily, looking over her shoulder at the guards who'd rushed in from the hallway. "Help—"*

*"She is responsible, my love. Would you have her lie to herself?" A dark-clothed man somehow like and unlike the old soldier stood in the inner doorway. He took a step toward them*

and held out his hand to Solstice, who was pale and trembling. "Come."

"I'm not your love!" Solstice snapped, and suddenly she had a dagger in her hand. That was when Snow realized the furious tremble as well as the afraid, and perhaps those who were both. "Run, Snow! Guards, kill him!" Solstice cried.

But Snow couldn't move.

The man laughed. "What can they do?" He flicked his fingers, and the guards hit the floor as violently as her father had. Still, Snow couldn't move.

Solstice dropped the dagger and held her hand straight out from her, palm up and fingers splayed. Ice began to form on the gold-rimmed mirror on the wall across the room and grow to the floor, a waterfall of ice built rather than frozen.

One of the guards lifted his head and began crawling stealthily toward a desk against the wall a few feet away. How had he survived?

The ice coating the mirror rushed its growth across the room toward Solstice's outstretched hand.

"Oh, come now," the sorcerer said. "Stop fooling yourself, Solstice. You're mine, and you know it."

"I know whose I am!" The ice that reached Solstice's hand crystalized into a sword. She jabbed her free hand at Snow's father. "His!" The sword broke free from the ice that forged it, and she touched it to the floor behind her, its point a nucleus for the wall of ice swiftly separating Snow, her father, and the mirror from Solstice and the sorcerer. Solstice raised the sword—Winter's Sword. No spell could touch its bearer. No one could resist its order of banishment. "I was never yours! I hate you and always have! I'm his as he is mine, and nothing will change that."

The man flushed, the veins on his forehead bulging. He sprang forward, drawing his wand. "You are mine!"

The guard rose to his knees, snatched a bronze statuette from *the desk, and hurled it at the sorcerer's head. It struck him as light burst from his wand. The light fizzled against the sword's tip, and he collapsed.*

*Drawing his knife, the soldier sprang up and sprinted for the sorcerer. Snow turned away. Solstice sank to the floor. The ice and sword vanished back into the mirror.*

*"Quick!" Rising as swiftly as she'd fallen, Solstice ran for the wall and yanked the mirror off it. "Help me move him!" She laid the mirror beside the king. It began to ice over again.*

*The guard, eyes questioning, hurried to them, lifted her father, and placed him on the mirror's surface. The guard jerked back with a gasp as ice covered her father as well.*

*"Stand back." Solstice pressed her hand against her husband's chest, the golden ball on her bracelet glowing. King Theodore disappeared. The guard gasped louder this time.*

*"Look at me," Solstice ordered. He obeyed. "There might be a chance to save the king. Give me an hour. Get rid of the sorcerer, and don't let anyone else in." Solstice grabbed Snow by her sleeve, and they were drawn into the mirror.*

*Birch was already bending over her father. He was waking, but something in Birch's expression told her King Theodore would never leave the mirror.*

◈

SNOW FELL in and out of memories, the taunts and cruel laughter always rising in the longer periods of darkness, always whispering even in her dreams. Did her father bear this torture constantly in his head? Or was Birch able to help him?

Voices, real ones, sometimes faded in and out as well, along with a strange, small patch of warmth against her neck, at her shoulder. The voices were the loudest, the laughter the quietest, when that warmth was there.

"You pocketed Lady Violetta's kiss this morning, didn't you?"

"The curse doesn't affect me as an animal."

This voice was closer, as if coming from right beside her. It took her a moment to put names to the speakers.

*Robert.* Robert was the one so close.

Could a cursed sleeper cry? Her heart was suddenly full yet could get no release through tears. He hadn't abandoned her. He'd kept a frog form just to be near her!

*They also didn't bury you, which is slightly more important at the moment,* her practical self chided.

"Does she hear us or know we're near?" someone asked. Cello?

"She would be the only one able to answer that." I Don't Know. The little man who rarely left the library, for "To know, is to know that you know nothing." He'd quoted Socrates or some other philosopher to her nearly every time they'd met. Were all the enchanters keeping vigil with her?

"Snow's curse, what can you tell me about it?" The warmth at her neck shifted. "I gather the curse was not originally concentrated in her lips?"

How did Robert know that?

"I had noticed the spell color there before this," he continued.

"When did you first notice it?" Colors asked, curiosity in his tone.

"When I saw her here. I'd not learned to see magic when last we met. I wasn't cursed then either."

"Ah." There was a thoughtful pause before Colors replied, "I don't know the details of her curse. Lady Violetta's note implied the same fate the sorcerer achieved in her father would have happened to her had not a visiting enchanter 'saved' her. Incompletely, as it turns out."

"I don't suppose sorcerers leave journals in the library here?" Robert asked.

"No. They openly reject the code of ethics we claim and so have no part of an enchanter's library."

"What about incompetent enchanters?"

Blatherskite, she assumed, snorted.

"Quite a few have," Colors answered with restrained laughter in his voice. His tone sobered. "And many who do not follow well, if at all, the ethics they profess."

"Queen Solstice wasn't sure of his name, not surprising given the shock and loss she endured that day," Today put in. "We've already searched for the name she thought he gave but had no luck."

"Pity I was dealing with a dragon curse in Gorlag at the time," Blatherskite said, with more seriousness and less bragging than she would have expected from him, "or I could tell you. By the time I got back, no one would talk about anything other than the queen's mourning clothes and her strange absence from her chambers, from the entire castle, on the night of a fire scare."

Robert sucked in a breath. "Wait!"

"Exactly, Your Grace!" Lyndon cried. "Blathersk—"

"Actually, Blatherskite," Colors interrupted, "that is something you should remedy. You and Who go to the palace and request an audience with Queen Solstice. Get her to tell you as much as she can about this incompetent enchanter: looks, mannerisms, methods. Talk to servants and anyone else who might know something, but remember, our January is in hiding. Enchanter names don't often mean much and sometimes change frequently, but if we could figure out who was there, we might be able to either find him or find his writings."

"Consider it done!" Blatherskite declared. "Get me a description, and I'll tell you who it was. Who's who, that's me. Don't even say anything, Cello."

❧❧❧

"EMPTY YOUR POCKETS, ALMOST-PRINCE." There was a thud of books onto a table to accompany Blatherskite's odd demand. "We got a lead on the rapscallion and know a couple of names he's used."

The warmth at her neck left, and the voices faded.

# CHAPTER 13

"**H**ow does the spell color look to you, Robert?" Colors, seated beside Snow's bed, glanced at Robert before sipping from a steaming mug, which was larger than the ones he had used before Snow's relapse into the Sleeping Death two days ago.

They were all taking coffee in Snow's room now. At first, the gentlemen had considered it somewhat creepy to watch her sleep, but then they decided they didn't like leaving her alone, like she was an abandoned corpse. They chose to consider staying with her as guarding her instead. Robert, as her almost-fiancé and the one she'd known the longest, would get the privilege of being the only one there when she woke. That was something they would know was coming based on the spell's coloring.

The red glow no longer engulfed Snow but made a dark halo around her shoulders and head. Her lips were a deep ruby.

Robert set his own coffee cup down and returned his attention to the book on transformation curses he was reading, his efforts aided by a Speed Reading Spell. "The spell color is moving back toward her lips. That's good, isn't it?"

"I hope so, for that is what I see as well."

A quarter hour later, Robert finished the book and his coffee, pocketed the effect of Lady Violetta's earlier kiss, and curled up as a frog at Snow's neck for a short nap. He didn't know if she could sense him or not, but just in case, he wanted her to know he'd not left her. No curse would scare him off.

He was awakened sometime later by a thud of books on a table.

"Empty your pockets, almost-prince." Blatherskite poked him in the side. "We got a lead on the rapscallion and know a couple of names he's used."

In retrospect, Robert was grateful Blatherskite had the sense and ability to move out of the way rapidly; otherwise, there would have been a nasty collision of the two of them when Robert transformed. As it was, Robert, the enchanters, and Lyndon were soon gathered round the table as Today divvied up the stack of autobiographies.

This particular incompetent enchanter, whom Blather-skite had been able to rapidly identify based on Solstice's description (Who had apparently recognized him as well), had, at various times, gone by Aureus, Ferlo, and Henry. They'd found books under all three names, undated, unfortunately.

Today handed Robert *The Life of Aureus*, Volume 2.

The man had either led a very interesting life or was full of himself, for the book was hefty. It was also glowing gray. "This book's got a spell on it, sort of steely gray? A lock?" Robert held it up for Colors to see.

Colors slipped *Ferlo* under his arm, then withdrew his

wand and tapped it on the book. The gray dissolved. "So it seems. Very good, Robert."

"Is mine gray?" Lyndon paused in his attempt to pry open the cover of *The Life of Aureus*, Volume 3.

"Yes." Colors tapped Lyndon's book, then eyed the others. Who had Volume 1, but it wasn't gray.

"I don't need to see spells to guess when one's about." Who hooked his finger under the front cover and flicked it up to indicate it was freely moving.

Colors chuckled.

"The rest are good," Robert said as he claimed his chair by the bed. "Let's get busy."

"I still don't understand how he does it." Blatherskite pouted as he drew a chair from the ether and sat. Robert shrugged and tried not to smirk.

"Maybe because he puts it to good use."

Who got a glare for that comment, but Robert doubted it bothered him.

Today, ever courteous and playing host, brought them more coffee, plus cakes. They settled down to read, aided by an Index Spell set for *princess, Snow, New Grimmland, apple, sleeping, poison*, and a few other words.

Sometime later, a third of the way through the book, Robert's weary eyes riveted to the phrase *Princess Snow*. With an excited cry, he pocketed the Index Spell so he could actually read rather than skim pages.

"Read aloud!" Blatherskite commanded as he slammed his own book shut.

Robert read of the enchanter's great honor in attending the king and queen in their hour of need, of single-handedly saving their heir from a poisoned apple. Aureus gave, in technical jargon Robert hoped the enchanters understood, an explanation of what he did for Snow.

Cello interrupted him during the account of Aureus's receiving a monetary reward, and Robert continued reading in silence as the enchanters discussed Aureus's methods.

Robert's jaw ticked as he turned a page. He really, *really* wanted to punch that man. He didn't seem to care at all about Snow, just the reward and the fame. Robert's dislike intensified as he read further.

*As I checked into the inn that night, I remembered that I had neglected to warn the king and queen that the curse wasn't completely gone, merely in holding at the princess's lips, the first spot to touch the poisoned apple, and that the princess shouldn't kiss anyone. But she's only ten, so there's plenty of time to fix her. I'll just have to find a way to see her without explaining. But, of course, as soon as word spreads of how I saved her, I'll likely be offered a position as Court Enchanter. I might accept. Or should I tell them now so they'll keep me on until a cure is found? I'm sure I could find one by the time she was ... say eighteen and old enough for them to be shopping her around to suitors?*

The next day:

*I have been used exceedingly ill. No mention of my heroics was made in the papers. The king may have died, to be sure, but I saved his heir. Does that count for nothing? This is a barbaric kingdom. I shall find one better suited to my talents and superior tastes.*

Robert slammed the book shut. "Is there any way I can get a hold of this enchanter?" Robert growled, interrupting the scholarly discussion still waging.

Everyone stopped talking to stare at him.

"Someone already did," Who said with a strange cheerfulness, and Robert fancied Who knew exactly what kind of a hold on the man he wanted—a strangle hold.

"He's not available then?"

"No."

Who said it with such a vicious briskness, his corner more shadowy than usual, that Robert, startled out of his desire for justice, couldn't help but lean toward Colors and whisper, "Is he safe to have around the house?"

Colors responded with a strangled laugh. "Yes, unless you're a criminal," he answered when he'd regained his composure. "He's not terribly useful against a fey prince though, in case you get any ideas in that direction."

Robert cast another glance at Who, looking for some sort of official insignia. "Retired enchanter law enforcement?"

"Something of that sort. Not retired. More like hunting."

A sudden interest, coupled with surprise, drew Robert's eyes to the watching Who. The shadowy enchanter's grin was wolfish. Robert grinned back, feeling as if he'd found a friend.

"When we've cured January," Robert said, "we'll have to discuss tactics. I've done some hunting of weak enchanters and poisoners myself."

Who nodded, but something in his expression was amused, as if he well knew what Robert had done.

"What about your own curse?" Colors asked.

Oddly, it took Robert a moment to register his question. Was he growing so used to the daily transformation and cure he didn't feel cursed any more, per se?

A glance at Snow's sleeping form not only made his heart ache but also made him think he didn't have it so bad, so long as he had friends to help him.

"If I had a wife to cure me every day, I wouldn't mind it so much. And being a frog could come in useful if I needed to get in somewhere I didn't want to be seen."

Colors's chuckles faded as Who stated a fear that had been niggling at the back of Robert's mind. He didn't usually ignore those, finding it best to acknowledge and address them whether he wanted to or not, but this one brought a deeper dread than most.

"The curse is lax," Who said, "in letting her kiss-slaps count to reverse your transformation to a frog, but there's no guarantee it didn't take that initial slap as a first kiss. You have to be a man for the first kiss to work as a curse breaker. You may have lost that chance."

Robert squeezed his eyes shut, knowing Who wasn't finished.

"The terms of a curse can be altered. Prince Dokar won't be content to let you seek the kiss of only one lady, especially not of your wife, or your aunt. He'll return and change it. The fact you're here, for we've warded the cottage and grounds, may be the only reason he hasn't already done so."

"I know," Robert said softly.

"You can't stay here forever."

He glanced at Snow. "I know that too."

"We can get you safely to your estate or the palace and ward that," Who continued, "but I don't imagine you want to live trapped."

Settling down on his estate, if he had Snow as his wife, had never sounded so appealing, but what if his uncle, Rupert, or Solstice needed them? Leaving would mean risking a meeting with Dokar and getting a curse that might force him into being unfaithful rather than merely threaten consequences.

Even learning all he could about fighting the fey prince and then facing Dokar as he'd planned might mean death, abandoning Snow after he'd finally, really found her. For the first time in his life, Robert was reluctant to fight.

"I'll worry about facing Prince Dokar after January is free," he said, his voice heavy. "Did the diary entry tell you anything useful?"

Colors shook his head, and Robert's heart sank further.

"That fool enchanter," Colors said with more censure than Robert had heard from him. "All he had to do was remove the bite of poisoned apple from her mouth and let her wake naturally, but that wasn't dramatic enough for him. His meddling transferred the Sleeping Death poison to her, focusing its power in her lips and effectively turning her into the poison. The sorcerer who'd tricked her into taking the poisoned apple had intended it for King Theodore. The king didn't eat the apple, but the princess kissed him, not knowing of her condition. No poisoned apple to remove, no known curse breaker for the altered curse: there was nothing they could do for him here. A few other enchanters tried to help the princess later, but no one could."

The blood drained from Robert's face. She'd killed her own father. *Oh Snow, I'm so sorry.*

Blatherskite picked up the discussion, though Robert scarcely heard. "Brief contact with her skin, away from her lips obviously, likely wouldn't have an effect. Holding her hand for a prolonged period might cause drowsiness, but no lasting affects beyond a longer than normal sleep when a rest is taken. Not wanting to risk testing that, however, she hasn't touched anyone, even an animal, in years, Queen Solstice said. I'd wondered at the princess's reclusive behavior and wardrobe."

"In short," Lyndon said, his tone holding a question, "you can't get a handle on the curse since he tampered with it, and others did as well? Her best hope is Lady Violetta's gown and time?"

Colors nodded, and everyone looked to Robert.

He forced a smile. It wasn't the quick cure he wanted, but it was one, and for that, he was grateful. "I'll wait."

❧

BY THE NEXT EVENING, Snow's complexion was a healthy pale again. Only her lips held the ruby glow. She even stirred slightly in her sleep. Robert couldn't stop a stupid smile taking over his face as she started to blink.

"Robert?" she asked groggily, cocking her head to study him.

"In the flesh—human flesh too."

Squinting in the mid-morning light, Snow looked about the room and then down at herself and at the dress hanging on the wall.

"What are you doing in my room?" she asked sharply, pulling the blankets up to her chin.

Grinning wickedly, Robert leaned back in his chair, folded his arms behind his head, and stretched out his legs. "I am exacting revenge, dear January—discomfort for discomfort, imprisonment for imprisonment. *You* are not properly dressed: you are now confined to your bed for as long as I am here, and here I intend to remain."

She gaped at him, then shook herself and said coolly, "I hope you're content eating Lyndon's cooking then."

"It's a small price to pay for sweet revenge."

As she gave him a seething look undergirded by uncertainty, Robert's grin brightened. When alarm entered her expression and she drew the blanket closer to her chest, he laughed.

"Alright, I confess. I wanted to be here when you woke, because, well, I like to be near you, and I wanted you to know a little curse wasn't going to run me off."

Snow's beautiful eyes flared wide, and no hint of repugnance shown in them. It was only with effort that Robert managed to keep his train of thought and continue on. Was she actually starting to like him?

"It seems the strength of Lady Violetta's dress was too high and awakened your curse, drawing it through your entire body rather than slowly siphoning it, mostly through the dress itself, into the Poison Stone. You've been asleep for three days. You gave us all quite a scare, you know. I thought you were dead until I remembered you were cursed too." Quickly shoving off the horror of those moments, he gave her a roguish grin, and her posture stiffened, as if ready for whatever nonsense he intended. "I wanted to kiss you awake, but they wouldn't let me. Kisses work for my curse. Why not yours?"

Her expression turned solemn, and suspecting he'd guided the conversation rightly, he rejoiced in a victory. "The intent of mine was to kill," she said, "not cause mischief."

Robert shrugged. "You never know." *Trust me. Tell me yourself about your curse and your father.*

"I know what happens to those I kiss."

"I'm sorry," he said, the words drawn out by the pain in her eyes.

Snow looked down at her hands, then met his gaze again, her expression growing determined. "That's how my father died, Robert. After I'd been cursed and 'cured,' I kissed him. That's why—that's what I wrote you about. I can't marry you: I might kill you!"

Biting her lip, she turned away, but he'd seen the anguish

in her expression as sure as he'd heard it in her voice, and that, he realized with guilt, cheered him.

"Even if we can't marry," she pleaded when he remained silent, "I still want to be frien—"

"Can't marry *yet*."

"What?" she asked, startled enough to face him again.

"Can't marry *yet*. We're both going to be free. Well, free of curses but bound to one another. If you're agreeable, that is."

"But the dress failed—"

"Trust me." He reached for her bare hand but drew back just before touching it, for a look of panic had flared in her eyes. He could talk with her about that later. Settling his hands in his lap, he continued, "Lady Violetta's dress will help after it's hemmed properly or something. And if not, somehow or other, I'll be your curse breaker, and you'll be mine. We'll work it out. I'm willing to wait."

Snow studied him a moment, her expression cloaked, but then she gave him a weak smile and leaned back against the headboard. It wasn't an agreement to hope, but she wasn't arguing. Not quite sure he'd say the same in a year or two, probably.

Still, she hadn't given any reason other than the curse for not marrying him.

"I'm sorry about your curses," she said. "We're a sad pair, aren't we?"

*We're a pair...*

Robert's face ached with the effort of restraining a smile. He forced a gruff tone instead. "Why, Miss January, are you trying to get free of the room on the grounds of good behavior?"

Her lips quirked. "Is it working?"

He winked at her and rose. "Lady Violetta left the altered dress. It should make you drowsy at once, but the sensation should fade in an hour or so. I'll be waiting outside. Don't lock your door, just in case."

Robert paced on the landing a few minutes, and when he heard no sound of movement inside, he called through the door, "Colors invited us to join the others and Lady Violetta in the sitting room, when you're ready. Everyone was concerned and wants to see you."

"I think it's working," she said, her words slow and heavy. "I'm not quite up to walking yet."

"But you're dressed?"

"Yes."

Robert let himself back into the room. Snow was sitting on the bed, blinking slowly as she turned to him. "You don't have to walk," he said. "I'll take you there."

Snow shook her head, the gesture sluggish. "That's sweet of you, but you can't carry me. You're still recovering. I promised Lyndon to look after you."

"Fortunately, I prepared for such an argument." He strode back out to the landing, grasped the cushioned arm of Snow's chair, and slid it into her room. It was glowing white with the Gliding Spell. He left it halfway between the bed and door and moved to Snow's side.

After studying the chair a moment, she laughed quietly. "I thought there was something suspicious about that chair." She slipped her gloved hand into Robert's, and he helped her up and led her toward the chair. "I suppose you could push me."

"Uh-uh." Robert released her as they neared the bespelled conveyance. He sat and patted his lap. "You'll ride. I'm not supposed to be walking much either."

"Robert…"

"You can sit very primly on my knee and pretend I'm extra cushioning. We'll be two invalids struggling along together. No one will think anything about it." He held out his hand to her. "And I will certainly *not* kiss you, though it would be a sweet way to die, I must admit. It's only your kiss that's dangerous, by the way. Not your skin in general."

Shaking her head with a fond smile, Snow took his hand and let him seat her in his lap.

"Wait! Did you say *only* my kiss—not any part of my skin or hair—is dangerous?"

"Yep." Thinking it better to ignore the tears shimmering in her eyes and flowing down her cheeks than tempt himself to brush them off, he kept his head down and scooted her to sit sideways, then tucked her voluminous skirts under her legs. "Well, here goes." Wrapping one arm loosely around her waist, Robert gave a light push against the floor. The chair glided swiftly onto the landing, and Snow gasped.

"Turn and left," he whispered as the floor beside them gave way to steps.

"Robert!" Snow cried, squirming as if she intended to get off. "The stairs!"

"That's alright. The chair can't lose *me*."

"What—" Realizing what he meant, Snow flung her arms around his neck and buried her face against his shoulder. He braced her with one arm around her waist and the other around her shoulders.

The chair tipped, and they sailed down the stairs and then glided through the house.

"Left!"

"Left again!"

"Straight!"

Robert guided their swift passage through the cottage to the enchanters' sitting room.

"Stop."

The chair eased to a halt before the carved wooden door.

"We're here," he whispered.

The tenseness left Snow, and she relaxed against him. More like slumped against him in a kind of jelly-legged relief, but still. Robert's heart was suddenly beating faster than it had been when they'd flown down the stairs.

"You're despicable," she muttered against his chest. But like him, she made no move to get up.

"I know," he whispered. Resisting the urge to kiss her hair, he hugged her to him and let them sit in the quietness of the hallway. The murmur of voices drifted through the doors.

"Robert?" she asked drowsily a few minutes later as she shifted to look up at him, careful to keep her face away from his.

"*Hmm?*"

"I thought we were there?"

"We are."

"Oh." She pushed up enough to look around. "We're still in the hallway."

"You seemed comfortable. I didn't want to disturb you."

Suddenly fully awake and blushing charmingly, she started to extract herself from his arms. Laughing, he caught her back to his chest. "When I found you on the kitchen floor earlier," he said softly, a bit of his terror slipping into his voice again, "all I could do was cry for help. *Colors* carried you upstairs. But now that I'm human again, I feel a strong urge to remind the gentlemen here *I* am the only one who should have the privilege of holding you."

Snow's breath caught, and when her gaze met his, it was slightly dazed. She made no effort to move or protest, so he stood, lifting her into his arms. He nudged the door with his foot until it inched open and then carried her inside.

"Our princess is awake, gentlemen, my lady."

# CHAPTER 14

"So *that's* how you cook eggs," Robert said with exaggerated wonder the next morning as he set the pan of water and eggs on the stove to boil. "What next?"

"Wait for it to boil, and then let them cook. When the eggs are nearly done, we'll make toast from the bread Lyndon bought in the village. I'll make fresh bread later." Snow hid a smile, then a yawn, behind her hand as Robert nodded seriously, dried his hands on her apron, which was rather small on him but charming in its foreignness, and went in search of the breadbox.

Stroking the soft fur along Charters's back, Snow nestled deeper into her comfy chair, the gliding one from Robert's room, and used the exquisite, almost-forgotten feel of a living creature under her touch to keep the weariness at bay. Her crimson gown, so wonderfully lovely, did indeed make her sleepy for several hours each morning. Due to which, Robert insisted on helping her make breakfast. She didn't mind at all—the help or the company—but she didn't want him watching over her as solicitously as Lyndon did him.

She'd promised Birch and her father another loaf of fresh bread and a meal. She'd been too tired to visit since waking from the curse, but she needed to go to them soon, lest they became worried. She also needed to find out if Birch had seen whoever was interfering with her and Robert's correspondence. She wasn't at liberty to divulge the mirror's secrets even to Robert, at least not yet. Another reason to visit the castle.

Charters's fur bristled, and he hissed just before a loud rap sounded oddly through the house. Snow blinked and shook her head to clear it of lingering sleep. "Was that the front door?"

"Yes." Robert raised his eyebrows at her before stuffing a scrap of paper into his jacket pocket. "Do we answer? We do our own cooking and laundry…"

Lyndon, sitting comfortably at the breakfast table beside the window, chuckled. "No need to stoop so low, Your Grace. I'll see to it. I'm certain I can pull off a crazy act to Cello's satisfaction, if the need arises."

Agreeing heartily to the latter, Robert went back to alternately checking the water for bubbles and scouring the counters, cupboards, and drawers for the bread knife. Charters recommenced purring under her touch.

A moment later, Lyndon returned with her guards, whom she had entirely forgotten.

"Oh! Is everything alright?" she asked in alarm. Charters gave a customary hiss at the two men, and she braced him under her hand, just in case.

"That's what we've come to find out, Y—" Brenner cleared his throat. "Forgive us for saying so, but we don't like being so far away from you. We can hardly do our job with you here and us in the village."

"We've been trying to get someone to answer the door for days." Sutton's brows were drawn in a scolding manner that forced her to hide a smile. "If your stepmother hadn't warned us of the place being like that, we'd have broken in days ago."

"Ah, yes, this house is a bit particular. I do apologize for your concern. I was unable to receive visitors until this morning, so we never heard your summons?" She glanced at Robert for confirmation. He nodded, then joined them and rested his hand on the back of her chair.

"It's a pleasure to see you up and about, Your Grace," Brenner said with a curious look between her and Robert. A blush threatened her cheeks. The reclusive, plainly dressed princess who'd refused to meet with her almost-fiancé at her own palace now wearing a ball gown and cooking breakfast with him at a distant cottage. What must they think of her?

As if considering the same, Lyndon cleared his throat, reminding them the cottage had at least one chaperone.

With something of an amused twist to his lips, Robert nodded his thanks to the guard. "I have had excellent care, and you can rest assured that between myself, my godfather, and the enchanters here, that Miss January is well looked after." He smiled down at her briefly, and she found herself returning his smile without thinking about it. He addressed the guards again. "However, as a soldier, I understand your predicament. Perhaps we can arrange for you to stay in the rooms above the stable?"

Sutton and Brenner lost some of their tenseness.

"Thank you, Your Grace," Brenner said with genuine appreciation. "We'll gather our things and tell the others immediately."

"We'll leave Mays and Gareth at the inn to receive the post," Sutton said. "The two of us will return today." He pulled a few letters from his pocket and offered them to her. "No silver salver, I'm afraid."

"That's perfectly alright, Sutton. Thank you," she said with a smile as she accepted the letters. The one on top was from Solstice, and the next from Annabeth Houen, her best friend. Her stomach sank as the mysterious blackmailer's handwriting came into view on the third note, but she managed to keep her face impassive. She didn't recognize the handwriting on the fourth envelope.

The guards left a moment later, and the house, apparently keeping them abreast of the strangers' whereabouts by sound, carried their whispered comments and footsteps back to them.

"Looks like they got things patched up alright."

"Aye. Almost dying for her must have done the trick. Good thing too. I was starting to worry that arrogant coward Bankor was going to wed her and claim the throne."

As if! With a contemptuous huff, Snow released her hold on the squirming Charters and began opening her letters.

"I like those two," Robert said cheerfully before turning away to inspect the pot of noisy eggs. "These are bouncing away nicely on the bubbles." He remained leaning over the pot for some time, watching, until Lyndon reminded him of the toast.

Jaw clenched, Snow opened her archenemy's message first.

*I don't make idle threats.*

*Neither do I.* Huffing, she moved on to the final letter.

With surprise did she realize it was also his, though the outward handwriting was different.

*I don't make idle claims either.*

Claims? Was he using that as a synonym for *threats*? What had he claimed?

*You are mine!* Snow shivered as the sorcerer's long ago assertion about Solstice was followed in her thoughts by a cruel laughter that was somehow both familiar and unknown.

Ordering her trembling hands to steady themselves, Snow slowly folded the two letters and set them aside. What to do with them? Burn them? Find a manure pile? She paused, a bit of maturity overcoming her old desire to offend the writer as much as possible. Was there some way she could use them to find the author?

She glanced at Robert and found him watching her, head cocked. If they were to marry one day, perhaps she should start seeking his support in her troubles now.

"Is everything alright?" he asked.

Swallowing hard, Snow rubbed her fingers over the golden sphere on her bracelet. "Remember that walk I promised? The one where I was to tell you Princess Snow's secrets?"

His eyebrows drew together in confusion. The poor man probably wondered what other secrets she could possibly have! "Yes."

"If you'll help me make bread and soup this afternoon, and don't question what I do with them, we'll take that walk. I … I need permission to tell you this particular secret of hers, which isn't all her own."

He nodded, concern and curiosity in his expression, before returning to the matter of slicing bread.

"By the way"—he paused to look over his shoulder at her, a fat slice of bread falling away from the knife blade—"how did you come to be such a fine chef and housekeeper? Is the education of princesses, and their maids, so different in New Grimmland than New Beaumont?"

"Remember that walk I mentioned?"

His brows drew together again before relaxing. "Ah."

He soon set a plate of toast on the table and returned to the stove for the eggs. "Any secrets you can tell me now? I already caught you riding astride at a pace that surprised me. Riding very well too, I might add."

"*Hmm*," she said, trying not to beam too much under his praise. "I did—on the sly—along with cooking and horseback riding, learn swordplay. I'm no warrior, but I enjoy the exercise and the sport of it."

Robert spun around to stare at her. His eyebrows were practically to his hair!

She grinned smugly as the corners of his lips began to curl. "I've been longing to tell you that for ages, for I knew you'd be pleased to know I wasn't the coward I pretended to be, but..."

"You'll explain tomorrow?"

"Yes."

"I look forward to tomorrow then." He placed the eggs on the table, and Lyndon the fruit, butter, and jam, and they enjoyed breakfast together.

BY THE AFTERNOON, Snow was feeling herself again and so consigned Robert to a mere assistant chef position rather than chef-in-training for the making of the bread and soup for the castle.

Later, when the kitchen was unpleasantly warm from the combination of baking and summer heat, and the sink was filled with dirty dishes and pans, Robert lifted his arms in a stretch that involved the cracking of enough vertebrae to make her shudder.

"That was a hard day's work," he said, lowering his arms. "I'm for a nap now, if only to forestall Lyndon's insistence on it as a condition of my walking tomorrow." He leaned out the open window briefly, his gaze searching the yard and forest.

"How well you know me, my lord." Lyndon rose from his table and gathered his books and paper.

"Oh, no you don't!" Snow gestured to the full sink. "We're not done yet, gentlemen."

His expression falling, Lyndon took in the sink and her hands on her hips. "I'll dry."

Robert, who'd been humming and murmuring something resembling a song, took off the spare apron he'd found in a deliberate manner and hung it on a nail by the pantry. He walked to the sink and glanced out the window again. "I don't think that's necessary, but if you wish, Lyndon," he said, facing them again.

Snow narrowed her eyes at him, suspicious. "What do you mean? Helping isn't necessary or cleaning isn't necessary?"

He winked at her and drew out a scrap of paper from his pocket. "The former. I found this handy spell song in your apron pocket this morning—for calling the woodland creatures to clean for you."

"Woodland creatures? Would that include you, Your Grace?" Lyndon asked wryly. His eyes suddenly widened, and he cocked his head as if to listen.

"Oh!" Snow cried, both remembering the spell and noticing the increased chatter of squirrels and twitter of birds. She leaned around Robert to peer out the window. A cloud must have eclipsed the sun, for it was unusually dark out. Her breath caught as her eyes made sense of the *moving* darkness hurrying toward them. It wasn't a shadow. "Look out, Robert!"

He ducked with a yelp and dashed further into the room as enough song birds for the dawn chorus dove through the open window, some diving between the bushy tails of the squirrels and the twitching ears of the rabbits climbing over the windowsill.

"That was one of Lady Violetta's spells," Snow called out over the honking of a goose. "Anything could happen!"

Robert blanched as a fawn, followed by its mother, leapt through the window, landing gracefully despite the clatter of hooves on the tile floor. "You're right."

"A retreat might be in order, Your Grace." Lyndon pointed to a waddling badger wrestling a raccoon for a dish rag. Five field mice and Charters were busy licking the bread bowl together, but there wouldn't long be enough batter to share. A goose honked loudly as the doe yanked out one of its tail feathers.

"Agreed." Robert, dodging the doe and the goose now fighting over the feather duster, grabbed a towel and the soup pot, Lyndon the bread from off a turtle's back, and Snow her heavy skirts from a floor being swept by squirrel tails. They rushed out, barring the door firmly behind them.

"What in the greenwood!" Blatherskite bellowed from inside the kitchen as they raced away.

As if the sight of her in a crimson ballgown wasn't enough of a shock, Snow, after handing Birch the soup and bread, flung her arms around her father, letting her hair touch his neck, and squeezed him in a tight hug.

He stiffened, but then quickly returned the embrace. "Is the curse ended, Snow? What is it?"

"No, but I can touch—for a short time—without harm, and Lady Violetta made me this beautiful dress to draw out the poison! I don't know how long it will take, but Robert said he'd wait!"

With an inarticulate cry, her father pulled her tighter and kissed her forehead. When he finally let her go, Birch, and then Solstice, newly arrived, also claimed hugs. It was only with difficulty that Snow limited herself to one round of such a precious treasure.

Taking a seat next to her father, Snow explained everything that had happened, then asked King Theodore if he remembered voices and laughter from when he fell into the Sleeping Death.

Sighing tiredly, he rubbed a hand over his face. "Yes. They're still there, in the background of my thoughts. Birch helps drive them away."

Grimacing, Snow gave his hand a quick squeeze.

"Why?" he asked.

"I had forgotten about them … until today. It took me a while to remember, but when I dreamed during this last Sleep, it was of that day and of a taunting voice." She managed something of a laugh and touched Solstice's hand, drawing a weepy smile from her stepmother. "I remember Solstice being so angry and ready to die with you, Father, that she pulled Winter's Sword from the mirror and threatened the sorcerer with it."

"I was also trying to defend you, dearest, since you seemed disinclined to obey my order to run."

"I couldn't move, much less run!" Snow protested.

"Then I am glad Schwan killed him before he reached me," Solstice said. "I have not been trained in any sword's use, much less that one. That thing is *very* heavy, Birch. You could have warned me."

Birch laughed. "You weren't ever supposed to need it. It's more for banishment than killing anyway."

"Did you actually see Schwan kill the sorcerer?" Snow asked, not for the first time.

"No," Solstice said. "But he'd have made himself known if he were still alive, and that one note—I'm sure it was a fake. Why?"

"Robert can see magic now. When we talked about it, he mentioned that Schwan has a bit of magic about him." She gave her father a wry smile. "Robert also adores Houen and detests Bankor."

"Man of sense."

"Schwan's risen a lot since he was our guard, somewhat dubiously in his methods too, I suspect," Solstice said musingly. "He'd have to have some magic of his own to control even an injured sorcerer." She frowned. "Not to mention some to survive whatever was done to him and the other guard."

"Birch." Snow held out her hand to him. With a smile half of amusement and half of pained understanding, he took her hand in his and gave it a gentle squeeze. "Did you find the one who intercepted my correspondence?"

"Yes and no. I made a sketch of the servant who intercepted it, but no transfer has been made to anyone else."

"Ah."

She looked to her stepmother, who gave the name of the

servant and indicated he was being watched by more than just Birch. "We'll keep an eye on Schwan too," Solstice said.

"Good." Clasping her hands in her lap to hide a touch of nerves, Snow met Solstice's gaze. As Keeper of the Mirror of Talvinen, Solstice was the one who decided who knew of it, though she would include Birch and Theodore in the decision as well. Snow took a deep breath. "There's something else I wanted to ask you. You probably already know what it is."

⁂

SNOW WAS tired the next morning, but happier than she'd expected to ever be again. Perhaps it was being too happy to sleep that woke her early. Or mayhap the tantalizing smell of food. She snuck downstairs to the kitchen, eschewing the gliding chair for slow, careful steps.

Robert's voice wasn't suited to spell songs meant for her apparently, which had caused the mishap of the previous day. Despite being told Colors and Today had kindly cleaned the kitchen with magic, she, half expecting to see a deer licking plates or a badger attempting to fry bacon, peered warily around the thick wooden door before entering.

No deer, no bacon sizzling, but there was a man seated at the worktable scarfing down the remains of her soup, as if ordered to clean the bowl. So much for leftovers for their lunch.

To her further surprise, the offending man wasn't Blatherskite. The stout, middle-aged man in a suit of indifferent quality now staring at her in wide-eyed guilt was a stranger to her.

"What—" *Are you doing here?* How did he get past all the alarms?

"Ha!" he cried, his confidence growing as he rose and bowed to her. "You found me!" He bowed deeper. "I was afraid I would be lost forever. *What* at your service, Miss January."

*What...* Oh. Snow raised an eyebrow at the formerly missing enchanter. "I suppose only food could draw you from whatever place you lost yourself?" she said drily, resigning herself to a lunch of cold cuts and fresh fruit to go along with the second loaf of bread they'd made.

The bread!

"It works like a charm."

Snow was fairly confident he winked at her as he said it, but she was hurrying to the breadbox and not in the mood to acknowledge him. The sight of the golden-brown loaf still in the wooden box satisfied her concern. Thank goodness the animals had left that alone. And the man.

"You're welcome to finish the soup then," she said with as much grace as she could muster for someone who could acquire food by magic from servants at home.

"Thank you, Miss January." What returned to his seat. "Perhaps there is something I could help you with in return?"

"That's kind of you, but I'm claiming dish drying."

Snow startled and spun around at Robert's voice. He practically flew in on the bewitched chair, barely stopping himself before slamming into the worktable.

"I don't believe we've met," Robert began, spinning the chair toward What, who was swiftly rising. Robert looked up, stiffened, and then was up, standing before What with a dagger dimpling the enchanter's shirt at his heart.

"Robert, this is What, the missing enchanter." Snow said it with a calm that surprised her, especially since she found herself inching toward the knife block for a weapon of her own. One knife wasn't sufficient for an enchanter, she was fairly certain. *If* one was needed at all, that is. She looked to Robert and decided she trusted him more than the enchanter, and that startled her.

Robert scoffed, stalking forward a step, forcing What backwards. "Are you now?" he said, his eyes a stormy blue she'd never seen before. She'd always heard Robert was a warrior, but she'd never actually seen that side of him, just the part where he fell off a horse unconscious or stared at her with blackened eyes and a bandaged head. At the moment, however, he was looking fierce, powerful, and alto-gether impressive.

Apparently, What thought so too, for he looked nervously between her and Robert. "Yes," he squeaked. He cleared his throat. "I am What. Lost myself during a tricky trans-formation."

Robert quirked an eyebrow. "Curious, for you bear a remarkable resemblance—even in the blue curse-line down your cheek and neck—to a swindler and weak enchanter my uncle's men and I exposed but failed to catch last year."

"I can—"

Robert inched forward again. What staggered back into the counter and snapped his mouth shut. He glanced at Snow, as if for help. In truth, she was more interested in watching Robert than him and didn't bother to respond.

"This swine," Robert said, his tone angry but controlled, "helped an illegitimate child steal a widow's home and inheritance."

"She was very sour and mean," What squeaked. "The kid was much more pleasant, and generous. He deserved it, the poor orphan."

Robert's eyes flashed. "If that 'sour widow' was sour it was because her husband was an abusive cad, just like the 'nice' person you helped steal the home. And this *poor orphan* was well provided for already, while the widow had nothing else. Well, now the widow is smiling and happy, as are the true orphans and abandoned young mothers she's helping at her home."

Hands raised and trembling, What turned to Snow again. "Isn't this where you're supposed to beg for mercy for me, tender-hearted female and all that?" His eyes seemed rather larger and browner than before, the image of truthfulness; his stocky frame thinner and hunched, pitiable.

"Is what he says true?" she asked coolly, focusing on Robert instead of the deceitful enchanter.

"Well..."

"Yes," Robert snapped.

Crossing her arms, Snow leaned back against the counter, announcing her intent to remain a cool spectator. "Then I don't think so."

"Surely you don't want blood on the floor?" he cried, his voice rising in pitch.

"I think you misinterpret the duke's posture. This is a bind-him-until-he-goes-before-the-magistrate posture, but with a sudden-death-if-necessary stance thrown in for good measure."

Robert half turned to her, his blue eyes wide with one of those sappy looks that made butterflies dance in her stomach despite herself.

"Robert," she hissed. His attention snapped back to What. The next moment the man was slumped on the floor, unconscious at Robert's feet.

"Did you really mean that?" Robert asked, turning to her again, vulnerability and hope in his eyes, which had the same effect on the butterflies.

"Mean what?"

He hesitated, then shrugged, but she doubted any

nonchalance was truly in the gesture. "Everything, I guess. You took my side though he seemed like the underdog and I the aggressor." His expression started to turn sappy again, but he cleared his throat and said gruffly, "After seeing you cowering under your carriage during the highwaymen attack, I was concerned you'd either faint or run away, or forbid justice to prevent violence."

"You saw me?" she stammered, then collected herself. "I was not—well, I suppose I was cowering. But it was only to prevent my men from being slaughtered defending me! I was safe and hidden; they had nothing to fight for."

There was a certain sneer to Robert's expression that made her think he considered anyone accepting that bargain as cowering, but he said nothing. He knelt beside What and began searching him for weapons and a wand.

"How did you see me?" she asked, suddenly realizing she still held a knife. She carefully put it away. "The cloak I was wearing was a magical one, a gift from an enchanter. And I have no objection to justice."

"I'm glad of that. As for seeing you?" Robert began to bind What with the cloth napkins. "I had to teach myself to see magic while seeking the ones involved in the assassination attempt on my uncle. That's when I met What. He's one of the few poisoners and unscrupulous magic-workers Rupert and I discovered who escaped imprisonment or death. He's not so violent as the others, but even a confidence trickster can cause much harm," he added sadly before meeting her eye again. "Thanks for not trying to stop me, for believing me." He looked away quickly, and Snow was glad of that. For some reason, she was finding it hard to breathe when he looked at her like that.

"You have a reputation as a just man, Robert," she managed after a moment, feeling the need to respond.

Solstice always let Theodore know how much she respected him as well as loved him, and Snow knew how much that meant to him, especially since he could do so little trapped in a mirror. "I didn't doubt you there, but since he is an enchanter, I was worried you might have bitten off more than you could chew. Obviously not, though."

"Why, Miss January, were you concerned for me?"

"For myself," she said archly, "as he might seek to harm me as a witness."

Laughing, Robert stood and toed the unconscious man. "He's not that skilled, and faerie curses tend to be jealous and run off other curses. I don't think he could've done me lasting harm." This time he did wink at her, and she was pretty sure she blushed. "But thank you for your concern."

Snow smiled in response, and kept smiling apparently, for she realized, when Who cleared his throat, that she and Robert had been staring at one another rather sappily for some time.

Certain she was as red as her gown, Snow backed up to the counter and began pulling out plates for a meal she'd not yet begun.

"Do you mind if I take him now?" Who asked, his tone amused. "The house itself will get hungry if I don't end that Tantalizing Smell Spell soon."

"Please do, partner," Robert said, confidence bordering on swagger in his tone. There was definitely a swagger to his steps as he walked to the pantry.

Who laughed, which was an unexpected sound from him. His back to them, he knelt beside What and began, Snow assumed, wrapping him in spells. "You could've let him talk a bit more though. That wasn't the best confession I've heard, but it'll have to do."

"Sorry." Robert leaned against the counter beside Snow,

flour and leavening in his hands. "Didn't want to give him a chance to be *persuasive*. He talked one of my men into letting him go last time." He handed her the sack of flour and whispered, "There's no reason to be so embarrassed. They all know I'm in love with you."

But was she willing for anyone, even herself, to know she was in love with him?

# CHAPTER 15

I t was raining. Robert was a leopard frog. The latter's name did not derive from any particular speediness or fierceness in the species.

Robert sat grumpily on the pillow the next morning, staring out the rain-streaked window until the hallway floor squeak announced a visitor. Lyndon watched him with amusement from his chair.

"My, you're looking unusually handsome today." Snow stopped just inside the doorway to cover a yawn with her armload of linens. "What fine spots you have."

The day suddenly felt brighter, and Robert hopped over to his chair. Working to keep his voice gruff, he said, "Very funny. Come on, pucker up."

Snow arched an eyebrow as she deposited the linens on his bed. "You're very demanding today."

"Your flattery has increased my confidence and made me bold. I also suspect you want help with the laundry, so it's I who am doing you the favor. And I don't want to spend my entire human day doing laundry, so let's get started, shall we?"

"And how do you plan to spend your free time?" she asked.

He imagined himself waggling his eyebrows. "Chasing the pretty maid around. We're going for a walk, remember?"

He wasn't sure how the eyebrow waggling translated into leopard frog, but Snow gave him a stern look. He hopped down to the laundry pile, tugged out a dishrag, and gripping it in his mouth, attempted to fold it with his webbed feet.

"I *don't* remember, and you, sir frog, are staying *as is* if you think human you is fit for going for a walk in the rain." She pointed to the cloth dangling from his mouth. "You're barely able to fold laundry."

After a few muffled words escaped him, Robert spit out the cloth. "Oh, come now! There are such things as umbrellas and cloaks! You're as bad as Lyndon."

"Which is why Lyndon trusts me."

"Exactly," Lyndon put in.

Snow nodded in agreement to his godfather before turning back to Robert. "You must be fully healed before getting into another scrape, even the danger of a summer cold. End of discussion." She tapped him gently on the head. "You will be babied, and you will take it, like it or not."

Robert was very tempted to like it, to be honest, so long as it kept Snow close. But he said, grouchily, "I bet my Princess Snow would never treat me like this. She'd probably say, 'Yes, Robert dear,' and let me do whatever I pleased."

Snow snorted. "You have a very low opinion of 'your' Princess Snow. Do you like spineless women who can't say *no* even when they need to? For your or their own good?"

"Well, now that you put it like that, she *does* sound a bit too yellow for my taste. Not a good thing for her, and certainly not for the children we'll have. She should work on that."

"But…" he added after a moment, during which Snow sucked in an offended breath and he tried to look as serious as a spotted frog could look, "as far as saying *yes* to me, she can keep that up."

Snow threw a folded towel at him. He hopped out of the way, across the bed, and into Lyndon's lap.

"Hey! Remember how feeble I am, barely able to fold laundry and all that."

"That's when you're human."

"Yes, about that…"

"You're staying a frog today," she said, a teasing glimmer in her eyes.

"But January!"

"I wouldn't want to be a spineless people pleaser like your Princess Snow."

"But saying *no* to everything is just as bad!" Robert tried tapping his webbed forepaw to his chin and found it worked well. He said in a low, thoughtful voice, "Reverse psychology is effective with this one. No laundry for me today. I'll just lounge around and catch some flies and maybe go for a swim."

Snow stiffened. "That's a wonderful idea, Robert," she said, stalking around the bed toward him in a manner that had him looking around for an open window despite the earlier humor in her eye. "I'll heat some water for you to swim in. I'll heat it real slow, so you don't even notice the change." Around the bed now, she lunged for him, hands out.

"January!" He leapt for the open window behind Lyndon and hit something hard and transparent. He slid down it with an embarrassing squeak and thumped to the floor. "You cleaned the windows, didn't you?" he croaked.

Chuckling, she scooped him up. "I got a spell for it."

As he moaned out imprecations against "retired" enchanters, she returned him to his chair, then kissed a finger and touched it gently to his head.

She backed away as Robert returned to his true form. He gave a disgruntled sigh. "That was not fair."

A hint of a smile curved Snow's lips. "Come, let's sing while we work. Join us, Lyndon. Before we know it, the sun will be out, and we can go for that walk."

"If not?"

"We'll walk around the sitting room."

THE SUN DID INDEED COME out that afternoon. Robert pointed out its first shy appearance.

"You know you're going as a frog, don't you?" Lyndon fixed a gaze on him as stern as those from his uncle King Patrick.

"I beg your pardon!" He'd really hoped Lyndon had forgotten that agreement.

As with King Patrick, Robert's outrage had little effect on Lyndon. "Out as a frog. Back as a human," his godfather said. "We have to be careful to stay within the warded perimeter of the Cottage Woods. Colors thinks you'll somehow sense that better as a frog, something about you being in a magical form."

Robert opened his mouth but then shut it with a huff of frustration. He was going to have it out with Prince Dokar one day.

"You can ride on my shoulder." Snow handed him her cloak. As Robert took it, he swept a glance over her billowing gown. She looked stunning, but...

"Impractical, I agree," she said with a knowing smile as he slipped the cloak onto her shoulders.

"Oh, I'm not complaining. The dress goes very well with my suit. You could pass for a princess in that outfit, and a princess and a frog are an odd pair to be seen together..."

"As *a frog*," Lyndon butted in, "a rather small creature, no one will notice you to think it odd."

Sighing, Robert pocketed his spell and let Snow place him on her shoulder.

Lyndon collected baskets for the berries, and they set out for the woods through the back garden. They were some distance along the trail when Robert realized Snow's guards hadn't followed them. Looking down at Snow's cloak, he could understand why. The men, from their stable perch, at only a quick glance from the rear, probably thought Lyndon was going for a walk alone.

"I hope one of your secrets involves the identity of the tailor of your cloak," he said.

"I'm afraid the name would do you no good, as he's long deceased."

"Didn't pass on the talent?"

"Not that I know of."

"Pity."

They meandered down the trail, admiring the wild roses, hydrangeas, and other summer beauties for some ways before finding the patches of blackberries Snow had discovered on her rides to the village.

"There's another patch beyond the trees there, if I remember rightly," Lyndon said, pointing to a thick growth of hollies and laurels. "I'll start on it."

The rush of a rocky stream to their right tempted Robert's membranous ears. "I'll be right back. I want to see how these flippers work in the water."

"Ro—Alright."

Laughing softly, he hopped off her shoulder and onto the side of a dogwood tree. "I'll be careful, and I think the barrier is on the opposite bank. I won't cross."

She nodded and began choosing the plumpest and darkest from among the berries and dropping them into the basket. Robert hopped off and was soon enjoying the cool water. His webbed feet worked well.

A scream came from the bank, a feminine one that left him trembling. It was followed by a man's inarticulate cry.

Robert bounded from the water and up the steep bank, from root to violet clump to laurel branch, until gaining level ground. He forced himself to stop there, to observe and plan.

Snow stood with her back pressed to a tree, a dagger buried hilt-deep in the leaves beside her, a man before her. Robert reached for his spell pocket, ready to grab his own dagger as soon as he transformed, but then he caught the smooth cheeks and trembling hands of the man not standing, but *cowering*, in front of Snow.

It was a boy. He held another dagger in his hand, but Robert couldn't bring himself to use his own, and if he transformed, the boy might spook.

"I didn't know it was you, Your Highness," the boy cried, his chest heaving in a fit of panic. "I didn't want to. They—"

"Put the dagger down," Robert said, putting as much warning into his voice as he could.

"Please! You've got to go!" The boy seemed not to notice him or care.

Robert hopped onto another tree and said in a slightly different voice, "If you want to live, boy, put the dagger down."

This time, the boy stilled.

"Drop it, please," Snow said, her voice strong despite a slight tremble.

The boy dropped the knife and fell to his knees at her feet. Robert would have breathed easier if that hadn't put the boy's hands back on level with the knives.

"Please! I—"

"Stop your excuses, boy," Robert snapped. "Tell us who sent you and why."

"Where are you?" he cried, turning frantically around.

"Wherever I need to be, and that might be at your throat with a knife if you don't answer me."

The boy settled for staring at the ground at Snow's feet. "There's a group of highwaymen in the valley beyond the village. They told me I'd find a dark-haired woman between the cottage and the village. I've been watching for days. I was to..." The boy hunched over as if about to empty his stomach. A sizable, waterproofed pouch hung at his waist, along with a string of garlic. Robert thought he might be sick as well.

"Killing and taking the heart is an initiation rite, isn't it?" he asked.

The boy hung his head, his shaggy, dirty-blond bangs brushing the leaves. "I have nowhere else to go. They said she was a witch."

Robert's jaw clenched at the all-too-familiar story. "Get yourself kicked out of the village?"

The boy nodded. "Stealing and ... not taking reprimands well."

"No one tried to help you?"

"The pastor got me an apprenticeship with the saddler, but I lost it."

"And you didn't mind because you wanted an easy life of freedom and adventure."

The boy winced but didn't respond.

"Cutting a woman's heart out is quite the adventure, isn't it?" Robert said, pressing in deeper, letting what the boy had almost done sink in a little more.

When the lad curled in on himself and began weeping, Robert let out a pent-up breath.

He caught Snow searching for him, and hopped to another tree to catch her attention. Once steady on the tree trunk, he waved at her the best he could. He didn't like her pallor, but he didn't think she'd faint. Good girl. He motioned for her to stay as she was.

"What will you do now?" Robert asked gently.

The boy quieted and wiped his nose on his sleeve. "They'll kill me if I go back emptyhanded. She was said to have bewitched our boss."

Snow cocked her head. "Who is that?"

"Some rich man named Guagin. He sells the stuff we get and takes a large cut. They don't like him but do what he says."

Snow gasped, but Robert hurried on, "Do you think they knew it was the crown princess he wanted killed?"

"I think they must have. Nobody wanted to go. They made me."

"They do what he says, though," Robert continued thoughtfully, "so they'll make sure the job gets done, won't they?"

"Yes."

"There was"—Robert's stomach clenched—"an older man nearby picking blackberries. Did you see him?"

"I snuck up behind him and hit him over the head. He should be fine."

Despite his relief, Robert's eyebrows rose in his froggy manner. The boy had skills, but not in the direction of saddlery.

The boy wiped his nose again and sat up. "You should go. I-I can wait here and-and—"

"No," Robert said forcefully. "You'll go back now. Kill an animal on the way and take its heart with you. They won't question you." He paused. "Do your tears indicate you'd take a different route in life if you could, an honorable one, even if it was hard and involved correction?"

The boy hesitated, then hung his head again. "Aye, but who would take me now?"

"Aye, who indeed? Those who understand repentance and grace perhaps. As soon as you've done what I asked, go to New Beaumont. Go to the estate of the Duke of Pondleigh and tell his steward the duke sent you. The old huntsman could use an apprentice. He'll work you hard but will take care of you—and I mean the latter in whatever way is necessary. Cause trouble of any kind and he'll know how to deal with you."

The boy stilled, then slowly turned in Robert's direction, expression questioning. Not daring to hope as well as fearful?

"Truly," Robert assured him.

"Y-yes, sir." The boy hastily collected and sheathed his knives, then staggered up.

"Be off with you then, and hurry."

"Th-thank you, sir." He gave Snow a clumsy bow. "Please forgive me, Your Highness. You're certainly no witch, though you are as beautiful as they say."

Snow gave him a weak smile, her face still dreadfully pale.

The boy ran off, and Snow sank to the forest floor. Closing her eyes tight shut, she drew her legs to her chest and wrapped her arms around her knees.

Robert leapt from the tree to the fallen leaves, torn between comforting Snow and finding Lyndon, but when he reached into the spell pocket and gained his long legs again, he ran through the bushes to hunt for his godfather.

He found him unconscious on the ground a few yards beyond the clump of hollies and rhododendrons. Robert's heart eased its agonizing worry at the steady rise and fall of Lyndon's chest. The wound on his head was clean, and at least he hadn't fallen into the thorny blackberry patch. "I know you'd rather me get someone else to do this, but you're not awake to scold me!"

Grunting, Robert hefted the smaller man onto his shoulder and carried him to Snow, who still sat with her head against her drawn knees. She startled as he lowered Lyndon to the ground.

"Is he alright?" she asked as Robert took off his jacket to use as a pillow for him.

"Should be. Will wake with a headache and a nasty temper."

Snow leaned back against the tree with a heavy sigh.

Robert settled down beside her, their shoulders touching, and leaned back against the beech with its peeling grayish-brown bark. "Attempts on your life don't get any easier to take, do they?"

"No," she said. It was a simple word, but he understood it. "Especially not," she continued slowly, her expression drawn in something like guilt, "when they're your fault and involve others. Boys being asked to commit murder."

"How is this possibly your fault!"

Snow gave a mirthless laugh. "I threatened to kill all the advisors."

Robert's response caught in his throat. That was not the secret he'd expected her to share today, not that he knew what to expect from her anymore. "Why?" he asked cautiously.

Without answering, Snow reached to her side and pulled two folded sheets of stationery from a hidden pocket in her dress and handed them to him. He opened the letters and read.

*I don't make idle threats.*

*I don't make idle claims either.*

"I don't understand." He dropped the letters to his lap and met her gaze.

She opened her mouth, frowned, then shifted to lay her head on his shoulder and look out at the laden blackberry bushes. He decided he didn't mind, just this once, if she didn't want to look him in the eye while talking.

"Solstice and I have gotten anonymous threats, demands, and 'suggestions' concerning various policies and royal appointments since Father … since the curse. They weren't death threats for us," she said hastily, forestalling his question of why this hadn't been addressed. "They mostly threatened to falsely expose Solstice as a sorceress and me as the cursed girl who killed her father and king." Her voice cracked, and Robert tucked her hand into his. She cleared her throat and continued on.

"They also threatened Solstice's mirror. These notes began when I was thirteen. Given the nature of the information in some, I guessed them to be from one of the advisors, or a group of them. I…" She paused to take a deep breath, her color rising. "I retaliated by sending anonymous letters to all of them, even those I thought were innocent, with a threat the perpetrator would understand. When I was fifteen and Guagin tried to force Solstice to marry him, I gave him the same threat verbally—I threatened to kill him with a kiss. I've repeated it since, as needed."

"That would be too good a death for him."

"Only if it truly killed."

"But—"

She held up her hand. "Guagin knows about my curse. He has a distant cousin who's an enchanter. Solstice asked him for help not long after I was cursed. He basically told me to become a nun and pass the crown to one of the nobles."

Robert snorted.

"Guagin may suspect about other things, yet I'm not sure he knows. Schwan does know, as he was there when the sorcerer attacked us. Sometimes it seems like there is something between Schwan and Guagin, so Schwan may have told him about those other things." She paused, her heart hammering with all the terror of a little girl who'd just lost her father and now faced his murderer. "Or maybe the sorcerer survived. One note suggested he did, though Solstice doesn't believe it. I—Anyway, I got two warnings almost immediately after arriving at the cottage. One was to tell me I'd never marry you, the other a threat against the mirror." Robert wove his fingers through hers, and she squeezed his hand. "I responded with a threat as usual. Apparently, Guagin saw my seclusion here as a chance to get rid of me. So this was my fault. And if anything happened to me, who would protect Solstice and the mirror, my father?"

She fell silent, and Robert, struggling to put off thoughts of justice until the time of comfort was done, shifted to wrap his arm around her and pull her into a hug. Her words finally caught up to him, and he jerked away just as she relaxed against his shoulder.

"Whoa. What? Your *father*?" he cried.

"My father." She raised her hand. The golden bracelet, the

one matching Solstice's and glowing with magic, dangled from her wrist. It held five golden charms—a ball, a castle, twin mountain peaks, a mirror, and a sword—and one bronze cube.

Robert sucked in a breath, his eyes widening with under-standing as they met hers. "Queen Solstice's mirror ... it's a *magic* mirror."

Snow nodded, more than simple acknowledgement in her eyes. "My father's alive, but only in the mirror. Birch, Lord of the Mirror of Talvinen, was able to save him, but only if he stays in the mirror. There's a castle there. No servants. Solstice and I spend a lot of time there." Hesitating, she looked down at their clasped hands. "For a while I—I gave up on ever being cured. I thought the curse might even be the only way to save Solstice from the sorcerer, if he survived. I got a Switch Spell so I could take her place if he came for her: I would kill him with his own curse. I'd do it to keep her safe and my father happy."

Not knowing what to say or think yet, Robert squeezed her hand again and considered what she'd said. As if someone had wiped a mirror clean, he thought he was begin-ning to understand—the reclusiveness, the skills most princesses didn't have, odd comments here and there in her letters. She'd given up a court life, a life of ease, to spend time with her father—helping with chores in a servantless castle and bonding over activities that allowed her to keep a distance from others, skills more likely to be taught by a father. How difficult Snow's and Solstice's lives must have been since the curse! King Theodore's too.

They weren't the only ones, actually. A suspicion niggled at him, rousing his anger. "The Duke of Houen and a few others of the nobles who were especially close to King Theodore have suffered strangely the last several years, both in personal illnesses and in inexplicable business fiascos. I'm beginning to wonder if those weren't coincidences. Magical poisons can resemble illnesses."

"I suspect not now. Guagin, possibly with his cousin's help, could be behind it all."

"Shall I take care of Guagin for you? His enchanter cousin? This sorcerer, if he's alive? I can get Houen to help as well."

Snow sat up to smile broadly at him, her eyes bright with fulfilled hope. "I would appreciate your help. You don't know how much it means to me, but I need to discuss this with my father and Solstice too."

"I take it from the bread and soup you disappeared with into your room two days ago that your bracelet allows you access to The Mirror from any mirror?"

"Yes."

"May I join you for this meeting? I'd love to see King Theodore again."

She hesitated, her gaze somewhere over his left shoulder. "Only the immediate family of the Keeper are allowed in."

Something in Snow's not-quite look at him and the blush to her cheeks suggested she was thinking the same thing he was—that one day, soon hopefully, he would fit that description. "January."

Snow's eyes met his, questioning. He brushed his fingers gently along her cheek, then lifted her chin toward him.

"Would Princess Snow be upset, do you think, if I kissed you?"

Panic, and then something very opposite of that, flashed through Snow's eyes. "Princess Snow would be heartbroken," she said, a slight tremor to her voice.

Smiling at what he'd seen, Robert tilted her chin slightly away and kissed her hair at her temple. "I'm glad."

"*Ohhh.*"

Robert stilled as Lyndon moaned and began to stir. Snow bit her lip, and when he met her gaze, her eyes were laughing.

Robert sat back, chuckling. "Right on cue." He hopped up and held out his hand to Snow as Lyndon sat up, rubbing the bump on his head.

"This is not where I was." Robert's godfather looked up questioningly, accusingly, at him. He didn't have quite the dazed look of a man who'd just woken.

Robert arched an eyebrow, but then assumed an innocent expression and raised his right hand. "I give you my solemn word as a man of New Grimmland that I did not carry you anywhere in my fragile state."

"You're from *New Beaumont.*" Despite his accusatory glare, Lyndon accepted Robert's help up and his arm until he was steady.

"Exactly," Robert said as Lyndon released him. "I'm glad to see your mental abilities are as acute as ever." He added in a mutter for only Lyndon to hear, "Your hearing too, I shouldn't wonder."

Lyndon's lips twitched as he brushed leaves off his jacket. "Tell me, Miss January, do you have enough blackberries?"

"Oh!" Snow looked around for her basket. It lay under the bush, its berries strewn about the forest floor. Robert collected it for her.

"I'll make a peach pie from the jars my stepmother sent instead," she said. "I've had enough of the forest today, if you don't mind."

"I'm for returning myself," Robert agreed, "as Lyndon looks overtaxed."

Ignoring Lyndon's rebuttal, Robert offered Snow his arm, and they set off at a slow pace back to the cottage, explaining the parts of the afternoon Lyndon had missed and which Robert didn't mind sharing.

They hadn't progressed beyond the nearest clump of trees before hoofbeats and cries for Princess Snow found them.

When Snow's guards rounded the bend in the trail and stopped before them, their disgruntled, hurt expressions were enough to make Robert feel scolded.

"Ah, there you are," he said. He cleared his throat at Sutton's glare. "We were wondering what happened to you. I've something for you to do later. Either of you ever trailed anyone in the woods before?"

# CHAPTER 16

Brenner and Sutton had enough tracking skill to follow the boy about thirty feet. The kid was good; the guards were not.

"You're not tracking the boy to the hideout yourself." Lyndon gave Robert a stern look that was, for once, hardly needed. They were in the sitting room with the enchanters late that night while Snow visited her family. She would return by midnight, as Lady Violetta was to join them with information on the timing of removing the curse via the Poison Stone after attending a dinner with the only other person known to have used the stone. "Prince Dokar," Lyndon continued, "would find you the minute you left the wards around the cottage."

"Someone's tried breaking through a few times. You're lucky six of us are here to uphold the wards." Paternal concern wrinkling his normally cheerful face, Today shook his head in warning. "Don't think he's forgotten about you. I dare say he's found new ways to use you or loopholes for your protections."

"I know." Robert sighed and ran his hand through his hair. Lyndon, bless him, had trimmed it for him the previous night so he wouldn't look so scraggly when escorting Snow. "I want the highwaymen taken care of, but it's not something I need to do personally. Houen has a good tracker. We'll okay it with Snow and send word to him to send the tracker and enough men to take care of the highwaymen. Brenner or Sutton can get them started."

"The princess's immediate danger," Colors said, "is from the highwaymen, if they doubt the boy's story or if Guagin sends someone to 'find' the body, possibly implicating you, Robert, in a murder. The wards weren't set up against mortals walking through, but the cottage has defenses. If they did try to attack here, she'd be safe."

*Attacked by wild beasts, Snow ran away, Robert murdered her...* Robert had considered all the possible stories Guagin might use for Snow's death or disappearance, and the latter accusation was sounding more probable by the minute. "Guagin, possibly with the help of Schwan and maybe a weakened sorcerer or his enchanter cousin, has been threatening Queen Solstice and Princess Snow for years. I suspect he's also been mildly poisoning and causing financial crises for Houen and a couple other advisors. If Guagin is starting to act boldly now, we need to do so as well before others die and he starts a conflict with New Beaumont."

"You'll need more than the word of a scared boy trying to save his own neck," Who said, sitting in his chair in the shadowed corner.

"Yes. We'll need someone who can see magic and sneak into places unnoticed." Robert felt Lyndon's intense stare and reluctantly met his eye. Conflicting emotions passed over his godfather's face before a pained expression settled there.

Looking far older than normal, Lyndon pushed himself

slowly from his chair. "My head aches from today's abuse. I'm going to retire early. Good night, gentlemen."

When Lyndon had shut the sitting room door behind him, the enchanters all looked to Robert.

"That must have cost him a lot," Blatherskite said.

Robert answered with a weak smile. Lyndon knew as well as Robert did his duty to protect his family and kingdom, New Beaumont's to aid New Grimmland, come what may. Lyndon had no say in this. Robert was only awaiting King Theodore's permission.

"What are you planning?" Who asked. "Given that you've declared the highwaymen not worth your notice, I assume you're going after the advisor Gaugin?"

Robert nodded and sat up, trying to regain his usual excitement at the prospect of adventure and danger, of aiding those in need. "I must find papers or other evidence connecting Gaugin to the highwaymen, the threatening letters, and the ills that have befallen certain of the other advisors. If I can't, I think I can scare them out of him. I need to know if anyone else is involved as well before we show our hand, or they show theirs again."

"And if Prince Dokar catches you first?"

Robert didn't answer for a moment. "How long do you think I can be outside the wards before he finds me?"

"It depends on how actively he's seeking you," Colors replied. "A half hour perhaps? But what can you do in that time?"

"What if I'm not where he expects me to be when I leave the wards?"

"Twice that?"

Robert kept his eyes fixed on Who. The enchanter cocked his head in question.

"I can't recommend this, Robert," Colors said, catching his line of sight.

"No. It's foolish and it's a risk, but I can't let Guagin kill or threaten anyone else." *And I told Snow I would help.* He gestured to the shadowy enchanter. "Who is leaving soon to transport What in a portable ward system. I could go with them, and we could take a detour to Guagin's estate. I can sneak in as a frog, find his study, and be out in an hour."

"Those wards aren't strong enough to keep a full fey out. I can't help you if Prince Dokar shows up." There was a strange intensity to Who's statement, but the enchanter hadn't outright denied Robert's request, so he was still hopeful.

"I don't expect you to face him with me. Can any of you put a spell on me that would force me to be faithful to Snow? I'd rather die than Prince Dokar succeed. Or Guagin. But I can't stay trapped here, not doing anything."

"Spells can be fickle things, Robert," Colors said, understanding and sternness blending in his expression. "Even if we broke our own rules to do a control-type spell on you, there's no guarantee it would work as you want. It might guard your thoughts but not your deeds. It might see your aunt, sister, or daughter as a threat and prevent you caring for them. *If* it took at all over your current curses. I'm sorry, Robert. Your godfather may not have the authority to stop you, but I do. Two kingdoms, at the least, could be dragged into ruin if Prince Dokar catches you. The faerie prince has been denied too many times lately to stop at light mischief now. He *will* find a way to control you."

"Who exactly are you," Robert growled, "that you can command me?"

A flicker of a sad smile passed over Colors's face. "I know your love and your courage, Robert," he said firmly. "I also know your wisdom. If you wish to protect Princess Snow and both your kingdoms, remain the honorable man you want to be, you *must* stay here."

Before Robert could reply, Colors locked gazes with him, and Robert found he couldn't move. Couldn't scream at the images passing through his mind, searing him with shame or pain. Couldn't stop his dream self from doing the things he did. From doing whatever Prince Dokar commanded.

The pressure holding him in place eased, and Robert buried his face in his hands. "I'll stay," he said, his voice choked.

"Thank you, Robert, and ... I'm sorry." Colors patted him on the back and left the room, his steps slow and tired.

Some part of Robert said he should thank the enchanter, but at the moment, Robert didn't want to talk to anyone. He felt vile, broken by loss, and altogether a stubborn, proud fool.

"What exactly did Colors—"

"That's none of your business, Blatherskite," Today reprimanded.

"Come." Who clasped Robert's arm, encouraging him to rise. "Rest in your room until your lady returns."

Robert mutely followed him out.

*How was my day? I went for a walk in the woods and was nearly killed by a boy who wanted to cut out my heart. How was yours?*

Snow groaned as the ice deposited her in the rose garden. How was her father going to take the news? Would Solstice ever let her out of her sight again?

More importantly, what were they going to do?

Wishing she could borrow some of Robert's courage, she

pressed on to the castle and soon had King Theodore and Birch corralled in the family sitting room.

"How's Robert?" Her father's grin made her blush, then her stomach clench. More than wanting to marry her, Robert *planned* to marry her. But how long would that last? Was it fair to make him wait for something that might not happen for ten or twenty years or more? If the dress worked? She shook herself. Now was not the time.

"He's fine. Where's Solstice?" Snow asked as they sat.

"On her way to visit you," King Theodore said with meaning, surprising her. "A guard rushed in on one of the advisor meetings the morning after you visited us saying you were terribly ill and that she should come immediately. Given the time delay of getting a message from the cottage to the palace, we figured it was from when you were in the Sleeping Death. Solstice couldn't explain, nor could she refuse to respond to so public an announcement, so she's joining you for a few days at the cottage." He gave her that grin again. "She promised she wouldn't interfere with a young lord's cooking lessons."

Snow didn't think the guards had known she was ill, but Solstice would enjoy the break from the palace. What was the harm?

"Lyndon's always with us, so she might as well join us too," she said with a chuckle. "She did carry the mirror with her, didn't she? Or any mirror? If she comes here before reaching the cottage, there's something I need you to tell her. Robert, Lyndon, and I had a very interesting walk in the forest today."

"She took the mirror with her, of course," Birch said. "Why don't we play cards for a while and see if she joins us?"

They agreed, and Snow and Birch quickly set up the card

table. After an hour, however, they set the cards aside, and Snow told her tale.

By the time she finished, her father was pacing the room. "I really, really want out of this mirror, even if only for an hour," he said in a low growl she didn't think he intended for them to hear.

Pained for her father's struggle with his helplessness, Snow looked to Birch. His eyes were shut, his metallic silver hair a shifting crown of colors.

Catching her focus, Theodore moved to stand beside her and took her hand. "Tell Robert to get Houen to join him and do whatever is necessary to capture Guagin. And those high-waymen. What can you see, Birch?"

"The boy is riding fast through the forest," Birch said without opening his eyes. "The highwaymen appear to be celebrating. Guagin is in a coach traveling through a forest not unlike the one where the cottage is. I still see nothing when searching for the sorcerer." He cracked one eye open to meet Snow's, a familiar reprimand there. Was it her fear that kept her from believing him dead? Had she let fear interfere with her reason the same way she'd let it guide her to assume Robert's guilt and desertion? Shame warmed her cheeks. Birch closed his eyes again.

"Schwan sits alone in his study—no, the servant who's been intercepting the messages is with him. The servant's upset about something, something he never agreed to be a party to. He distrusted the foreign queen and strange princess but didn't hate them. Guagin had boasted to him of not needing the messages intercepted anymore. Concerned, the servant did some snooping to discover why. Guagin had Snow followed to the cottage. Realizing his highwaymen associates were near, as was the Duke of Pondleigh, he arranged for her murder. Schwan was once a guard, so the servant came to him. Schwan's furious. He's strapping on a sword and leaving the room. The servant's running after him, still talking." Birch looked up at her father, his face stricken. "Guagin plans on saving Solstice and thereby earning the kingdom's favor to marry her."

"Saving … Where is she, Birch?" Theodore cried. Snow had a horrible feeling she already knew.

Birch closed his eyes again. "She's tied to a chair in a darkened room. Her head is on her chest. She's asleep. This cottage is one of several ramshackle ones in a valley."

"The highwaymen have her," her father said flatly. "Guagin faked the message." He spun away from them, his fists clenching.

"Where are we?" Snow asked. "Where's the mirror?"

"It's at the cottage. A different room. It's too far for me to pull her through. I can't use my one day of freedom a century to help her unless she wakes and wills it."

*If Guagin really did break the mirror...*

Snow caught her too-fast breath and forced herself to hold it, then slowly release it. *Breathe. Hold. Breathe.* She wasn't powerless. She was the only one of them who could do something. She *would* do something—something more useful than panicking.

But what? She could use the Switch Spell, but then she'd be tied up and unable to retrieve the mirror. Bring a knife with her? No, she'd lose that in the switch.

*Bring...* What a fool she was! She didn't have to do this alone.

"I'll get Robert, the enchanters," she said, hope daring to color her words. "We'll save Solstice and the mirror." She clasped her father's shoulder in encouragement, met Birch's worried gaze with one of forced hope and determination, and ran from the room.

She didn't stop running until she burst into the cottage's sitting room. Surprisingly few were there to greet her.

"Where's Robert? Colors?" she asked as the enchanters politely rose at her entrance.

"In their rooms, I imagine," Cello said with something of an odd look at the others. He offered her his hand and guided her to a seat. "I'll fetch them for you."

Rather breathless from her haste, Snow nodded and allowed him to settle her into one of the comfortable wing-backs. The cuckoo sang its midnight notes, and a violet haze appeared around Lady Violetta's chair, positioned next to hers.

Lady Violetta materialized, elegant in a deep-violet gown, and smiled as her gaze swept the room. Her smile faded as quickly as the glow about her. "You're all very glum tonight, I must say."

"I'll explain in a moment," Snow said. "Cello is fetching the others."

Lady Violetta's brow furrowed, but she remained silent. Today offered them tea, which Snow took as a welcome distraction.

Colors joined them, his smile of greeting more serious than normal, and they waited for Robert, Cello, Lyndon, and Who. It was some minutes before the door burst open. Cello was alone. His bloodless face sent a chill through Snow.

Cello sought Colors's gaze. "Robert's gone. Lyndon's under a Sleep Spell, and I can't find Who or What."

# CHAPTER 17

T he squeak of the hallway floor outside his room brought no smile of amusement as it normally did.

Who stopped him outside the door. "Try to sleep, Robert. Remember those things in the visions Colors gave you did not happen, might not have happened even if you'd left."

*But I was so close to making them possible. I knew the risks—how high they were, who I could hurt—and was willing to ignore them.* Robert patted the enchanter's arm and turned to the door, but Who blocked his path.

"Don't get trapped in the past, or the almosts either." Who's eyes—pale green, perhaps, under the shadows?—conveyed a painful experience. "It doesn't help." He held out his hand. "Farewell, spell seer. Perhaps one day we can hunt together again."

Robert managed a nod as he shook Who's hand. "Goodbye, enchanter."

Who cleared his path and walked away. Robert, steps dragging as if he wore Snow's fatigue-inducing gown, pushed open his door and walked inside. He stopped just shy of the bed, tiredness and visions all forgotten.

What, the rogue enchanter with a talent for persuasion and transforming into objects, stood by Robert's window, his blue curse-line more prominent than normal. There was a cocked pistol in his hand.

"How did you get in here?" Robert cried, loudly enough, he hoped, for Who to hear.

"There is no *How* here." What sneered. In his hand, beside the grip of his pistol, was a familiar green handkerchief.

The door burst open as Who ran in, and then they were both frozen in a bubble of magic that felt, horrifyingly, of Prince Dokar.

What laughed as he tucked the crumpled handkerchief into a pocket of his jacket. "That's not a curse-line you see, Your Grace, that's a divide-line. The mark of a half-breed. *I* don't hide mine." He smirked, vindictive malice glittering in his eyes. "When I heard who had cursed you, I sent word to my prince offering my assistance. The cottage wouldn't let me out after *Who* tracked me here and told it not to, but no one ever said mice couldn't leave, or cross the wards. They're very easy to enchant, and very fast." He patted his jacket pocket. "My prince sent a number of useful aids back by them to recover you. You should be honored."

Robert felt he was going to be sick. He cut his eyes to the side, trying to see Who. Could enchanters not fight this magic either?

"Oh, he can't help you, Your Grace."

The magic in the bubble pushed Robert's face to the side, straining his neck until Who came into view. The enchanter was frozen mid-sprint. At a word from What, his arms slapped to his sides, his ankles cracked together, and his lips pressed together in a muffled cry but then vanished behind a darkening of the shadows always about him.

"Who!" Robert shouted, straining to move but unable to do more than yell. Somehow, he doubted the sound would reach the others. He both feared and hoped it would. *Keep Lyndon out of this mess, please. And make me cunning.*

"Come now, old friend," What said, addressing Who with a malice worthy of the fey prince's minion. Robert fervently wished the man had given him reason to kill him earlier. "Shall you tell him or shall I?"

The shadows about Who thinned, darkened, and then vanished, but by whose command Robert wasn't sure. Uncloaked by shadows, the enchanter beside him didn't look at all as Robert had envisioned, but he'd suspected that already. Who's face, scrunched in pain, was unnaturally pale, narrow with prominent cheekbones. A thin, gold divide-line ran across it like a scar. His hair was a pale gold as well.

"I'm sorry, Robert," Who said hoarsely. He opened his eyes and met Robert's stare with a golden gaze. "You are bound by your king's authority, so am I. No matter what kingdom the half-fey choose, we cannot unchoose the fey."

Who vanished. The clock struck midnight. And the room swayed as Robert fell.

"Come along, frog."

What scooped Robert into his pocket, and the bubble of magic burst.

⚜

ROBERT WAS DEPOSITED on his webbed feet in the middle of a forest glen lit by glowing orbs. It was empty save of two stone chairs, one throne-like, the other merely regal. Nostrils flaring, Prince Dokar rose from the throne. Lucrezia, seated in the second chair, gasped. Forcing away the memories of Colors's visions and the fear they birthed, Robert allowed himself one contemptuous huff. Portable throne room for watching the ruin of mortal lives? Pity he was going to disappoint them. Wars weren't waged solely with swords. Some of the visions could be turned his way—thanks to the forethought of his courageous Snow and her desire to save her stepmother.

"What sort of a rescue is this?" Robert snapped. "Where are the women?"

Dokar actually paused mid-stride and blinked before continuing toward him. "Lucrezia, Robert should know that—"

"You said two days for a married woman, didn't you? Do I get more if she's a queen?"

Lucrezia's gasp was of a different sort this time, and Robert hoped frogs didn't blush.

A slow smile spread across Dokar's face as he knelt before Robert. "Lucrezia, our noble warrior must not like the taste of flies."

From behind him, that swine he should have killed a long time ago scoffed. "Doesn't like women he can't—"

Dokar shot What a glare. "Don't interrupt, half-breed. Your usefulness is over. Be gone."

The traitor's face darkened, but he bowed and left, quickly disappearing into the forest. Robert hoped a wolf ate him. Or Who caught up with him again, for he doubted whatever loyalty kept Who from helping Robert against Dokar applied to What.

The smile of interest returned as Dokar focused on Robert again. The faerie prince was silent, apparently intending Robert to continue.

His stomach roiled, but Robert remembered what he had to fight for—to lie for.

"I need your help," he said, hopping forward once. "I have unfinished business with the royal family and advisors of New Grimmland. Gather the ones I ask for, and I will kiss Queen Solstice in front of them." *Please let Snow's Switch Spell work! She's a betrothed princess—kissing her might free him of his curse. If not, and if he fell into the Sleeping Death, she'd take him into the mirror, where Prince Dokar couldn't force him to hurt anyone. Where Snow might marry him and visit him as Queen Solstice did King Theodore.*

Lucrezia gasped again and may have said something, but Robert couldn't hear her.

Dokar quirked an eyebrow, more in skepticism than disgust. "Though you're engaged to her daughter?"

"Yes." He drew on the bitterness he'd felt at Snow's supposed snubbing of him all those years. "Snow's put me off too many times—I know all about her and that Bankor. She expects me to be faithful, but—" He met Dokar's eyes, his expression hardening. "I know her stepmother's ambitions too. King Theodore lives—magically, but he breathes, trapped in a mirror. Since Queen Solstice *is* married, that means two days for me."

Dokar's thin lips spread in a smile that turned Robert's stomach.

"The advisor Guagin intends to marry Queen Solstice," Robert rushed on. "Guagin will duel with me. Snow and Solstice will hate me. Before the night is over, I'll have kissed a married woman, broken an engagement, killed a foreign advisor, revealed a trapped king, exposed a traitorous wife, and started an international incident. What more chaos can you want?"

"Done." Dokar's eyes sparkled with all the malice present

around a thousand enemy campfires. He paced around the clearing, rubbing his hands together and muttering to himself, ignoring Robert. Searching the mortal lands for those Robert had asked for?

If only Robert were a beast ferocious enough to kill a fey lord. Now would have been the perfect opportunity.

"Going to make me human again? I don't imagine anyone would be jealous of a frog. I'm *speckled*."

# CHAPTER 18

"**G**one! Where?" Snow exclaimed, confusion and fear dragging her gaze to Colors, where everyone else's had gone.

The silver-haired enchanter's jaw was clenched, an unfamiliar anger in his eyes and a sternness about his face.

"He gave his word!" Today cried, bewildered. "I fear—"

"He broke it too," Colors snapped, rising. His crimson suit melted into one of black leather, a close-fitting, armor-like style reminding her of a warrior of old. A crest was stitched into the front and was also present on the sheath of his sword. Colors was a lord among the enchanters?

"No!" Snow cried over the clamor of voices. She caught Colors's arm, stopping his march out, forcing him to turn to her. "If Robert promised something, he'd stick to it. I am proof enough of that. Tell me what is going on. I can find him for you."

The hardness of Colors's eyes flickered but didn't give way. "He wanted Who to take him to Guagin's despite what Prince

Dokar would do to him if he found him—and the fey prince will find him. Who is gone, as is Robert. I am not allowed to interfere with the affairs of kingdoms except when those gifted with magic seek to cause chaos." His eyes flickered again, pain exposing his fury for what it was. "Robert is a spell seer, and he is cursed and is likely to gain from Prince Dokar whatever magical abilities he needs to fulfil Prince Dokar's schemes. Because of that, Robert is under my domain, and I must stop him." He paused, turning his gaze from Snow to Lady Violetta, who was looking older and more serious than Snow had ever seen her. There was a pained understanding in her expression. "It is easier to stop a man than a fey prince."

Snow's hand trembled as she realized what Colors's warning meant about Prince Dokar's interest in Robert—he intended to ruin Robert and as many mortal kingdoms as he could through him.

Putting aside her fear and focusing on what she knew of Robert's character, she looked from Colors to the others. "Then Robert's not gone of his own accord—someone took him. And Guagin's not home for him to go to. He had Queen Solstice kidnapped. He's riding to meet her at the highway-men's hideout. Schwan is going there with his own men. There will be a fight." She swallowed hard. "The Mirror of Talvinen is with her—it is not indestructible. My father and Birch…"

Fear for her family, for Robert, the ache of a dream dying, all settled in her chest and nearly stole her voice, but she forced herself to continue, "I can locate Robert using the mirror. If you can take me to him, and if Prince Dokar has corrupted his curses with worse ones, I will kiss him and take him into the mirror. Prince Dokar's magic cannot touch him there. But you must help me save my family. Take

Houen's men and my guards to the hideout if your laws don't allow you to fight yourselves."

Colors studied her but didn't respond beyond an additional tightening of his jaw at her news.

"Traveling armies is forbidden," I Don't Know ventured quietly, as if he didn't want to be heard.

"That fey is forever interfering with my fairy godchildren," Lady Violetta hissed to herself, her fingers tapping briskly on her wand, shooting a myriad of hues along its shaft. The others remained quiet, for once, waiting for Colors's decision.

At last he sighed and patted Snow's hand in his old manner, which cheered her. "We will do what we can, around the rules. Go find out where the young lord is, but hurry."

"I think you'll find you're going to the same place." The statement was followed by a wet cough and a hiss of pain that brought Snow around to face the opposite side of the room. Who was slumped in his chair in the corner. The shadows about him were weak enough to reveal torn clothes, bits of twigs and leaves, and enough blood-smeared gashes for some sort of animal attack.

"What happened to you?" Today cried, bustling over to him, a teacup suddenly in his hand.

"Where's Robert?" Snow cried, feeling guilty for being more concerned about him than the injured-but-obviously-still-breathing enchanter.

"I had some unfinished business to take care of." The enchanter, who seemed younger than she realized, and somehow different in the thinner shadows, gave them that wolfish grin of his that made her think he *could* transform into the creature. It disappeared behind the teacup.

"Drink this," Today ordered, shoving the teacup at him. "You're losing fluids."

Taken aback, Who obeyed. The shadows darkened about his face, and he looked up to meet Snow's gaze. "Robert's a clever liar when the need arises, my lady." A corner of his mouth quirked before he flinched. Today, along with Cello, examined his wounds, clucking like mother hens.

"*What* made a bargain with Prince Dokar," Who continued through gritted teeth, "and got the magic needed to get both him and Robert out. Robert's convinced Prince Dokar to help him kill Guagin, among other things. I don't think Prince Dokar will change his curse terms for a while, but if Robert is being as clever as I think he is"—his gaze focused on Snow's wrist, on her bracelet—"Prince Dokar will not be pleased when he realizes it. You should beware."

Snow wrapped her hand around her wrist, clasping her bracelet against her skin. What was Robert planning? Her stomach knotted. How did one fight a fey prince bent on mischief in addition to highwaymen and a traitorous advisor?

"Well," Lady Violetta exclaimed in a bright voice, clasping her hands in front of her, "now that we know where everyone is going, I feel a celebration is in order. A festival— for the summer solstice. Rose garlands for the hair, I think, should do it." Her grin was sly as she snapped a crimson rose into existence and tucked it into Snow's hair before glancing around the room. She frowned at Colors. "Don't look at me like that. I see no reason why we can't have a saber dance at the festival. Naturally, we'll bring what's needed for it. Traveling large groups for *parties* isn't forbidden, after all."

Colors actually grinned at her. "I'd forgotten how clever you are, Lady Violetta."

To Snow's surprise, the enchantress's expression sobered

again. "I'd forgotten it myself, for a time," she said softly before shaking herself and adding a few more roses to Snow's hair.

"I'm beginning to like the sounds of this party," Blatherskite said as the men began to plan.

"I'll give out invitations to the Duke of Houen and his men," Today volunteered.

"Blatherskite," Cello said, "invite Schwan and that servant. His men too."

"We'll have a pleasant chat on the way," Blatherskite said. "Guard to royal advisor. That will be an interesting story."

"Somebody wake Lyndon."

"January—"

A sudden tingling worked its way up from her feet to her head. The words blurred as the hues around her smeared, streaking as if the world was spinning faster and faster around her. A woodsy odor filled her senses, then blackness.

◈✦◈

ROBERT HAD EXPECTED a human king's throne room, not a ramshackle cottage in a valley. He'd expected Guagin and Solstice and a few guards he'd have to subdue without killing (he couldn't conscience killing men doing their duty, even if they were in his way), not a gang of celebrating highwaymen. He'd expected Prince Dokar to watch visibly, not disappear with a sinister laugh.

As he stood on the doorstep where Dokar had dumped him, Robert was half tempted to rap on the painted wood to see how his expectation of the door being opened by a drunken rogue would be thwarted.

But more importantly, why was he here? Was Dokar playing a joke on him? Was he planning for him to wear himself out defeating highwaymen so he'd be killed later dueling with Guagin? Why would he take them on when others could do that?

Not wanting to stand in indecision, Robert eased nearer to one of the lighted windows. Inside, the highwaymen— twenty strong and all armed—drank, danced, played cards, and bragged of riches, of a queen's ransom even. The same instinct that told him he'd never outrun Dokar back to the enchanters' wards from here also told him the highwaymen weren't so far gone in their revelry as to be easily overcome. Biting back a curse, Robert crouched and moved swiftly to the next window, his gaze set on the dark one beyond that. The rattle of carriage wheels sent him scrambling toward the bushes under the lightless window. What fool would stop here?

*A queen's ransom...*

As Robert slipped behind the rose bushes, the swaying light of the carriage lanterns nearly searching him out, he understood: Dokar left him here because *Solstice* was here. Because Guagin was about to arrive. His jaw clenched. If that fey brought Snow to this mess ... as he needed. *Merciful Lord, help me save her and Solstice and cause no lasting harm this night. Foil Dokar's plans for me.* He'd asked Dokar to bring Snow, Solstice, and all the advisors together so they'd all know the truth about Guagin and any others on the louse's side. He hadn't wanted the gathering to include the highwaymen!

Forcing his thoughts into strategy, Robert rose enough to peek into the window, but it was too dark to tell what was inside. Kneeling, he felt around the ground beside him, his fingers finding an old rock border covered with dirt and moss. He began digging out the stones, snapping grass roots and ripping moss in his haste. Gathering four hefty rocks, he watched as the carriage drew to a halt and one of the footmen hopped down to open the carriage door. Guagin stepped out, a crisp military uniform on and a sword at his waist. Robert scoffed. An accidental rescuer indeed. He probably had a fake bandage ready to cover a 'head wound' gained while bravely rescuing the queen.

Rising quietly as Guagin spoke to one of the four men with him, Robert sprinted a dozen feet forward and launched first one dirt-and-moss encrusted rock, then another, at the men's heads, until two of them had crashed unconscious to the muddy lawn. Guagin and the remaining two drew steel, their cries for assistance drowned out by a rousing song counting bottles of beer.

Robert pocketed his humanness, fairly disappearing into the night, and crept behind the searching, spooked men. He transformed, grabbed the two guards, knocked their heads together, and tossed them into Guagin, toppling them all. Before Guagin could escape from under the men, Robert drew his dagger and rapped him over the head.

"Seventy-eight bottles of beer on the wall," he sang along softly as he began divesting the men of their weapons. He loaded the guards and servants into the carriage, then shoved their weapons—all but four pistols, which he loaded—into the bushes. "Thirty-two bottles of beer on the wall," he whispered as he hopped onto the driver's seat, released the brake, slapped the reins to get the horses into motion, and jumped off. He sprinted for Guagin, tied his hands together with strips of the man's fancy shirt, dragged him up, and slapped him.

"Wake up just enough to stand." Robert slapped him again. "I don't know how long you told your remaining men to wait before rushing in to help you 'save' the queen, but I'm sure you brought some, so we need to hurry."

Guagin moaned, and some of his weight eased off Robert.

"Good enough." Shifting Guagin to one side, Robert fired a pistol just to the right of the lead horse as the matched pairs began to slow. The poor creatures bolted. Robert stuffed the gun into his belt, dragged Guagin to the front door, and drew the next loaded pistol.

The singing stopped, and the door opened, filling with two bandits. Not the unexpected, after all.

In a glistening kind of invitation, Robert showed them the barrel of his gun.

"Your gold is in the carriage dashing away, driverless. You might want to go after it." He pulled the blinking Guagin aside and waved the pistol at the two men. "I don't shoot men in the back, so don't turn around as you go."

They looked from him to the gun and took off running.

Robert shoved Guagin inside and slammed the door shut behind them with his foot and kept his back to it. It was a large, open room with a fireplace, tables, chairs, and a smattering of villains. If he'd been that fool boy, just the smell of the place—alcohol and unwashed bodies—would have been enough to set him on the straight and narrow. He pulled a dagger from his belt, wrapped his arm around the nearly steady Guagin, and pressed the dagger's tip into the advisor's belly, daring him to move. The pistol he kept open for the room to see. "Good evening, gentlemen."

A dozen and a half highwaymen glowered, gaped, or blinked at him, depending on how many bottles of beer they had personally taken off the wall.

"What do you want?" one man growled, his foreign accent answering one of Robert's questions as to why the highwaymen would agree to abduct a queen. Thickly built and red cheeked, the bandit's eyes held a hard, shrewd look promising trouble and showing little fear of it.

"There's a loose carriage you might want to catch." Robert

glanced around the room, ignoring the leader and making eye contact with the others. "You can buy yourself a better hideout with the reward money in it. This one is going to be overrun with the Duke of Houen's men in under an hour. Guagin's *evidence removers* in less than that, I shouldn't wonder."

Apparently awake enough to sputter a refusal, Guagin did so, but Robert doubted any were willing to believe the scoundrel.

"Quiet!"

The angry snarl of words and tangle of moving men reduced in intensity at the window-rattling roar from the leader.

"Why warn us?" Aside from his dagger, the man's muscled arm was such that even Robert knew better than to get in a wrestling match with him should words or swords fail.

"Because I want Queen Solstice for myself. Guagin is using you to gain a kingship by marriage. Do you think he'll let you live, knowing what you do? I want the queen and am willing to give you a sizable head start in return."

The man sneered. "Then there's no gold in the carriage, is there?"

Robert smiled wryly. "You are not as drunk as you should be. A carriage that fine would summon a high price. Guagin here might fetch a price once his treachery is known—or now if his son is loyal."

The man huffed, then nodded to a couple of the more stable-looking bandits. "Bring the woman ... and the mirror."

"But, Stan—"

"Get them," Stan barked. The pair hurried off down a narrow corridor.

The mirror? *Snow's father...* Robert's stomach knotted. The mirror was not light or fitted with a handle. Could he get Solstice into the mirror so he'd only have to run with it? Was she in a condition to run on her own?

"What do you know about the mirror?" Stan demanded as the two bandits returned, one burly man hauling Solstice in the chair she was tied to. Solstice, appearing drowsy but otherwise unharmed, was placed at the bandit's right. The mirror was leaned against her chair. Stan gestured slightly to another couple of bandits, who slipped out the rear door.

"Nothing you need to know." A tingling on his back painted a bull's-eye there. Robert used his elbow to slide the latch bolt into place and then eased just to the side of the door and a potential bullet's path. The bandit leader smirked at him. "But I fancy taking it with me when Queen Solstice and I leave," Robert finished.

Dazed, or drugged, Solstice tried to lift her head to find him.

Scoffing, Stan eyed him thoughtfully. "I'm sure you do, *Your Grace.*" He flicked his hand toward Robert and Guagin. "Wound them but make sure they'll live long enough for ransoms to be paid. Take the mirror, leave the queen. We're going."

"Wake up, Solstice!" Robert shoved Guagin into the charging bandits and pocketed his humanness. As men cried in astonishment and Robert slipped between their feet, he had to admit that though he'd rather be a ferocious beast, a frog small enough to make him seemingly vanish had a certain advantage.

So long as he didn't get stepped on.

Robert leapt for a baggy pantleg to avoid an unusually heavy-looking boot, then continued up to a greasy head and hopped from it to another toward the queen.

"Wake up, Solstice!" he yelled as Solstice's unfocused gaze roved the room.

"He's using magic!" someone cried.

"The frog!"

The sudden movement of the man under Robert nearly sent him skidding off, but he half slipped, half jumped for the next head two feet over. A thick hand swatted him from the air. He hit a shoulder before tumbling to the floor. Gathering his webbed feet under him, he leapt out from under a descending pair of hands.

"Stop in the queen's name!" someone commanded as light flared through the room. Startled cries and oaths followed this.

Robert's hop ended with a bellyflop onto the stone floor, his human head knocking into a knee. A highwayman went tumbling back. Momentarily too dazed to remember how to work whichever body he had, Robert scrambled ineffectively to rise.

"Your Majesty!" someone cried in shock and concern. Houen?

"Lady Lucrezia will see to the queen. You needn't move," said a horribly familiar voice. "Unbind her, Lucrezia, then guard her."

Robert went limp on the floor and looked around, his gut tightening with dread.

Prince Dokar, in the guise of a New Beaumont general, stood some ways to his right, in a clear spot near the inner door. Houen stood next to him, eyes wide. Bankor cowered at the fey's other side. A highwayman was backing away from them but drawing a dagger.

"Keep still, everyone, until we figure out what's going on!" a steady voice yelled amid the panicked questions. Schwan crouched by the door, sword in hand, looking the soldier he'd once been. He faced the swarthy giant of a highwaymen leader.

Robert kept turning, fearing what he'd see but needing to know.

New Grimmland's advisors were scattered about the room, highwaymen crowding around them or backing away, depending on whether the advisor was armed. Only three were.

"Robert!"

Two highwaymen were dragging Snow toward the rear door, her puffy crimson dress tangling with her feet, hindering her efforts to free herself.

His mind finally remembered which body he had, and he jumped to his feet, drawing two of his loaded revolvers and firing one. "Leave her!"

One bandit collapsed, and the other backed off, putting an abandoned, card-and-tankard-filled table between him and Snow. She stumbled but caught herself on a chair. As she pulled herself upright to lean against the table, she looked to Robert, her mouth opening, but he gave a discreet shake of his head and turned away. *Don't spoil my deception, darling, by thanking me. Be a cold January a bit longer.*

Needing a solid barrier behind him, Robert backed slowly to the inner wall, by the fireplace, his gaze darting around but going frequently toward Snow, who was standing proud now. How brave she looked as she watched, so still, that resolute set to her jaw. Like all the recent arrivals, she was paler than normal, a bit greenish. Being snatched by magic had that effect on one. The highwaymen, as well as the advisors, kept glancing warily at Dokar, as if sensing a power they shouldn't tangle with, a performance not to interrupt.

"Robert! What's going on?" Houen bellowed in a tone equal parts outrage and confusion as he glanced between the highwayman still too close to Snow and Lucrezia guarding an unbound Solstice with a drawn revolver. Another revolver hung at Lucrezia's waist.

"The Duke of Pondleigh," Dokar said smoothly, preempting Robert's reply, "possesses some little talent for magic. He wanted you to witness Guagin's treachery for yourself."

He swept a hand toward Guagin's body near the door, the bandits having done more than wound him in the chaos. Schwan, who stood beside it, looked down on it with distaste. Robert noticed for the first time a faint divide-line under the man's hint of magic. So that was how the former guard had survived the sorcerer's assault. Robert prayed Dokar wouldn't notice and try to take advantage.

"For Guagin had the queen kidnapped," Dokar continued. "The duke risked much to rescue her."

"Then why is that woman holding my queen at gunpoint! Those swine trying to take my princess!" Houen bellowed. The tautness of his body indicated he was ready for a fight, though he held no weapon.

"Peace, Houen! Things are not as they seem!" Robert cried, fearing his friend would get himself killed. Robert felt a hint of Dokar's power brush by him with a warning crackle, and he clenched his jaw.

"His Grace will explain," Dokar said smoothly. "Won't you, Robert of *Pond*leigh?"

Though feeling Dokar's gaze on him, Robert focused on Houen, willing his old friend to trust him. But the look of sudden hope in the man's eyes didn't give Robert the satisfaction he'd expected. He'd kill that before he was done tonight, and he'd never get a chance to explain. *Please, Colors, Lady Violetta, do something! I didn't mean to go back on my word.*

A flash of gold caught his eye as one of the bandits between him and Snow picked up a golden bracelet glowing with magic. Snow gasped and clutched her wrist, her eyes briefly meeting Robert's in distress and a silent plea. He returned a slight nod.

"Your Grace," Dokar prodded.

Dropping the spent revolver to the floor, Robert swallowed hard. "I—I need a word with Princess Snow first."

Snow narrowed her eyes at him, cunning in their depths. Sadness too. His heart ached with an understanding of it. If he succeeded tonight, he might have her, but only in a kind of half-life. He'd never see his family again, never fence with Rupert or give his niece piggyback rides. Never again serve his king or protect his people. He'd never leave an empty castle in a mirror. *If* Snow got him into the mirror at all. If his curse wasn't too jealous to accept the Sleeping Death and worse things befell him.

With a prayer for deliverance or death, Robert strode to the highwayman pocketing a priceless trinket. Reaching him, Robert held out his hand. With one glance at his face, the highwayman silently dropped the bracelet onto Robert's palm. He closed his fist over it and brushed past him to Snow. Stopping a foot from her, he bowed formally. She held herself stiffly, her eyes carefully shuttered.

Calling up all his anger at Dokar, he infused it into his tone, willing his voice not to crack, and held out the bracelet with the golden ball. "You'll regret not marrying me when you had the chance, Princess Snow." As she slowly reached out to take it, he mouthed, "Switch with Solstice." Shoving the bracelet into her palm, he sneered. "I know all about you and that pipsqueak Bankor. What were you thinking?"

As her hand closed over the golden charms, her hard expression cracked, and she looked from the bracelet to him, her eyes shimmering. "Of you, Robert," she whispered. She met his gaze, everything he'd been yearning to see in her look. "Always of you."

Robert swallowed hard.

"Your Grace," Dokar called, his voice smooth despite the warning it carried. "If you're plotting something other than our agreement, you might want to reconsider."

Taking a step away, Robert focused on a spot beyond Snow's shoulder, where it was easier to concentrate. "Princess Snow of New Grimmland, I hereby release—" Fear cut through him. If he broke the engagement as he'd told Dokar in his desperate ploy, would the mirror let him in, since he wasn't engaged to Snow, if even that was connection enough? "Do what you will with the engagement," he snapped, spinning around. "I have business with the queen."

Heart pounding in his ears, Robert strode through the watching men. They parted for him, giving a view of the unlit fireplace and its companions.

The mirror leaned against the stonework hearth, out of the way of clumsy feet. Lucrezia and Solstice stood a few feet from it, Lucrezia between the queen and the mirror, tears streaming unchecked down her cheeks. A revolver, directed at the queen, trembled in her hand. He saw her struggle in the line of her jaw, the crease between her eyes. He knew how hard, and ultimately how useless, it was to fight the magic of a control spell.

Ignoring the girl, Solstice watched him, wariness in her gaze, something of a wild animal not sure whom to trust and ready to do whatever it took to save her loved ones in her stance.

"Switch with Snow," he mouthed as he neared her. Her gaze darted to her stepdaughter. "I want you all to know," he called out with a brief glance around, "that Queen Solstice is married. Her husband is not dead." Solstice flickered with magic, the look in her eyes more sad now than desperate. *Snow.* He reached for her, forcing himself to see his betrothed rather than the queen before him. "I'll let you guess to whom." He pulled Snow into his arms, determined to make their one true kiss count.

"Shoot her, Lucrezia!" Dokar yelled. "That's not the queen!"

"No!" Robert pivoted Snow away from Lucrezia, but the spin felt wildly out of control. Robert stumbled and seemed to be falling backwards, Snow toppling with him.

"Robert!" she cried as a sense of green welled up in him.

Dokar was reclaiming his allowance for humanness without a kiss.

A bullet blasted the stone floor beyond them, sending bits of rock flying. Lucrezia's broken cry pierced his ears.

Robert slammed into the floor as a frog. Snow hit it a few feet beyond him, her glamour disappearing to reveal her true face and that enormous, crimson gown. Had Dokar forced the Switch Spell to reverse?

"Shoot the mirror!" Dokar cried. "It's the source of the witch's power! She's blocked the doorways with magic and bewitched the prince!"

"No!" Three shouts sounded together, warring with the yells of desperate highwaymen.

Lucrezia, muscles taut and still crying, turned to the mirror. She exchanged her spent revolver for the fresh one at her waist.

Pulling his webbed feet underneath him, Robert leapt for the gun, knocking it aside as another boom blared through the room and stone from the fireplace flew. Stunned by the noise and the kick of the gun, Robert toppled to the floor and lay there, unable to move.

"Catch him, Lucrezia!"

A thin-soled slipper pressed him to the stone. High-waymen surged forward, but Robert couldn't move, could hardly think.

"Enough!" Snow pushed herself up with one hand and held the other out toward the mirror. The bracelet dangling from her wrist glowed golden. "It's not sorcery but the power of a keeper!" Ice shot from the mirror.

# CHAPTER 19

As men cried out in alarm, Snow pulled ice from the mirror, forming a barrier around it and sending a line toward Lucrezia and Robert, blocking them, Solstice, and her, from Prince Dokar and the others. Solstice, back in her true form, shoved Lucrezia off Robert, sending her tumbling into the fireplace. Lucrezia's head cracked against the stone, and she fell limply to the floor. Though Snow recognized Lucrezia's struggle against a control spell of her own, Snow couldn't find it in herself to feel sorry the *blonde curse* had been removed from the chaos. There was plenty of that without her. If they survived, what would the advisors think of her and Solstice's magic? Would they be in danger as sorceresses, or the mirror's power in danger of being abused?

Ignoring the burning of her hands, Snow sent jagged walls of clear ice through the room, scattering men, not stopping to think beyond the distraction she caused as she strained to resist the mirror's attempts to pull her through. She hadn't the same control Solstice did as keeper.

"I've got to find my bracelet! They stole it!" Solstice cried, rising from beside a human Robert. "Snow, protect the advisors. Robert, help me." Somehow, the petite queen managed to haul Robert to his feet as Snow walled off the frail Duke of Mourin.

Staggering as Solstice released him, Robert shook his head, as if still dazed. Solstice grabbed his hand and passed with him through Snow's wall of ice, doubtless intending him to bully her bracelet from whomever had stolen it. He glanced over his shoulder at Snow, but a clamor of voices raised in song stole her attention. The sound carried through the windows, half war chant, half summer dance. They'd come! But the door didn't immediately burst open with arriving help. What was keeping them outside?

As Snow sent a wall of ice between a courageous but unarmed Houen and a dagger-wielding highwayman, the sound of a fight outside interrupted the song. Were more highwaymen outside? Or had Guagin hired men to attack the bandits after he'd gone, and they were battling with whomever the enchanters had brought?

Snow yelped as several feet of the ice walling her and the mirror off shattered. The largest of the bandits crashed to the floor amidst the broken crystals, blood seeping from his chest. Heart pounding, Snow worked to rebuild the wall, but her hands burned from the cold. She'd never held the ice this long, and the tug to travel was almost sickening in its intensity.

"You interest me, mortal."

Snow's heart sank, and her concentration, her connection to the mirror, snapped. The ice stopped flowing.

Standing within her walled chamber, Prince Dokar cocked his head to study her. "So you are the Daughter of Winter," he said, his slow walk toward her graceful in a predatory way. Rubbing her hands on her dress to warm them, Snow watched him silently, willing herself to stand tall and hold his gaze. If Robert could face the fey prince, so could she.

But Snow wasn't the Daughter of Winter, not until Solstice passed that duty and honor to her. Yet until Solstice found her bracelet, Snow would have to serve, and she wasn't about to admit anything to Dokar. Would the mirror treat her as keeper though, for now?

"I'd wondered where the land and its keepers had been hidden all these years."

Snow stiffened at his interest, her gut tightening with unease. Then something cool and solid touched her hand, and her fingers automatically tightened around it. She listed to the side as the full weight of Talvinen's Sword hit her. Solstice hadn't been lying about how heavy it was. Had Birch sent it to her as a bluff, or did it sense a threat to the mirror?

For a moment, Dokar seemed to hesitate, fear flashing through his eyes as they took in the sword. Was it the weapon or the sounds of battle intensifying beyond their chamber? For men bearing Houen's and Schwan's colors, and rose garlands in their hair, had burst into the cottage. Dokar's gaze swept the room, landing briefly somewhere she couldn't see, before focusing on her. His eyes glittered with mischief now.

"You have an exceedingly fine weapon, my lady." He flicked his wrist, and a sword as black as a moonless night appeared in his hand. "Would you care to spar?"

"No!" Snow blurted, but Dokar lunged forward anyway. She brought the sword up to parry the blow, but the ebony blade never came, and Snow found herself following through with a swing that would take her blade through Dokar's chest.

Horror and hope warred within her, but the blade passed through the fey as through a mist, and Snow stumbled, following the heavy sword. With laughter as cruel but not so mad as the sorcerer's, Dokar stepped back, allowing her to crash to the floor, landing on her knees in a puddle of fabric, her grip on the sword lost. *No*, she cried as the sword clattered to the floor beyond her reach. Not that she could wield its powers anyway, it seemed.

"So you're not Winter's Daughter. The queen is. How interesting," Dokar mused. He chuckled, but there was something unsettling in the sound. "It was a good bluff though. I was concerned, for a moment. But you *are* the heir—you may bear the sword but you cannot banish anyone with it. Perhaps," he said, eyeing her as she pulled the mass of red fabric away from her feet to rise, struggling against a new understanding of what it meant to not take defeat lying down. Dokar still had his sword and more than enough magic to defeat even the enchanters. "Perhaps we could arrange a trade," he continued, still somewhat musing. "Yes, I think so. Swear allegiance to me as heir to Winter. I have no desire for your mortal kingdom."

"Nev—" Snow bit back her angry refusal as Dokar continued, smirking.

"And I will give you the Duke of Pondleigh, his curses gone or under your control, whichever you wish." He stretched out a thin hand toward her, a king waiting for the kiss of submission, sure it would come.

Snow's gaze shot from Dokar's outstretched hand to his eyes. She couldn't give away a kingdom to him, not even one such as Winter, not even for Robert. Through the ice wall behind Dokar, she could see Robert and Solstice running toward them, a golden glow about Solstice's wrist again.

What would Dokar do to Solstice, knowing who she was now?

*For once, let my curse be useful.*

Saying nothing, Snow knelt before Dokar, lightly took his hand, and leaned toward it, quickening her movement at a hiss from the prince. His hand slipped from hers to find her cheek. Her head jerked to the side at the force of his slap. Snow bit her lip against a cry as she struggled to regain her balance.

"Fool mortal to think you could curse me!" Dokar grabbed her face in his hands, his fingers cold and too strong to fight. "I will show you how little your mortal-wrought poison affects a fey prince."

Tiredness swept through Snow, a bitter cold and cruel laughter following it. Her throat closed up, and she couldn't breathe.

He shoved her away and stepped back, wiping his hands on a green handkerchief. Behind him, Robert and Solstice passed through the ice. Together, they reached for the fallen sword.

"Sleep, princess!" Dokar commanded.

Robert and Solstice raised the sword.

Snow's head hit the floor, her eyes closing. For a brief moment, a heart-piercing scream replaced the sorcerer's cackles, then the swish of a sword through the air and a man's outraged cry. Then all vanished but the cruel laughter.

꧁꧂

DOKAR DIDN'T BLEED as Robert wanted him to as Solstice's sword pierced him. There was no satisfying hiss of iron against fey skin. The immortal prince simply cried out in anger and disappeared, allowing Robert and Solstice a clear view of Snow collapsed and pale as death on the floor.

Robert was numbly aware of Solstice's scream of despair as she ran to Snow, of her sword crashing to the floor, too heavy for him without Solstice's presence to give him the right to lift it. A part of him recognized the fight still raging beyond the swiftly melting walls of ice and his own need to join the advisors and the men the enchanters had brought. Even as he leapt into the fray, even as six enchanters, Lyndon, and Lady Violetta appeared, his thoughts stayed on the woman in the crimson gown.

Robert and the men the enchanters brought made quick work of clearing out the remaining highwaymen and Guagin's men. The enchanters apologized for taking so long to arrive as Robert led them through the cleared cottage to Snow and Solstice, but he barely heard. It had taken time to convince Houen's and Schwan's guards to come along and then to find the right highwaymen's lair, they said. He couldn't find it in himself to be surprised at that, or when Lady Violetta produced a wet cloth and bathed Lucrezia's face as Lyndon checked her head. Or when Solstice called a strange man with mirror-like hair from the mirror.

He was vaguely aware of the crowd gathered around him and Snow as Colors and the man with the mirror-like hair— whom Solstice called Birch—knelt beside Snow and examined her. The spell color about her was different than it had been when the Poison Stone worked too fast. The hue wasn't the same; the color was more settled into her.

"I don't think the dress will help her this time," Colors said, his voice cracking as he rose. He shared a glance with Birch, who nodded, regret in the gesture. "The spell has finally set. She's not a child and accidental victim this time." Colors met Robert's eye, genuine grief there. "I'm sorry." He patted Robert's shoulder and walked away, the others following silently until only Robert, Solstice, and Birch remained.

Robert sank to his knees beside Snow, so many things he'd wanted to say jumbling together and blocking his throat, burning it with the need to speak but not allowing it to. He smoothed her hair away from her face instead, memorizing the feel of her soft skin under his fingers.

"Robert," Solstice said gently, "we have to take her into the mirror. She'll be well there, with her father."

He didn't respond but took Snow's hand in his.

"Robert." Lyndon echoed Solstice's quiet plea as he moved to Robert's side and laid a hand on his shoulder.

Birch knelt across from them. Expression apologetic, he reached for Snow.

"No." Robert gathered Snow into his arms. Suddenly he understood what it meant to leave all others for one's wife. He loved his aunt and uncle, Rupert, his sister, but his life ultimately wasn't with them. It was with his betrothed, with Snow.

"I have to take her into the mirror," Solstice said firmly. "Please, Robert. We can work together to find a way to free her and her father, if there is one, but for now, she has to go."

"I can't follow her there? I have to find a betrothed princess to break my curse. As long as Snow lives, I don't want it to be anyone else."

"It's only for the Keeper to come and go from the mirror, and her family," Solstice said gently. "The mirror decides who is family."

Robert shifted Snow in his arms, holding her head so that she faced him. She was so limp, growing cold so rapidly. "Snow is mine," he said, his voice cracking. "She always has been, as I have been hers. Where she goes, I go." He drew her closer.

"Robert!" Lyndon's cry of alarm blended with Solstice's.

Before they could stop him, Robert pulled Snow to him and kissed her. But there was no life in it, no return of his love.

No sleep.

"You're..." Solstice slowly lowered her hand from her mouth.

"I have a jealous curse," Robert whispered, his arms loosening their hold.

Birch took Snow from him and carried her toward the mirror. Robert would have hated the way the man's slow steps sounded of a funeral march, but his heart ached too much for hate, and a familiar slimy feeling was welling up in him. He doubled over as a wave of nausea hit him, then left as suddenly as it had come. As he uncurled, he dully noticed he could feel no trace of the greenness. Even his Pocket Spell had vanished.

"Birch?" asked a sleepy voice.

Robert stilled. Solstice gasped.

"Yes, Princess?" Birch's reply trembled.

Robert clenched his fists, his eyes scrunched against a sight he feared he wouldn't see. *Please don't let me be dreaming.*

"What happened?" Snow's voice was croaky with sleep, confused.

Beautiful.

He opened his eyes. Birch was staring at Snow as she blinked up at him, but it wasn't him she should be seeing just now.

"Give her back! Please!" Robert sprang up, stepped over dropped weapons and toppled chairs until he stopped in front of the man with the mirror-like hair. Focusing on Snow, Robert held out his arms.

Her gaze met his, and the confusion in her beautiful eyes vanished. She reached for him.

As if he had been waiting for that, Birch gave her up to him.

Barely had Robert put her on her feet and hugged her to him when Solstice threw herself at them, embracing them both.

"What happened?" Solstice asked, wiping away tears as she released them and moved away to stand beside Birch and Lyndon.

"It was the kiss." Snow touched a hand to her lips and stared with wonder at Robert. She was steady on her feet now, but he kept an arm about her waist anyway, and she didn't seem to mind. "I remember a kiss. It stopped the laughter."

"The laughter?" he asked.

Her face twisted briefly with pain. "There was always a cruel laughter in my cursed sleep. A voice saying only love could break the curse but I'd never had that. The love was his." Snow cocked her head to look at her stepmother. "I think it was the sorcerer mocking Father. He thought you loved him, not Father, that you only wanted Father's crown." She leaned into Robert, though she stayed focused on Solstice, and he tightened his arm about her. "Robert loves me, and his kiss broke my curse. If you had kissed Father goodbye, as was the ancient custom here, then he would have woken."

"All it needed was a kiss?" Solstice cried. "On this side of the mirror?"

Snow hesitated and looked to Robert before breaking into a grin, which he returned. "I think so."

"Birch," Solstice ordered, pointing to the floor at her feet. "Bring me my husband."

Birch, his expression a mix of joy and something else, loss perhaps, spun away to the mirror.

As if taking that as a sign the private time was over, Houen, Lyndon, Lady Violetta, and the others all crowded round, expressing their joy and bombarding them with questions.

Though not even Solstice fully understood the sword, she and Colors seemed certain Prince Dokar was banished to his own realm for quite some time. Robert and Snow, and even the still-unconscious Lucrezia, were safe from the fey prince. Schwan, while admitting having done many shady things to gain his current position—partly for the power and partly for love of his wife—assured them he truly had killed the sorcerer that day. He was no fool, he told them. He had not killed his father-in-law. Guagin, having learned of Schwan's mixed heritage through his enchanter relative, and suspecting other things, blackmailed him while also helping him gain his position, intending to force him into supporting whatever he wanted. Schwan and Blatherskite felt certain they could figure out what Gaugin had done to harm certain of the other advisors and their families and undo what could be undone. With one of his wolfish grins, Who promised to deal with Guagin's enchanter relative, a greedy man who'd doubtless aided him in some of his schemes.

Birch soon returned with King Theodore, dragging the unconscious man over a swiftly forming ice path to Solstice. She quickly woke him, to the additional shock and joy of those present.

The questions and excited chatter continued, and Robert finally dragged Snow away to a quiet corner of the main room.

"I'm not cursed anymore," Robert began, "so you don't have to kiss me every day, not—" *Because of my curse anyway.*

"Cursed or not, Robert of Pondleigh, I'm going to kiss you!" Standing on tiptoes, Snow took his face in her hands and kissed him full on the lips. She broke away quickly with a gasp, her face as red as ever the curse had made her lips.

Robert, too shocked—in a pleased kind of way—to respond properly earlier, caught her round the waist as she backed away. "Don't stop. I think I deserve three proper kisses for every slap-kiss you ever gave me as a frog."

"I never slapped you," Snow protested, half-heartedly pushing against him.

"Oh yes, you did." Robert caught her hands against his chest. "And I intend to claim every kiss you owe me, starting now."

⚙

LADY VIOLETTA SURVEYED the room of smashed furniture, distasteful odors, and unsightly stains with a satisfied smile. Robert was kissing Snow. King Theodore and Queen Solstice were likewise engaged—and on this side of the mirror too. The remaining advisors were planning how to announce the exceptional news of a returned king and a betrothed princess to the kingdom. The good people of New Grimmland had quite a pleasant shock coming to them.

Birch, with his magnificent mirror-like hair, was gently lifting the unconscious Lucrezia into his arms. Birch, like King Theodore, looked more gardener than royalty. She would soon fix that. Was it possible to create an outfit that changed to match Birch's varying hair color? Or would that be too distracting?

Lady Violetta felt a pleasant kind of warmth as Colors

moved to her side, looking handsome and formidable in his ebony uniform. As he should, for she'd designed it for him centuries ago.

"What are you going to do with her?" Colors asked Birch of Lucrezia.

If only Lady Violetta hadn't allowed herself to be tricked into giving the girl that control spell! Doubtless it was that mischief which drew her to Prince Dokar's notice. Yet, perhaps, the noblewoman, raised by a hard father to be selfish and demanding, and so easily blinded by her own desires, would turn out better for her current struggles. She could never return to the land of her birth, though, or New Grimmland, since Robert would be here as king one day.

Birch looked down at Lucrezia's gaunt face, his own appearing weary and old beyond measure. The room quieted to watch him.

"It's time," he said, more to Queen Solstice than to anyone else. "I'm wearing thin. You said my brother's heir seeks a wife of noble blood, an alliance with a summer kingdom. She is the one—I can see it in her. She is destined to be a queen. I will take him his bride. If she is willing. This time I will not fail." Hugging Lucrezia to his chest, he strode to the mirror. Solstice met him beside it and spoke quietly with him.

"Snow! Robert, my son!" King Theodore barely gave the young couple warning before embracing them both in a hug as large and strong as his heart. He would probably be setting a wedding date for them before the night was done, good man. She would design a new gown for Snow and an outfit for Robert for the occasion, of course. Fashion, comfort, and usefulness in clothing, those were her true talents.

"Well, Lady Violetta." Colors, still standing close beside her, lifted her hand to his lips and kissed it. For once, his pale skin was free of curse colors, and there was something different about his eyes as he looked at her which she rather liked. It had started to bloom there a few centuries ago, just as circumstances drew them apart. "It seems happily-ever-afters do exist."

Blushing, Lady Violetta smiled up at him and slipped her arm through his. "I've always thought so, though it does take a bit of work to start them and to keep them going."

# ACKNOWLEDGMENTS

This was a fun, albeit challenging, story to write. Many thanks to my beta-readers—H.L. Burke, Elizabeth Kraiser, Amy Bryant, Sarah Levesque, and Kate Endres—for their helpful feedback, my kind ARC readers, and all those enjoyed *Midnight for a Curse* and talked about it, which inspired me to push up writing Robert's story. To Victoria for her gorgeous covers. To Susan for her continuous encouragement and for the title. The biggest thanks to God, who gave me a talent and passion for creating fictional worlds and characters and who let me share them with this world. *Soli Deo gloria*

# ABOUT THE AUTHOR

E.J. KITCHENS loves tales of romance, adventure, and happily-ever-afters and strives to write such tales herself. When she's not thinking about dashing heroes or how awesome bacteria are—she is a microbiologist after all—she's enjoying the beautiful outdoors or talking about classic books and black-and-white movies. She is a member of Realm Makers and lives in Alabama.

May she beg a favor of you? You've already kindly read her book, would you also leave a review? Those gold stars can power more than fictional worlds: they encourage, inspire, and help authors through hurdles so we can seek out the people looking for books like ours. It's a daunting quest, and without you, fearless reader, it would fail. Will you join it?

To learn more about E.J. Kitchens and her books, visit her website and sign up for her newsletter.
www.EJKitchens.com

You can also connect with her and other fairy tale authors in the Facebook group Faith and Fairy Tales.

**The Mouse King Has Taken One Crown too Many**

Janawyn Stahl is convinced there's a connection between her godfather's suspiciously talkative automaton named Theo and his lost nephew, but can she protect Theo from the evil Mouse King long enough to find out?

This short story retelling of "The Nutcracker and the Mouse King" is available for free when you sign up for my newsletter.

## A CURSE KEEPER, CURSE BREAKER Fairytale

Belinda Lambton knows a curse when she sees one. She also knows the wisdom of agreeing with a powerful enchantress. So when she gets mixed up with a cursed Beast and his enchantress, she finds herself tasked with the role of Curse Breaker. That's not an easy position, for Beast has reasons of his own to keep his curse. There's also someone determined to break it by whatever means possible and claim Beast for herself, and she doesn't take competition well.

With wit, clean romance, and a touch of danger, *Midnight for a Curse* is a retelling of the beloved "Beauty and the Beast" tale.

# Jane Austen Romance Meets Fairytale Adventure

*When a prim, proper enchantress attempts to bewitch a magic mirror, she ends up cursed—powerless, penniless, dumped in a strange land, and stuck in the body of a hag. But the cure to her curse isn't what she expects, for one curse won't cure another. Or will it?*

*He's a non-magic who wants a respite from all things magical. She's an enchantress hiding a secret that could lead to her enslavement by the sorcerers. Together, they find themselves in a game of cat and mouse with the notorious Magic Thief.*

ADVENTURE AND ROMANCE IN A FANTASY WORLD

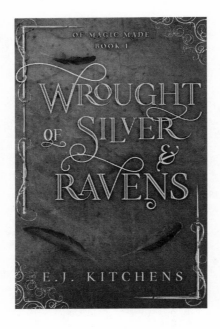

Book 1 of OF MAGIC MADE

With a malevolent prince stealing her kingdom and her magic one dance at a time, Princess Thea must win the loyalty of a mysterious guard to save her kingdom.

*Wrought of Silver and Ravens* is an adventure-romance retelling of "The Twelve Dancing Princesses" and is set in The Magic Collectors story world.

# Adventure and Romance Are Only a Page Away

E. J. Kitchens